P9-AZX-970

Four Ways to Wear a Dress

GILLIAN LIBBY

sourcebooks
casablanca

Copyright © 2022 by Gillian Libby
Cover and internal design © 2022 by Sourcebooks
Cover design by Stephanie Gafron/Sourcebooks
Cover illustration by Sarah Dennis

Sourcebooks and the colophon are registered trademarks of Sourcebooks.

All rights reserved. No part of this book may be reproduced in any form or by
any electronic or mechanical means including information storage and retrieval
systems—except in the case of brief quotations embodied in critical articles or
reviews—without permission in writing from its publisher, Sourcebooks.

The characters and events portrayed in this book are fictitious or
are used fictitiously. Any similarity to real persons, living or dead,
is purely coincidental and not intended by the author.

All brand names and product names used in this book are trademarks,
registered trademarks, or trade names of their respective holders.
Sourcebooks is not associated with any product or vendor in this book.

Published by Sourcebooks Casablanca, an imprint of Sourcebooks
P.O. Box 4410, Naperville, Illinois 60567-4410
(630) 961-3900
sourcebooks.com

Cataloging-in-Publication Data is on file with the Library of Congress.

Printed and bound in the United States of America.
VP 10 9 8 7 6 5 4 3 2 1

For my parents, Jim and Debby. For all the books and always encouraging my own reinvention.

Chapter 1

IF THIS IS THE REAL world, you can take it and shove it right up your ass.

Maybe it was naive of me not to be better prepared for this outcome. And maybe I should have understood I might be the one fired if I didn't keep my mouth shut instead of being the voice of the marketing department trying to explain to my boss at Butterfly Bridge that even if the toys his company makes are sustainable in environmental terms, the company he was running was not. But then I wouldn't be me.

The toys my former employer is attempting to bring to the world are made of beautiful blond wood—minimalist, sleek, and way too expensive. The kind of thing a parent will put on a shelf and photograph in a half-hearted attempt to show how chic parenting can be, but they're not the kind of thing a kid is going to beg for or play with for more than fifteen seconds. Plus, they're heavy, solid wood, making an excellent weapon for any toddler with a new baby sibling and something to prove. But Bob the Job had a specific idea of how he wanted to do things and wasn't going to budge from that. I don't think my parents are going to find any comfort in this explanation when I tell them I've been laid off. To them, it will be just one more reason to be worried that their daughter isn't a capable, functioning adult. Which, in a way, is fair.

I exhale, long and slow, a breath of disappointment as I shift the weight of the small box containing whatever was in my desk to my hip. On top of everything else today, I don't need to spill the little terrarium of succulents I received last year in the office Secret Santa exchange. I reach to push the button for the elevator and squeeze my eyes shut as I feel them welling with tears. Now what am I going to do?

"I got it," a voice calls from behind me. I'm in no mood for human interaction, but when I see it's Joss, a member of my former marketing team, reaching around me to push the button, I hand over the box for him to carry in relief. I wonder why he doesn't have more stuff, though he only started a year ago and still works remotely most days.

"I'll help you get a cab," he says. I can't believe he's still smiling. But he's so young this is probably his first time being let go from a job. He's probably thinking about cashing those unemployment checks on a beach somewhere. Honestly, there are worse plans.

"It's fine. I'm meeting some friends nearby," I tell him.

"In that?" He looks me up and down, fighting a smirk. At least I'm amusing as I hit an all-time low.

I don't blame young Joss for that look of amusement on his face. Not with the outfit this layoff has set on my body. I'm wearing all the clothes that have been cluttered under my desk for the last three years on top of what I wore to work today. Leg warmers (a long-forgotten Christmas gag gift), my very old Chapel Hill T-shirt (my backup gym clothes) over my button-down shirt, and a high-waisted faux-leather pencil skirt.

"Failure is very in this season," I grumble as my stomach seizes. I freaking hate that word. Especially when it's accurate. I'm trying really hard not let this layoff feel inevitable just because I was on the team. I may not have believed the product I was marketing was particularly meaningful, but I always felt the value in trying to create something that would last. Not just helping to build the company, but producing a toy that would be handed down for generations. That's what I tried to focus on, but clearly it didn't make any difference to anyone. This job also marked the first time I ever felt I had my life and attention issues under control, and losing it is one big wallop to the self-esteem.

The elevator reaches the ground floor, and Joss holds the door open, unnecessarily, as I pass by him. "Well, it looks good on you."

I stop and shoot him a sharp look. Can he just not?

Joss bites his lip. "I didn't mean that the way it came out." I take the box out of the former junior associate's hands and make my way through the lobby to the street. I'm really done here.

"Where's your stuff, anyway?" I ask him. "Where's that electric mug warmer you loved so much?" His mom sent it to him for his birthday, and he talked about it from September until March last year. I hate that I know this much about his relationship with hot beverages.

"Still at my desk. Listen, before you go, I was hoping we could make a plan to see each other again. So we don't lose touch."

Pass. Joss is a nice guy and everything, but it's not like we were super close before this. He probably just wants to make sure he can use me as a reference when he's job hunting.

"Don't worry, Joss. We don't have to hang out just so you can use me for a reference." I tug one-handed at the leg warmers that keep sliding down my legs.

Joss tilts his head. "A reference? Oh, no. Millie, I'm not being laid off. I thought Bob would have told you."

Poor kid, they just haven't gotten to him yet. "Joss, the entire marketing department is being shut down. I hate to be the one to have to fill you in." But someone needs to prepare him. This is his first job, after all. It was mine, too, but after three long and dedicated years, I'm still his senior. Or was.

"Right, the entire department except for me. I'm staying to run it. I'm reporting directly to Bob now."

I'm not a violent person, but as I stand here on the sidewalk looking at Joss's dark-blond hair and blue eyes, imagining him and the three other *guys* I know from other departments that haven't been laid off laughing with Bob the Job around the stupid office Ping-Pong table, I wonder what would happen if I kneed him between the legs.

"But you're the most junior person in the department." And the only guy, which I'm starting to feel isn't a coincidence. Seriously? Freaking start-up bros.

"I know, and you did great work with all the blogger outreach. You shouldn't feel bad."

My eyes widen at his patronizing words. I know I did great work. Or at least I was pretty sure before I was laid off and replaced by someone with less experience and none of my contacts. I straighten the terrarium I'm carrying and brush a few loose stones from the leaves. I hate that this is just the kind of thing that I would expect to happen to me.

The only reason I moved to New York was for this job, and I've regretted it nearly every day since. But the big-girl job where I wore big-girl clothes (except maybe right now) made my parents think that I had all my attention issues under control. That I had outgrown my impulsive behavior. Three years ago, their opinion was really important to me. The job had a few other perks, but I never looked around and thought, "This is exactly where I want to be." Maybe Joss did. Maybe that's why he's staying. Or maybe it's because he has a dick in his pants, however micro it may be.

"I'm meeting friends," I tell him. "I'll see you around." Or not. Which would be my first choice.

"Wait, before you go." Joss hurries so he's standing in front of me on the sidewalk. What hint does this guy need? "Let's get a drink this weekend. My treat, obviously." He smiles. "Since I'm the one still with income, right?" He laughs at his own stupid joke.

"Are you trying to get into my leg warmers, Joss?"

He laughs, and I immediately regret making a joke. It makes him think I'm not fighting the urge to push him in front of a cab.

"We can start there, sure." He wags his eyebrows while my stomach lurches. If only I could vomit on command. That might be the hint Joss needs.

Instead, I reach into my box of dearly departed office accessories and pull out the little terrarium. As much as I enjoyed the collection of cacti, I want zero reminders of this day and was planning on giving the terrarium to Kate, my most understanding friend, when

I met her and Bree at the bar. With one swift movement, I tip the contents of the little glass pot over the head of the guy who just last week was making appointments for me and watch as twenty-five dollars of dirt, pebbles, and tiny green plants tumble from his shiny blond hair to his limp shoulders.

"Have fun going down with the ship, Joss. That cactus is better at marketing than you are, and it's probably better in bed."

I sidestep around him and dump the rest of the box into the nearest trash can.

The twenty-minute walk gives me a chance to cool off, and when I pull open the door of my favorite West Village bar, I heave a huge sigh of relief at the sight of two of my closest friends, Kate and Bree. We met in college along with my best friend and former roommate, Quincy. But Quincy moved back home after graduation, while Kate, Bree, and I all found jobs in New York. So, naturally, we moved there together. Or, in actuality, they moved together and I followed about a year later because I had a little trouble pulling the trigger.

I wanted to move out to California with Quincy. That had always been our plan, but my parents were sure I'd become a waitressing surf bum, so when I landed the job at Butterfly Bridge, I went to New York to join Kate and Bree instead. Joke's on my parents, though, because as of today I am a surf bum, just without the surf.

"Oh, Millie," Kate says, shaking her head upon seeing my odd outfit. She's disappointed in me. Kate is like the prim mom I already have, but I still love her to death. She just wants us all to meet our hedge-fund husbands and move to the suburbs together.

It's the main reason she moved to New York. But she has a lot of great qualities too.

"It's a look, I guess," Bree says, then purses her lips and rolls her dark-brown eyes up to the ceiling.

"It was this or never see the contents of my desk again. Though most of that stuff just got dumped on Joss's head," I reply, then blow the air out between my lips, letting the reality of my day settle in. "How fun are start-ups?"

"You liked it so much though," Kate says. I shoot her a look out of the side of my eyes.

"Back up. What about Joss's head?" Bree asks.

"Joss gets to keep his job, the only one from marketing sticking around. So I dumped some succulents on his head." I shrug, trying not to show my regret at yet another impulsive choice. "That was after he tried to get into my leg warmers. Who knew this would be a look that works for douchebags." I gesture down at my ridiculous overlayered outfit.

Bree's eyes widen as she raises her arm and signals to the waiter to get me a drink. Sometimes you need a Kate and sometimes you need a Bree.

When the waiter comes over, I order a beer and then at the last minute shout at his back, "And the tater-tot poutine!" Because one, it's amazing, and two, cheese-soaked carbs are good for sorrow and confusion. It's a fact.

"And yes, Kate, I liked my job when I got to talk to Quincy during business hours for work. Or when I was able to think of a creative press release that might get the company some attention. But no one wants a plain wooden police car for their kids for one hundred and fifty dollars." I raise my eyebrows at the obscene number. "No matter how ethically or sustainably made it may be. They want the cheap plastic thing for twenty bucks that lights up and makes noise until it drives you to smash it with a hair dryer, and then when your kid cries about it, you buy another." I shake my head. "Now that's a business model."

"But all those mommy bloggers loved them," Kate chimes in.

"Yeah, they loved them when I sent them for free. But sometimes PR and marketing don't translate to sales." It's a sad fact that I'd repeatedly told Bob the Job for the last year. I had to keep explaining to him that even though I was doing my best and getting our products plastered all over Surf Shack Dream House, one of the biggest lifestyle blogs (and the corresponding Instagram account), and many others, that didn't mean regular people were going to buy the toys. I might have good connections with influencers, but I can't make people spend their money.

"What a waste," Bree adds. "You busted your ass all through the work-from-home time and this is the thanks you get? I know you felt some loyalty or whatever after such a weird first few years with them, but come on."

"Was it loyalty or lack of other options?" I reply. I don't know the answer, but I do know I want to put this all behind me as fast as possible.

My phone dings with a text, and I flip it over to check it.

> **Quincy**: That sucks, Millie! So sorry!

I look back up at my friends. I texted our ongoing group chat after I got the news from Bob the Job and may have vented a little aggressively. It's how Kate and Bree knew I needed to meet for drinks. Our other friends are just catching up now.

"Quincy," I tell Kate and Bree, explaining the text message. They flip their phones over and read the message for themselves. "I don't want her to feel bad after she helped me out so much with Alana and her blog. It's not her fault Bob had to use wood that cost more per ounce than actual gold."

"You don't have to make jokes you know," Bree says. "You can be pissed for real if you want to."

I shrug at her. It's what I do. Make a joke, sprinkle any situation that makes me feel like a flaky loser with enough sarcasm to deflect from what's really going on. I learned pretty young that if a teacher caught me not paying attention or doing something I wasn't supposed to, if I made a joke, I could probably escape trouble. But I know I don't have to do this with my friends, so I say the thing that's been ringing around in my head since I heard the big news. "This never would have happened if I had moved out with Quincy in the first place. You know I love you guys, but New York just isn't for me."

Bree gets it immediately. "Yeah, maybe you'd be a big influencer like Quincy instead of marketing useless stuff to them."

"Doubtful, but thanks." There are a lot of what-ifs about California. Quincy and my long-buried dream of not working in a corporate job are two of the three biggest.

Our friend Quincy is what we call in marketing a micro-influencer. Someone who has between ten thousand and fifty thousand followers. They make up one of the most important influencer levels because of their high follower-engagement rates. Meaning more of their followers are actual people who care about what the influencer is saying and not just someone shouting into an internet black hole of bots and hate followers.

The funny thing about Quincy is that she doesn't seem caught up in all of it. Which is why I love her so much. She updates her blog when she feels like it. Posts daily pictures of her cute kids and her rustic-chic beach cottage. Her ruggedly handsome surfer husband, Ari, doesn't hurt things either. Blogging really took off for her a few years ago when she became mommy friends with Alana Tatamo, the founder of Surf Shack Dream House. But unlike Alana's, Quincy's blog isn't a business; it just happened. Which I guess is pretty easy when you live somewhere as beautiful as Peacock Bay, California. Where every day has perfect waves to surf and golden hour lasts all afternoon.

So while Quincy has made a career of just being Quincy, I'm unemployed in New York with its heat waves and lockdowns and blizzards that last until spring.

God, I need to get out of here. But the waiter has returned, so while I might not have the sun, sand, and surf that my best friend has, at least I have tater tots.

"You guys want some?" I ask my friends while ignoring the texts I hear rolling in on my phone.

"You do realize how disgusting that looks don't you?" Bree asks, while still helping herself.

"Who cares what it looks like?" I ask her, shoving a few more of the cheese-covered tots in my mouth. "It's just us who have to look at it, and we know better than to judge something on outward appearances, don't we?"

Bree laughs. I love throwing her teaching methods back in her face whenever I get a chance. She's a kindergarten teacher at a fancy Upper East Side private school. Luckily, parents love her no-bullshit approach to their kids. It really could have gone either way there.

"So, do you have any idea what you're going to do now?" Kate asks.

"She just lost her job thirty seconds ago. Give the girl a chance to catch her breath," Bree says.

I wince. Just hearing the words makes my vision blur with shame and unshed tears.

"I don't know. I have a little saved. Plus, the lease on my apartment is up next month. If I have to, I can find a cheaper place." I really don't want to talk about this right now.

"Or move in with us!" Kate exclaims. I smile at her because I know she would happily take me in if I needed it, but I don't want to need it. What I really need is to find a new job right away so my parents don't start panicking and pushing me to get my real estate license so that I can work with them back in Nantucket. I may not love the city, but that tiny island life isn't for me either.

"What are you going to do? Get bunk beds? You guys are squeezed in as it is." I appreciate her offer, but no, bunk beds will not be in the next chapter of my life, and I'd prefer if endless days shut in an office weren't either. "Maybe it's time for a change of scenery?"

Kate looks around the city streets, but I shake my head. "Bree is right. While everyone else worked remotely from somewhere better, I stayed here and busted my ass in my tiny apartment trying to help the company. Maybe it's time I went remote myself. Like really, really remote."

I jiggle my foot against the leg of my chair. People leave the city all the time, especially in the last few years. It's actually stranger that I didn't, but I didn't have a reason. Maybe this layoff could be my reason. A reason to start fresh, to begin again and to do something completely different than before.

I pick up my phone, thinking this over. I scan a few texts from my mom, who predictably is freaking out about her newly unemployed daughter, and a few more on the group text. I only see the most recent one from Quincy that just reads YESSSSSSSSS! so I open that one up to read the entire chain from where I left it.

> **Quincy:** That sucks, Millie. I'm so sorry!

> **Quincy:** Let me know if I can do anything to help.

> **Quincy:** Maybe now would be a good time to take that trip out to visit us you're always hinting about.

> **Pete:** Yeah, Mills. Waves upon waves out here. You know you want to. Unless you can't surf anymore.

Pete. Pete Santana. The third what-if. My entire body goes cold, even with a belly full of gravy and covered by a wool poncho. He doesn't pop into the text chain much, but when he does, my stomach plummets like I've just dropped into a twenty-foot wave. Everything stands still, my blood stops running, and my heart floats in my chest waiting for another sliver of his attention.

Quincy: Of course, she can still surf, Peter. Give the woman some credit.

Pete: Prove it. Get out here.

Quincy: YESSSSSSSSS!

Get out here. Just reading those words is enough to melt the clothes off my body. He might as well have told me to get in his bed. Which is unlikely. He's Quincy's brother, older by just over one year, and another of our best friends from college. I spent a lot of college hours thinking of ways to casually cross those boundary lines, but my feelings of longing always appeared to be firmly one-sided. However, I can't really argue with *Get out here*, can I?

"What's with the face?" Bree asks. I have my hand fisted over my mouth, and I must be grinning like a lovesick schoolgirl. I nod my chin toward my phone. She picks hers up and reads the messages too.

"Pete and Quincy think I should go out to Peacock Bay to visit them." I shrug, trying to keep my cool and not run from the bar directly to the airport. They've invited me before, but I was always too busy or too out of cash. Plus, I'd always hoped Pete might drop any kind of hint that he was looking forward to me moving out to his hometown with Quincy after graduation, but it never came. Which may have been another reason why I took the safe job in New York. But *safe* hasn't lived up to its name, now has it?

"Oh my god, how hot is Pete these days?" Kate asks. She picks up her phone to begin what I know will be a fruitless search.

"Don't bother," I tell her, while scrolling through my mom's panicked messages. "He's unstalkable online. It's infuriating. No Facebook, no Instagram, nothing. He's like a ghost." I flip my phone facedown after scanning my mom's texts. God, does she really think I wasn't trying at Butterfly Bridge? I can't deal with her right now. I tried it her way and ended up out of a job and missing my best friend. Why can't I try it my way for once?

"But what about the hotel?" Bree asks. Pete is a part owner in his family's business, a chic beachside boutique hotel, but you'd never know it because there's no mention of him on the website or anywhere else online.

"I think their older sister, Amelia, runs the website and social media. Pete does more of the operations from what I understand," I explain. Pete and Quincy are the fourth and fifth kids in their family (Quincy is number five, like quint. They're very cute, this family.)

"Whoa, you're right. You can't find anything about Pete when you google him. Santana is a pretty common last name, I guess. Some guy in Birmingham is all I can find, and that is not the hot Pete I remember," Bree says.

Although the five of us were really close in college, Kate and Bree don't keep in touch with the Santanas the way I do. Quincy and I were roommates all four years, and being without her now is like missing a limb. Luckily for me, my (former) job required me to create contacts with influencers and Quincy unexpectedly found herself becoming one. So, except for the group text, Kate and Bree get their information on Quincy and her siblings from me. The group text also has the benefit of being the only way I could stay in touch with Pete because of his social-media darkness. If I want to know what's going on with Pete, I have to actually ask.

"So, do you think you'll go?" Kate asks. She's grinning from ear to ear. My crush on Pete isn't much of a secret, and it's one of Kate's favorite daydreams. But I'm here and he's there. It's not like there is much to do about it.

"Plus, it has been a while since you've been surfing. I know you miss it," Bree says.

She's right, I do miss surfing. I miss having a place to tuck myself away and let everything go. Everything loosens up on the water. Pressure from my parents, losing my job, missing a friend. It all fades into the background. I don't have to try to concentrate because I already am. There's no other time my entire body and brain will focus so completely without a struggle than when I'm surfing.

Not to mention Peacock Bay looks amazing. Quincy's hometown is a small coastal town full of surfers and small-batch iced coffeehouses. A town that's also, oddly, launched a number of influencers' careers since Alana moved there years ago. I hustled for three years at Butterfly Bridge and look where it got me. Unemployed and sitting at a bar stuffing my face with consolatory tater tots. I followed my mom's advice three years ago and shoved aside my blog while Quincy's took off. I watched her and the other influencers I've been sending toys to live their dream lives out there with their perfect husbands and beautiful children all under a clear blue California sky. Why couldn't that be me too?

"Maybe I could visit Quincy for a little while. Aside from you guys, there's not much for me here. Maybe...I don't know, but maybe there's a job for me there."

"Maybe you could be an influencer like Quincy." Kate beams.

"Doubtful. That kind of thing takes years, but it would be nice to visit for a while."

"You might as well," Bree adds. "You're not doing anything else."

"Thanks," I snipe. "That's probably not the key to all successful new experiences, but I can work with it."

At the very least, I can justify an extended stay in Quincy's hometown by saying I'm firming up my contacts with those influencers I've only met through email. If and when I'm interviewing for marketing jobs in the future, I can describe the trip and honestly say my connections with the top lifestyle bloggers are neatly within my grasp. It actually makes perfect sense.

"So, I guess I'm going." I grin at my friends. "I might have to store some stuff with you guys." My lease is up next month, and I might as well wait until I get back to find a new place.

"Of course," Kate exclaims. "How long are you planning to go?"

"I don't know. Maybe a month? Quincy has always said I could stay at the hotel whenever I wanted. Now sounds like the perfect time for an extended vacation."

"Slash blogger trip, right?" Bree adds.

I give her a finger point and a wink. "Exactly."

I pick up my phone and form my response carefully.

Millie: Fuck it, I'm in.

Okay, so maybe it wasn't that careful.

Chapter 2

I PROP MY PHONE ON my newly vacant bookshelf so I can regain the use of my hands. What's left of my crap isn't going to pack itself.

"But what are you going to do about money?" my mom asks via FaceTime.

I slowly exhale and try not to take the concern in her voice the way she probably intends it. To freak me out enough to do things her way. Leave it to parents to press that one spot you're already worried about.

"And you're just leaving New York after you worked so hard to build a career there?" my dad asks.

"Is sleeping your way to the top still considered hard work?" I ask out loud and brace myself for their reactions. Sadly, my shock-and-awe approach to distracting my parents no longer works. Not when I changed my major three times in college and had to suffer through two consecutive summers of classes just to graduate on time. Though there was that summer when Quincy, Pete, and I had a class together, which wasn't terrible.

"Millie, please. I'm not in the mood. I have a ton of my own work to do, you know. And we're catching the four o'clock ferry. We need to check on our rentals after the storm last night," my mom responds. My parents are never in the mood for my jokes, but even less so when the Nantucket ferry is boarding. My mom has been a real estate agent my whole life, but after I went to college, she and my dad moved off island to Boston. Instead of retiring, however, my mom decided she was tired of making money for other people and wanted a piece of the rental market for herself. So they sold the house we lived in when I was a kid and bought two small beach houses that they rent out for the summers. She still works the rental market all winter, and my dad's years as a plumber really help now that they have two rentals to maintain.

As for me, I would rather die than be trapped on that tiny island for another second. Sure, the summers are beautiful and the surf is pretty good, but it's an island. You're cut off from everything there, which I get is the point for people there for a week in the summer. But try growing up with the same fifty kids on one hundred of the same square miles and let me know if you might spend the rest of your life with a fair amount of wanderlust.

"Guys, New York will still be here. It just so happens my lease is also up. I'll stay with Kate and Bree if and when I'm ready to come back." I'm trying to sound confident about it all, but inside I'm churning with nerves.

I look up at my friends, who nod and continue to help pack the last of my tiny closet. Which isn't much after the purging that took place this week.

"Plus, I have some money saved, and I sold a ton of my stuff online this week."

"You sold your things?" my mom exclaims. She trades a look with my dad, and I know they're thinking this is a sign I'm spiraling into chaos. Which I could be, but a tiny part of me is okay with that. Let me be chaotic for a minute and see what comes of it. I've always had to fight against the tide of my own personal spaz. What would be so bad about seeing what happens when I don't for once?

"Just my old work clothes, stuff I don't wear anymore anyway. A few pieces of furniture. Nothing important. Don't worry, Mom, the family jewels will still be passed down to your future heirs." Bree titters in the background. My family has no jewels to speak of. Not even fake ones. "I can replace what I need when I come back, and Kate and Bree have very kindly offered to store a few boxes for me at their place."

"But isn't this just a vacation? Why are you selling so much?" my dad asks.

I don't really know how to explain it to my parents without causing alarm bells to ring out over my apartment in Bed-Stuy. It might look to them like I'm selling my stuff to go live on an ashram, but Peacock Bay isn't a commune. It's a fresh start. It felt horrible to work so hard and still feel like a failure at Butterfly Bridge. And I don't care if it freaks my parents out this time. I'm leaning into my failure, or maybe leaning out. I don't know, but I have to do something else.

"This isn't *just* a vacation," I explain. "Spending time with the bloggers in Peacock Bay will be good networking. This is basically a work trip. I could almost write it off on my taxes." That's all true, and if I need to come back and interview for jobs sooner than later, this will be the perfect explanation for my time away. But what if I don't want to explain it? What if I'm okay just being a beach bum selling coconut water or handmade bracelets on the beach? That's what everyone's expected of me anyway, and personally it sounds way better than anything I've done in the last few years in New York.

Bree makes a typing motion with her fingers, and I nod as Kate pulls a dusty cardboard box from the back of my closet. She makes a face asking what she should do with the box, and I nod my head to suggest tossing whatever is in the box. I'm guessing I never unpacked it when I moved in, a classic Millie move, so if I haven't missed whatever is in there by now, I'm guessing I don't need it.

"Plus, I've got a new Instagram account. It's called Here to Stay, and I'm going to chronicle my time away. Maybe there's something I can do with that," I tell them with a shrug. It's not as if I expect to become an influencer like Quincy, but it does give my trip a bit more purpose. Not that I need it. I'm doing this, with purpose or without, and I won't let anyone stop me! I hold up my phone to the computer screen and point to the pretty blue circle on the corner of the screen. "See? Kate designed an awesome logo, and I've written a few posts about packing up. What I'm keeping versus what I don't need anymore."

My mom looks at my dad who doesn't even try to hide the sarcastic raising of his eyebrows. I should be used to this, but it still stings in a way that makes me want to start unpacking and trolling the web for any job that will make me look like someone responsible.

I hold open my laptop closer to my phone. "Isn't the logo cute?" I point again to the blue-green circle with the font that took hours to choose. Kate was so patient with me while I made her try what felt like hundreds of different styles of type before we selected the cool seventies-style writing that almost looks like it's melting from the heat, a nod to what I hope will be many sunny days ahead.

"Okay, okay, I see. Very nice work, Kate," my mom calls to my friend. At least she likes the logo. We can build on this.

"Thank you, Mrs. Ward," Kate responds, as she ignores my instructions to toss the box she found and digs through its contents. I give her a look and she mouths, "Sorry." I wave her off because it's not her fault my parents think I'm a flake. That's all on me.

"Mom, it's going to be fine. Quincy really missed me, and I think she needs some friendly support." My parents love Quincy. There's nothing not to love, but it irks me a little that while Quincy married the boy next door, surfed, and worked as a waitress at her family's hotel for awhile before her blog took off, I was out here freezing my ass off and killing myself in an office—and my parents still think she has things more figured out than I do. Though, she definitely does, so they have a point.

I know there's not much hope of convincing my parents this trip isn't just the unemployment version of breakup bangs. There have been plenty of moments in the last few years when I've wondered what might have happened if I had moved out with Quincy like I wanted too. Maybe I could have waited tables somewhere while I worked on building something of my own the way Quincy did. Maybe I wouldn't be wondering what was going on with Quincy's extremely hot brother because we would actually talk on a regular basis in person.

"I guess Instagram is something to do other than just surfing," my dad says.

Of course, "just surfing" has been the chorus of my parents' song to me most of my life. During the summers in Nantucket, it was all I ever wanted to do. I get that I was never going to go pro, but they never even considered that I could do something related to surfing as a job. And I know why. A kid who can't sit still during class, makes jokes when she "loses" her homework, and just wants to surf all day can only be seen as one thing. A slacker. I know surfers get a bad rap as beach bums contributing nothing to the world, but that doesn't have to be the case. Surfers are also environmentalists, ocean conservationists, and some of the bravest, most badass people you will ever meet. I'm not saying I'm any of those things, just that being a surfer doesn't have to mean that you aren't anything else.

"You know that Instagram influencing is an actual job now, right? People make way more money with it than I will ever make in marketing."

"Sure, and some just post into the ether."

Sigh. I know that my working at Butterfly Bridge made my mom feel like I had finally reached some checkpoint of adulthood, but getting laid off is a clear signal I wasn't cut out for that life.

"So, I guess I won't sign you up for my newsletter, huh?" I grumble. This is going about as well as I expected. "And when I start getting sheet masks by the crateful, don't come begging, Mom."

Kate stifles a giggle while Bree gives me a look and points at her chest. I wink at her to let her know she'll get first dibs on those imaginary sheet masks.

"It just seems really impulsive. Jumping from job to job. Flying off to California…" my mom says.

I know what she's really saying. It sounds just like the kind of thing a grown woman with ADHD would do. And I get that. But this isn't like when I was seventeen and got fired from the giant pretzel stand for goofing around and twisting the pretzels in shapes that were "unsuitable for sale." Penises. I made penis pretzels. I'm not proud of it. But I didn't let Butterfly Bridge go down without a fight. I really tried. I might still have to fight against distractions and reckless impulses sometimes, but this isn't the same thing.

"You're still taking your medication, right?" my mom continues.

I roll my eyes and glance quickly at Kate and Bree, who pretend not to be listening to something so private. I started taking meds for my ADHD when I was twelve, and while I'm grateful for how they've made things easier for me in a lot of ways, my parents think because the medication helped me that it's the answer to everything. Fired from a summer job? Maybe we should up the dose. Struggling to get college applications done on time? Let's discuss it with the doctor. Luckily, I've always had good doctors who haven't increased my dose whenever my parents brought me in, but it would be nice if that wasn't their immediate answer for any behavior they found unnerving.

"Yes, I'm good. Really," I say quietly.

They trade a look that tells me they're not convinced. "Okay, well, just let us know if you need anything."

Hopefully, I won't.

I hang up the FaceTime call after a few more minutes of trying to soothe their anxieties about me "throwing away everything I've worked for." Their words, obviously. Then Kate, Bree, and I sit on the floor of my studio and dig into the pizza I ordered for us.

"I bet the pizza in Peacock Bay won't be as good as this," Kate says.

"Which is probably the only thing you'll miss," Bree adds. "I started following some of Quincy's friends last week. That place looks amazing. Like the most picturesque coastal California town ever. I wonder why it hasn't been built up more."

"I guess it's pretty far from any major airports. Kind of hard to get to, so it doesn't attract much tourism. And it's possible all those pictures just look amazing to us because we're surrounded by concrete."

My friends nod. I've done a fair amount of geotag searching myself in the last few days. I wanted to learn as much as I could about where I was going, but oddly, it wasn't that easy. It's a pretty small town a few hours south of Santa Cruz, but there isn't much else to learn except from the few bloggers who've made their careers posting about their beautiful surfers' paradise. I found websites for the Waveline Hotel, the one Pete and Quincy's family owns, and what looked like a few cheaper hotels—or maybe motels, it was hard to tell—and a few other local businesses. It's going to be a hell of a culture shock going from New York to such a remote town, and I say as much to my friends.

"Isn't that the point?" Bree asks.

"Yeah, it wouldn't be very relaxing to go to another New York just in California."

"You mean LA?" I joke.

"LA is not the California version of New York," Bree scoffs.

"And I'm not going there just to slack off."

"We know," Kate says carefully. They're not new to my parents' lack of faith in me, and I know she's trying to back me up. "We actually got you a going-away present." She pops her last bite of crust in her mouth and wipes her hands on a napkin before getting up to retrieve something from her bag.

She returns and hands me a long brown box a little smaller than a loaf of bread.

"Open 'er up." Bree grins.

The smell of freshly printed plastic hits my nose. A smell I recognize from the dozens of different press materials I've worked with in the last three years.

"You made me stickers?" I smile up at my friends and pull out one of the round stickers with the Here to Stay logo Kate designed on it. I smile at the very specific shade of blue-green we chose, fittingly called Hawaiian Blue.

"We wanted to show you we believe in you, plus maybe you could sell them," Kate says.

"When things take off for you, people are going to want to support you, and we wanted you to be ready," Bree adds.

I clutch the box to my chest. I'm so touched by this show of support. "You guys, this is amazing. Thank you." I turn one of the stickers over in my hand. I can't believe they did this for me. "This makes it so real."

"It *is* real, Millie." Kate beams at me. Even if my parents can't understand why I need to make this change, my friends are behind me, and that's more than enough for now. "By the way, that box you suggested I toss? When was the last time you looked inside it?"

I pull a face and shrug. "When I moved into this place? I probably got sick of unpacking and shoved it out of sight. Why?"

"Oh, only because it has the key to all of our happiness inside, that's all." Kate rises from the floor and grabs something out of the sad, neglected box.

My eyes go wide instantly. I trade looks of wonder with my two friends, whose expressions range from murderous to gleeful.

"You almost threw that out?" Bree exclaims.

"I didn't know it was in there. I…forgot about it," I answer honestly as my stomach twists in a knot of guilt.

Black silk cascades from Kate's fingers. No worse for its years of hiding. Our dress.

It was Quincy who found it at the vintage store near campus, and the way she turned the simple piece of clothing into a million different outfits made it the coolest thing any of us had ever seen. I'm not even sure how I was the one left in charge of it last. We started passing it around whenever one of us had a date, or an important meeting, exam, or interview. When we needed to look a little more special or feel a few degrees better than normal.

It never really worked for me the way it did for my friends though. While they were meeting their future husbands (Quincy) or landing their dream internships (Kate) or discovering their callings (Bree) in our dress, I was simply wearing a cool black slip dress. Sure, the knowledge that my friends had these major milestones in our shared piece of clothing meant something to me. Their successes seemed woven into the fabric, and I wanted to believe that the dress would have some effect on me when I next put it on. But it just never happened.

Maybe that's why I shoved it into a box when I moved and never looked at it again. Maybe I didn't want to be reminded of another way I'd failed or had something fail me. While my friends have moved on to the achieving stage of our twenties, I'm right back at the beginning again. This time I'm willing to try anything to make sure things are different.

"I thought Quincy had it," Kate says, holding our dress up to her chest and letting the skirt swish just slightly back and forth.

"Yeah, I figured it was in California with her or in a dumpster somewhere."

"It almost was." I shake my head. I almost blew this too.

"Millie, it's okay," Kate says, seeing my distress over nearly losing something that once meant so much to us. "We all forgot about it, and it showed up at the perfect time."

"Yeah, you have to wear this on the plane," Bree adds. "If I were heading to California for a quarter-life reinvention and about to see the guy I've been crushing on since college, I know what I'd want to wear."

I take the dress from Kate and hold it against my shoulders, but when I see myself in the mirror it all comes back. I'd wear it and he wouldn't see me. I'd wear it and still bomb the test.

"It never worked for me the way it did for you guys though," I admit. "I liked wearing it, and it will be nice to have it with me to keep me connected to you, but I didn't have the life revelations in it that you guys did."

"Yet," Kate says, and I shake my head.

I wish I could believe she was right. That this dress has been sitting in this box waiting for me to need it so it could come out and work its magic on me the way it did for my friends. I have nothing to lose by giving it another shot. It does look great on me, at the very least.

"Weren't you wearing it for your interview for Butterfly Bridge?" Bree asks. I wore it with a sweater over the top in my Zoom interview, and I can't believe she remembers. Though it was our classic interview outfit. Bree even wore it under a blazer for her interview for her first teaching job.

"And look how well that turned out."

"That job might not have been your dream, but it brought you to New York and back to us." Kate smiles at me. That's all true, of course. New York wasn't a waste of time, but it never felt like home to me. Not the way it did to my friends. Probably because the things I always hoped would happen seemed impossible here. Things like finding a career I loved while at the same time not being stuck in the corporate world, having a community of friends—not just a few. And then there's Pete.

Bree runs her fingers over the thin black silk, then looks at me with wide eyes. "This is what you should do," she says.

"Make dresses?" I ask.

"Wear this dress. For your Insta. One, it would be like an anti-fashion-influencer thing if you are mostly wearing the same dress, and it's a hook. Showing off the magic of this dress. Something different and special. And this dress is magic. There's no way it will let you down."

I hold the dress by its delicate straps and try to match Bree's enthusiasm. I love the idea and her faith in it, but if anyone can fail, even in a magic dress, it's me.

"It's a good idea," I tell her. "You guys have been so supportive of this entire massive life change. What am I going to do without you?"

"You won't be without us." Kate nods toward the dress. "So, luckily you won't have to find out." She takes the dress from my hands and packs it neatly into the open suitcase near the door. She looks up at me and says, "By the way, I can't believe there are no pictures of Pete online at all. You weren't kidding when you said he's a ghost."

"Right?" I say. "There are a few pictures that Quincy posted, but nothing in the last year." My friends both stare at me. "Not that I've been looking that hard or anything."

Bree laughs, while Kate does a search for Peter Santana content. "Do you think he still has that long hair?"

A collective sigh fills the room while we remember the Pete we knew in college. He had light-brown hair with streaks of blond mixed in from all his exposure to sun and surf, and it hung down to his massive ocean-sculpted shoulders. His skin was naturally dark from the Mexican side of his family, growing even browner by the time he'd return to school each fall. He has the look of a true California surfer guy, at least in my memory, but there's nothing about him that would lead anyone to call him a slacker. Pete was more often found tucked in a corner of the library with his laptop than out at the bars. In fact, I can remember more than one night when Quincy and I stormed the library to drag him out with us to do disgusting dollar shots that we deeply regretted the next day.

"I can't confirm knowledge of his hair length," I say. That's not exactly something I can innocently ask his sister for an update on. "But I do know he's not married. He's the only Santana sibling that's still on the market." I shrug as if this isn't something I think about almost daily. Pete Santana is still available. It goes against the laws of nature that no one has snatched him up yet, but there it is.

"The last Santana standing," Bree says. "Maybe you can change that, Millie."

"Only if I was setting him up with a high-powered lawyer or senator or something." Pete is too serious to think any romantic thoughts about his sister's flaky, unemployed friend who's come to hang out for a little while. Pete has never taken me seriously before, and now that I'm the least impressive I've ever been, he has even less reason to.

"You never know." Kate brightens with an idea. "Maybe it's such a small town that he's run out of options."

"Kate," Bree scolds. "Millie is no one's last resort."

"Thanks." I smile. Though I have to admit, I wouldn't mind being the shiny new toy in town for a little while. I look over to the suitcase now holding our talisman of unleashed potential. I know I'm way too old to believe something like this, but what if this time really is my turn for the dress to sprinkle me with its magic? It did turn up just when I needed some extra something.

I pull the dress back out of my suitcase and lay it on the floor near the window with the best light. I snap a picture to upload and try to come up with a caption that explains my excitement in finding this special item while admitting to how I almost trashed it forever. Even if your life is a full-time dumpster dive, you don't have to dress like it.

I add a few hashtags before uploading, then watch as the new photo loads on the screen.

Chapter 3

I PACKED LIGHT. ONLY ONE medium duffel bag on wheels and a carry-on bag with a few fragile things including my computer. I don't even own a surfboard anymore. That's how long it's been since my toes have touched surf, but that was part of why I sold so much stuff before I left. I didn't want to feel guilty about getting a new board. Picking out a surfboard is a little like meeting a litter of puppies when you're looking to adopt a dog. When you see the right one, you just know. I don't want to be held back when I find the right board to cruise around the waves in Peacock Bay.

But board shopping, while on my mind, will have to wait. Right now I need to find my ride. Quincy said she'd pick me up at the airport, but now that I'm standing here in the beautiful but blinding California sun, there's no sign of my equally beautiful but absent California friend.

There's no denying the beauty of this place. The sky is a crystal-clear blue, something it feels like I haven't seen in years. Dotted so sparingly with clouds, it seems like Mother Nature added them at the last minute because she felt like she couldn't leave the sky so plain or it would look fake. She was right.

I snap a quick photo, framing it so I get a nice sliver of palm tree but avoid anything that would give away that I'm only at the airport. I kicked things off on my new Here to Stay account this morning with a few photos of me in my long-forgotten dress, which felt cute with the denim shirt I had layered over it and tied at the waist. It took about a dozen tries to get a picture I was happy with, and I thought it might be funny if I posted some of the bad ones along with the one where I look halfway decent. So, after scrolling past my smiling face, I find one with my eyes closed, one where I'm midsneeze, and one where I'm actually holding my plane tickets upside down. I've gotten a lot of comments and lol's, so I'm glad people got the joke.

I attempt to smooth out the wrinkles of my dress and check my texts again, but there's nothing from Quincy. I sent her one after the plane landed, but I still haven't gotten a reply. That was thirty minutes ago. I don't even know what kind of car I should be looking for. I think I remember seeing a picture Quincy posted of a very cool mint-green vintage Ford Bronco, but who knows if that's really her car. It doesn't seem like the kind of car a young mom of two would drive, but I'm not a mom so what do I know.

If she's not checking her texts, maybe a notification from Instagram will get her attention. I post the picture I just took, tagging Quincy with a caption: I flew all the way to California and all I got was deserted at the airport. I put a geotag on the post so Quincy can see I'm here and waiting for her. Clearly, I'm getting desperate.

Though, not desperate enough to text Pete. He knows I'm

coming today, but I feel weird texting him about Quincy being late if she's just held up in traffic or something. I could take a taxi, though it's far and the fare could be the same cost as my budget airfare.

I'm just about to text Quincy again when a light-gray station wagon pulls up beside me. It stops nearly at my feet, and I'm thinking this nondescript car might be here to abduct me and force me into marrying a cult leader who wears sneakers the same color. I start backing away just in case, as Pete Santana hops out of the driver's seat and jogs around the back of the car to open the trunk.

His hair is short.

It's so short that it's hard to even call it a haircut. It's more like a buzz cut, except for a little extra length on top that he pushes to the side, a reflex that must be left over from the days of his longer locks, because there's hardly anything to push. It makes no difference, though, because he's still just as hot—if not hotter—than he was in college. Dark skin, those gray-green eyes, and full pink lips. It's all still there, and it's infuriating.

"What are you doing here?" I say. I internally kick myself, but blame the shock of his short-haired, still superhot presence for my lack of a better greeting.

"Nice to see you too." He shakes his head at me, already annoyed as he approaches. Still, he wraps his massive arms around me and gives me a light hug.

"Sorry, I was just expecting Quincy," I say into his wide chest. I go to hug him back, but it's already over. I missed it. *Damn.* "Hey, Pete. It's great to see you."

He drops his shoulders with a small sigh. "Hey, Mills." He gives me a tight smile. It's very rare for Pete to let it rip and allow a big genuine smile to fill his face. He smiles, he's not a gloomy guy, but his smiles are small and controlled. Like he's worried if he gives one out, he won't be able to get it back. A familiar feeling rushes through me of wanting nothing more than to make Pete Santana so thrilled he can't help grinning from ear to ear. "Quincy's car broke down. Nothing new, it happens constantly. It's completely impractical that she still keeps that piece of junk around."

"The Bronco? It's such a cool car. How dare it break down on my first day here," I argue, as Pete, without asking, grabs my luggage and starts loading it into the back of his bland wagon.

"She should have planned better. The thing is more or less useless. She keeps it just for the 'Gram." He shakes his head, then closes the trunk. "But it doesn't run. She says it's not that important because she walks most places or borrows Ari's car. But she's a mom. She needs a reliable car."

Ari is Quincy's husband. He runs a landscaping business from what I can gather, which likely means he needs his car every day.

"Why doesn't she just get another car and keep the Bronco for, as you said, the 'Gram?" I ask when we're both seated in his very boring, but very here-and-working car.

"Who knows? Money is a little tight for them, I think. Ari just started his company and everything else. So, she just borrows a ride from me or Amelia when it comes up." Pete shrugs and then turns on the car and cranks the AC. "Or sends me on her errands." He's annoyed. Of course he is. I'm sure he has a life and things he had to do today, none of which involved picking me up from the airport.

I'm suddenly back in college, his sister's sometimes annoying friend who needs help loading stuff in the dorms on move-in day, dragging him away from the library and the studying he needs to do. I always thought we were doing him a favor when we did that or that he liked the reminder that college was supposed to be at least a little fun. It felt important that we, as a group, made sure he graduated with not just a killer GPA, but some actual fun memories. With, you know, people in them.

But I don't feel like that today. I feel like an inconvenience and a chore. But Pete was on the text when Quincy invited me to come here. He was the one who said, "Get out here," so maybe it's not about me. Shocking to admit, but maybe he's not as focused on me as I am on him. He could just be annoyed with Quincy since this seems like something that happens frequently.

I let the car fill with silence. Pete doesn't turn on the radio. So I don't either. Instead, I stare out the window and start getting used to the endless reality that is the California sun while trying to ignore Pete's scent flooding my scenes. He smells like that first gulp of salty sea air after being held down by relentless waves. Inhaling him now is bringing me back to life.

"I think I'm going to have to wear two pairs of sunglasses. Is it always this bright?" I say after a few minutes.

"Pretty much. It's kind of what people like about this part of the country."

"I'm not complaining. I'm just pointing out something completely obvious in a blatant attempt to get you to make small talk with me."

Pete chuckles and shoots me a sideways glance that makes my

breath catch. I may have gotten a laugh out of him, but that's it. He's as annoyingly unreadable as he is invisible online. But I can't sit here and not say stuff for the entire ride. Some people get nervous when they feel like they have to make conversation. I freak out when no one is talking. This is due to the fact that I have so many thoughts racing through my head at any given moment that if there's no direction to the conversation, there's no telling what might get out. And it's worse with Pete right there. After all these years, he's there with those shoulders that look even broader than I remember and thighs that are straining against his well-worn jeans. Surfers are often long and lean, but Pete's natural build looks more suited for rugby than riding waves. He looks so good and he's over there thinking thoughts and it's killing me.

"Do you really want small talk?"

I want anything from you. Luckily, I'm able to keep this thought nonverbal.

"Fine, how about you tell me about Peacock Bay. There wasn't much information online for me to dig into before I left. All I know is it's a great surf spot and people like it there. That leaves a lot of blank space to fill in."

"Yeah, there isn't much online because there's really not much there. The town is tiny, but it's growing. Over the last few years, new businesses have been opening, and closing, pretty regularly," he grumbles.

"But the hotel is doing well, right?"

Pete makes a face. "It's been doing better. The last few years almost killed us, but we're starting to get back on track. Quincy and Alana's outreach has a lot to do with that. They've turned the

Bay into what looks like a surfer's utopia, and I'm not complaining because I'm not sure we would have survived without them."

"But…"

"That's not the real Peacock Bay. It is in a way, but it's a small town and it's struggling." Pete thinks for a second as we approach a traffic circle. I didn't know they had those out here.

"Maybe they're just highlighting the good parts," I say. "A struggling small town in the middle of nowhere isn't exactly going to keep readers coming back for more, but a charming surfers' village…" with guys that look like Pete for residents. Well, that would keep me tuned in.

"I'm grateful. Don't get me wrong," he continues. "But don't you think there's something weird about presenting your entire life to strangers like that? I think Alana even posted pictures of her last home birth." He shivers and I roll my eyes at him.

"Which part skeeves you out the most? The home birth or the lack of privacy?" I want him to address his internet darkness without letting him know that my search history is a list of combinations of his name plus anything I could think of that might lead me to some information about him.

"Both. Her husband is a great guy, and I actually really like Alana too. It's just weird going to a BBQ at their house and then seeing photos posted everywhere the next day."

"Aha!" I exclaim and point a finger nearly in his face.

"Can you put that away?" He waves a hand at my accusatory finger. "I'm trying to drive."

"You admit you are on some kind of social media. You wouldn't know about the photos on Surf Shack Dream House otherwise.

Why can't I find you?" I pick up my phone and start to dig into the Surf Shack Dream House followers. Why didn't I think of that before? While I scroll, I notice I have a few new followers to my new account. I check out their profiles. They look like real people, other bloggers looking for follows back, but they still count. I follow a few back, then check my comments, and I'm surprised to find quite a few waiting for me. Wait, what was I looking for?

"Of course I am. But that doesn't mean I post pictures or want anything to do with followers or friend requests or any of that stuff. I just keep an eye on the hotel stuff and a few local friends. My account is set to private."

Oh right. I was looking for Pete. "Ugh, why even have an Instagram if it's going to be private?" I scoff at him. "Well, I'm a local friend now. You can follow me. Did you see I started a new account? It's called Here to Stay."

His eyes shift from the road to me, quickly. "But you're not here to stay. You're just visiting."

"Way to throw your old friend some support." *Seriously, what's with the technicalities?* "And for now I am. So, for now you can follow me."

"Do I have to?" He narrows his eyes at me, but the corner of his mouth turns up and my stomach warms, thinking I'm close to getting a real smile from him.

Now it's my turn for the side-eye. "Don't worry, I won't include how grouchy the co-owner of the Waveline Hotel is in my posts, if that's what you're worried about."

"I wasn't." His eyes flick over me quickly. "You sit in some paint on the plane or something?"

I look down at my lap and the tiny flecks of paint and scowl at Pete. How did he even notice that? "It's vintage," I explain.

"You paid extra for it to look like that?"

I roll my eyes. Of course he wouldn't remember. Why should he have any memories of me swishing around in this dress trying to get his attention? It's not like I snuck it out of Quincy's closet any night I thought we might see him or anything.

"Man, the California sun doesn't have any effect on *your* mood, does it." Pete Santana is the only person who could maintain his rain-cloud-over-his-head persona in all this sunshine.

He smiles his tiny smile. Still not giving in to it. "I'm just more used to it than you."

The car climbs a large dusty hill, and when we reach the top, Pete pulls over to the side of the road, puts the car in park, and turns off the engine. I turn to him for an explanation. I'm getting warmer after a few seconds with the AC off, and the stillness of the air in the car feels stifling.

"Why'd we stop?" I ask. I'm suddenly really nervous and hyper-aware of the fact that after many years I am now very much alone with Pete Santana. I was not prepared for this today. I thought it was going to be Quincy picking me up, and I didn't think I was going to be parked cliffside with a sexy yet grumbly hotelier.

"You'll see," he says, unbuckling his seat belt. He waits for me to do the same, but I'm not moving without an explanation.

"What's happening? Is this some teenage make-out spot? Are you going to put on the slow jams now?" Why do I have to joke about things I actually want to happen?

Pete's eyes widen and I smile at him. I've forgotten how enjoyable this could be. It used to be one of the highlights of my day to see how uncomfortable I could make Pete with any number of suggestive comments. Once I asked him to button a complicated set of buttons on a dress before we hit the bars, and he nearly lost control of his verbal abilities. It was no coincidence that under my dress was a very elaborate lacy bra in full view during the buttoning. It was fun.

"Get out of the car," he says. It's soft, but low and direct. Exactly how I pictured him saying, "Get out here," over text, and the same way I could imagine him ordering me into his bed. Even though it's unlikely I'll ever hear such an order from Pete, I still like knowing how it would sound.

"Is this some kind of initiation? Do you have to paddle me over the hood of the car before you deliver me to Peacock Bay?"

Pete shakes his head with a hand over his eyes. Then he drags the hand down his handsome face. "Millie, enough with the dirty talk. Get out of the car. I want to show you something."

"Is it the secret Peacock Bay handshake? Are we going to be blood brothers now?" I'm so nervous I can't stop this stuff from tumbling out of my mouth. I must be making him crazy. Clearly, he's having that effect on me.

"Does it get exhausting being you all the time?"

"Sometimes," I tell him with a grin, but I know he's reaching his limit with me so I unbuckle my seat belt and hop out of his sensible automobile.

"Come this way," Pete says, waving me over to his side of the car.

A breeze hits me in the face when I reach him, and the scent of the air is like nothing I've known before. It's crisp but warm at the same time somehow, followed by a salty sweetness that reveals the ocean nearby.

And then I see it. Down below I can see the ocean stretched out to the horizon line, the clear blue sky meeting it at oblivion. Perfect waist-high waves curl one after the other, then chase each other toward the shore. I spot a few lucky surfers bobbing in the lineup waiting for their turns. It's one of the most serene sights I've ever seen, and I'm itching to get down there.

"Welcome to the Cove," Pete says. I turn to him and beam with excitement at the idea that not only will I finally get back on a board, but I'm going to get to do it in this unbelievable setting. It barely looks real. "This is my favorite surf spot in Peacock Bay." His fingertips find the small of my back, guiding me up the slope to get a better view while my throat constricts at his touch.

"Do you surf here every day?" I manage to get out. I'm not sure if I'll murder him out of jealousy if he says yes, or offer to be his live-in maid so I can do the same.

"Most mornings," he answers as a fresh breeze meets our faces.

"I've got to get out there," I murmur. Here's one thing about surfing that I really enjoy. I look fucking great doing it. I look better carrying a surfboard under my arm than I do in a formal gown. I feel sexier balanced on the face of a wave than most women probably do on their honeymoons. I didn't stand out in New York where a woman's success is a part of her appeal. But on a beach, on a wave, in the ocean, that's where I excel.

There aren't that many women who surf well. The numbers keep climbing, but it's still heavy on the dudes. So, when you're a lady who knows what she's doing dropping in on a wave, you feel insanely powerful. I was never going pro, as my parents constantly pointed out, but when you watch *Blue Crush* ten thousand times in your middle school years, you can't escape dreams of surfing as a job. Maybe with this move I could have a career that's surf adjacent. Seeing the waves below curling toward the shore makes me even more determined to make this happen.

"You will, but I have to show you around a little first. There are three parts to the Peacock Bay area. The Hill, the Cove, and the Bay. The Cove is there," Pete's hand lands just under my shoulder and turns me slightly to the right. The heat sears straight to my skin while I say a silent thank-you to the material of this dress for being so thin.

I can hardly imagine waking up every morning and gazing out a window that faces this break. I've never been that big a fan of dawn patrol—I like my sleep—but that view could change my mind. "The Bay is that way. That neighborhood is closer to town and the other beach, which is more crowded, but the waves are usually bigger since it's not as protected as the Cove. And the Hill is north of town, farthest from the beach, but less expensive."

"So the Cove is where you want to be?" I say, turning my head to him. I didn't realize he had leaned in slightly, and we almost bump noses.

"At least you get it." Pete smiles. And I'm nearly knocked over. It took about seven years of friendship and close to three thousand miles of travel, but I have finally seen a huge, sincere smile from Pete. I'd say the trip has been worth it just for that, but I still have some surfing to do.

I take out my phone and snap a few pictures of the Cove, the surfers below, and one with a sliver of Pete's profile in it as he looks out over his home. I couldn't help myself. His eyes are so full of pride and contentment with that smile still playing on his lips as he looks out over the water. I just had to capture it. For Kate and Bree if no one else.

"Can you take a few pictures of me?" I ask him, holding out my phone before he can answer. "Wait, are you sure you can handle this?" Pete's look tells me I have about thirty seconds of his patience left.

"Don't worry." He takes my phone. "I know what I'm doing," he growls. "Just take your stolen apparel and stand over there."

My breath catches in my throat. He remembers the dress. He must. If he knows it used to be Quincy's, he knows I used to wear it. Or that we all did.

Relax. The only thing he's admitting to remembering is my tendency to forget to return borrowed items. He is in no way admitting that he ever noticed the way I looked in this particular dress.

"We shared it. All four of us. It was a communal piece of clothing. I found it while I was packing for the trip." In a box that my brain put a block on and almost never opened again, but you know…details.

"You never offered it to me," he teases.

"You don't have the ass for it," I say and immediately want to smack myself on the forehead. Though his ass is dynamite, I don't need to bring it up this soon upon reuniting.

"That's debatable." He shrugs. "Okay, Sisterhood of the Traveling Dress, let's get this done."

If it weren't for the hint of a smile on Pete's face, I would have immediately reconsidered being here and everything that led me to ask him to take my picture. This has always been our relationship. We're friends, but he can only deal with me in limited doses. I'm always bugging him, always asking just a little too much of him. Always pushing for a little more than he wants to give. As I smile and try to look like this isn't incredibly awkward, I make a silent vow to do things different this time.

Once finished, he hands me back my phone, then digs into his pocket for his own that starts pinging with texts. "I better deliver you to Quincy. She says she's dying to see you."

I smile and take one more look at the waves that are waiting for me down below. I say a silent thanks for Quincy's car trouble because it means this was the way I first got to experience Peacock Bay. Getting a first glimpse of this stunning piece of the California coast, seeing the pride Pete has for the place he grew up and has since returned to. The whole experience has been sort of dreamlike, and I know if I told Kate and Bree about it, they would immediately point to the magic of the dress.

Maybe there is a tiny hint of magic involved. After all, Quincy's car did break down, forcing Pete to pick me up and give me my first introduction to Peacock Bay, and now I'm about to be reunited with my best friend. Okay, dress. I see you. Keep up the good work.

I text the picture Pete took of me to Kate and Bree.

Millie: Proof of life. I'm here!

Kate: The dress looks good in California!

Bree: Send proof of Pete. No one cares about you!

I bite my lip and raise my phone to Pete's back as he walks to the car. I quickly snap a photo, but of course, just as I do, he turns and catches me mid-photoshoot.

"Kate and Bree wanted a picture of…my surroundings," I explain.

"Sure, Mills." Pete rolls his eyes. So much for looking cool and confident in front of Pete. That lasted all of thirty seconds, which is pretty typical when I think back on our time spent together.

Back in the car I'm determined to act less like a spaz, but the only thing I can think to say to Pete is, "Why'd you cut your hair?"

He runs his fingers over the top strands without thinking. "That bad?" His eyebrows pinch together, and I get the sense he's actually asking if I hate it and now I feel guilty. Because *bad* is not even close to the word to describe anything about him.

"No, just a surprise."

"My dad." He shakes his head and rethinks. "He didn't think I could be the guy in charge with long hair. If I wanted to take over, I had to cut it. I waited as long as possible, just to bug him, but last year just before he officially retired and handed things over, I cut it."

I'm dying to reach up and brush my fingers over the back of his neck. I want to see if those short strands are as soft as they look. Instead, I say, "It does make you look very serious."

The smallest corners of Pete's pink lips turn up. "That was the idea."

It's funny that Pete's dad didn't take him seriously with a few extra inches of hair. Pete has never been anything but serious, at least as long as I've known him. I can understand that taking over a big job like running the family business may require a few changes, but I'm surprised that it hinged on a haircut.

We get back in the car, and I start to upload a few of the pictures I took into my Instagram stories. I'm surprised to see a few more new followers and some comments from people I don't know. I wasn't really expecting that.

One thing is for sure.... The grass here actually is greener. Not literally, because it's pretty dry everywhere, but none of this disappoints. Not the ocean or what little I've already seen of Peacock Bay and definitely, most certainly, not Pete.

Chapter
4

IT'S ANOTHER TEN MINUTES UNTIL we reach the Santanas' hotel, where they've so kindly offered me a room at a friends-and-family rate, and where we're supposed to meet Quincy. Quincy wanted Pete to give me a room for free since she felt bad about not having space for me to stay at her house, but I insisted on paying the kindly offered discounted rate, though I don't want to overstay and wear out their generosity. This puts a little extra pressure on me to figure out my life quickly, but I don't want to think about that right now.

When we pull up to the white clapboard hotel, I barely have a chance to look around before I hear a familiar voice calling my name.

"Milllllie," Quincy exclaims as she jogs toward me with a blond baby on her hip. Her light-brown hair is streaked with blond and twisted into a loose side braid that bobs along as she joins us. She looks so cool. She's always had great style, which made her the best kind of roommate, but she seems to have really found her truest fashion inspiration living back in her hometown. She's dressed in a pair of mustard-colored wide-leg pants and a loose white top tucked in just at the front. She has a velvet ribbon in the same French's hue as her pants tied at the base of her braid and a long necklace that looks like it has a pouch on it. I instantly want everything she's wearing. Such is the power of a natural influencer. I immediately feel I have no business being here or trying to join her ranks on social media.

Quincy squeezes me tightly with one arm, jostling the baby in the other, then holds me at arm's length to take me in. Her eyes widen with recognition when she sees what I'm wearing.

"You found the dress," she exclaims.

"I feel like it found me, to be honest." I wish I could say that I was looking for it. That I believed in its power the way my friends do. So far, the only thing I feel about this dress is the guilt I have for forgetting about it and therefore unknowingly keeping it from my friends.

"Well, it's here now. With you in it. You look great." She's trying to boost me up. Quincy is that friend so secure in herself and her ability to ooze coolness that she throws compliments over her shoulder as easily as spilled salt. I haven't even had time to return the compliment when she adds, "I'm sorry about my car and sending Pete to get you. I would have taken his car, but he refuses to get a car seat."

Pete rolls his eyes.

Quincy gives her brother a look, then turns to me. "He prioritizes his surfboards over his own family. Can you believe him?"

"Quincy," he warns. He's reached his limit with our teasing. "I have to get back to work." He turns to head inside.

"Millie?" she asks. Pete stops and turns around to see my

response. I squint and tap one finger to my chin like I'm really thinking it over. Pete rolls his eyes, but I see one corner of his mouth turning up.

"I don't think I can go against Pete here. Dude did just pick me up from the airport. Rescuing me and helping you out."

"Ugh, you always side with Pete," she says. I feel a blush heating my cheeks. I don't, but the guy has some decent ideas sometimes. The Cove was pretty sweet. But I refuse to let her comment hang in the air.

"Though I guess he could get a roof rack and put the boards up top if he had some car seats. How hard is that really, Pete?"

Quincy throws her empty arm around my shoulders and pulls me up next to her. "My girl is back," she exclaims to the sky. The two of us united against the mean big brother. I should be more into it than I am.

Pete stuffs his hand in his cropped hair, exasperated after only a few minutes of being reunited with us. He knows there's a lot more of this to come in the next few weeks, and he must be dreading it.

"Okay, I can see this is headed into a super-fun round of pick-on-Pete, so I'll bring in your bags, Mills, and then I'm getting back to work." His face falls and I think he's more bothered than he's admitting. This has always been our dynamic though. The teasing and joking with each other. The two against one.

I can't let him go without at least thanking him, so I chase him for a few steps and lightly grab his arm. He stops instantly, eyes flicking to my hand, making my whole arm tingle.

"I just wanted to say thanks for the ride and showing me a little of the town. It was really nice."

His face barely changes, but I can almost make out a hint of relief. "I'm glad you thought so," he says. "I'll probably see you later?"

I look back at Quincy, not sure what the plans are for tonight.

"Alana is having a thing. She's really looking forward to meeting you," she explains. I guess Pete already knew about this. Funny, I thought he said he didn't like going to dinner parties at Alana's because of how pictures would show up on social media the next day.

"Great. I can't wait to meet her too." I turn back to Pete. "So, yeah, I'll see you later."

Pete nods, then calls, "Later, Quincy."

"Later, Petesy," she answers, and he's gone with my bags before I can say anything more.

"I forgot about 'Petesy,'" I say about the nickname he hates.

"You probably should try and forget it again. He'd really hate it from you too."

"Yeah, I know. He has enough sisters already. He doesn't need me too."

Quincy looks at me and smiles while she shifts her baby to her other hip. "Right," she says with a shake of her head.

"Anyway, who is this little lady?" I ask.

"This is Clay. Who is a boy," Quincy says, laughing.

"Shit, sorry. I forgot." I can't really keep her kids straight. They both look so much alike. "Tell me the other's name before I embarrass myself more."

"My oldest is Monrow, who is also a boy, just so we're clear."

"You know the names could kind of go either way though, right?"

"That's the way in the Bay." She laughs. "Any kid with a name like Tom or Jen would stick out. We like to be a little more creative around here."

"How old is Monrow?"

"Four," she says, running a hand absentmindedly over the baby's hair. I haven't been in the same place as my friend for years, but I can still tell when something is bothering her.

"What?" I prod.

"I don't know. He's going through a stage right now. He's been so difficult. He's never really been easy, but I'm still hoping he'll grow out of it." Quincy shakes her head like she's trying to shake the thoughts away like cobwebs.

"I'm sure," I say, because what do I know about kids? Pretty much nothing, so I'll side with the mom here.

She sighs. "Anyway, Alana has been planning this pig roast to shoot some Friendsgiving content for the blog and she wanted me to be sure to invite you."

"That's cool of her to include me. But, Friendsgiving? Like Thanksgiving? It's August. Isn't that a little early?"

"Blogger life, Mills. You have to plan and shoot these things months ahead. This is why I will never be as successful as Alana. I just can't be as disciplined as she is. She has everything on a schedule. August is even earlier than she needs to be, but with her pregnancy, I think she wants it all done and ready to post so she's not scrambling when the baby comes."

"You're doing great, Quincy. You have a baby and another kid to be worrying about as well as the blog."

"I'm not doing that great. Plus, Alana has four kids," she counters. "And another on the way."

"But isn't she almost ten years older than us?"

"Sure, sure." Quincy chews the inside of her cheek.

"What?" I ask. There's a piece she's not telling me.

"I haven't exactly been bringing in a lot of revenue on my blog lately. With Ari just starting the landscaping business, we're a little stretched."

"But all those companies sending you things has to help a little."

"In a way. I mean, a free couch is great, but it doesn't buy diapers." She shakes her head, trying to move on. "I have a few things in the works that will hopefully help if they come through. It'll be fine." She doesn't look that sure, but I choose to believe her.

"I'm sure it will be. Where is Monrow by the way? I can't believe I've never met him."

"It's Alana's day for the homeschool rotation. I'll get him when we all meet up for the pig roast."

"Oh right, the homeschool. I remember she featured some of the toys I sent her during a post about it." Quincy, Alana, and their friend Sage take turns hosting a day of homeschool for all their kids during the week. I don't know much about homeschooling, but I do know it must take someone way more patient than me to manage all those different-aged kids and hopefully teach them anything other than how not to kill each other. Frankly, if I had half a dozen small children in my charge for a day, I would consider their survival a victory. "How's that been going?" I know Quincy had reservations about it before they started it last year.

"Fine, I think," she says, but her lips tighten. "They're only together a few times a week" I give my friend a look and wait for her to share more. "I'm not sure it's right for Monrow... He just has so much energy. Or maybe just a different kind of energy…" She lets her thoughts drift, but doesn't elaborate. "Anyway, I got my car working. How about I take you for a drive through town and then show you the beach?"

"Cool, but Pete showed me the Cove already."

Quincy rolls her eyes. "Pete is such a snob. The Cove isn't the only place worth seeing around here."

"It looked pretty great to me," I say.

"It is, obviously. But Pete is so old school. When we were growing up, the Cove was, like, it. But that place is a ghost town. Unless you can drop some serious bank or you don't care if you live in a tiny shack like Pete, no one can afford to live there. Turtle Beach has better waves, and it's easier to get to. Come on, lady. I'm taking you on a tour."

"Better waves for a shortboard, you mean? You want those big glory waves," I tease her. Pete and I always preferred longboards and smaller waves to cruise on. I likely won't be hunting big waves anytime soon, especially since I'm a little out of practice.

"To each their own." She grins and I follow her out to her car, which she's parked in the lot for guests around the side of the hotel.

If I were Quincy, I wouldn't give this car up either. It's mint green with no top, just a white roll bar and cracked tobacco leather upholstery. I just hope it can make it to town and back without breaking down. I'm interested in seeing more beaches, but something tells me I've already seen the best one.

After settling baby Clay (a boy) into his car seat, Quincy tosses that enviable long caramel-and-honey-colored braid over her shoulder and hops into the driver seat. She reaches behind us and grabs two wide-brimmed straw hats. She tosses one on my lap and plops the other on her own head.

"You're gonna want this. Rides in Monty get a little breezy," she says, checking her reflection quickly in the rearview mirror. I check my own reflection in the side mirror, and while I don't look quite as effortlessly cool as Quincy (who really can?), I have that casual coastal vibe that feels right in this place. That's actually not it at all. It's not so much a feeling I'm getting about this place; it's a feeling about myself. I'm not quite sure what it is yet. Maybe it's just being with old friends I haven't seen in a while. Maybe it's the excitement of being somewhere new. Maybe it's just the proximity to the ocean. Or Pete. I'm not sure what it is that has me smiling at my reflection right now. But I'm definitely not mad at it.

Chapter 5

QUINCY TAKES ME FOR A ride through town. She points out a small fair-trade coffee shop, an independent bookstore that buys back your used books when you've finished with them, and an organic, homemade baby-food store.

"How can that place possibly stay in business?" I ask. "Do you really buy your baby food there and not online or at a grocery store?" I give her a look.

"Well, sometimes I do. But usually I make my own." Of course she does. What was I thinking? "That's not all she sells anyway. She has bamboo swaddles, lots of kids' clothes, and hand-knit sweaters. Toys made from recycled plastic or sustainable wood." Quincy glances at my skeptical expression. "It's really a nice shop. Don't look at me like that."

"I'm not looking at you like anything. It sounds exactly like the kind of place the sales team would have tried to sell the Butterfly Bridge toys to. Which means no one is actually buying anything there."

"Well, people around here buy stuff there." She lifts her chin in a fake huff.

"Who's 'she' by the way? Are you friends with the owner? Is that why you shop there? Because you have to?"

Quincy rolls her eyes, then checks on the baby in the back seat. She gives him a grin before answering me. "It's Sage's shop. I'm surprised you don't follow her too."

The name does sound familiar. "I think I follow her, but not the store," I say, opening Instagram to check. Sage doesn't have a blog so I never reached out to her for placements for Butterfly Bridge, but I followed her since she is one of Quincy friends who I've heard so much about. She isn't very active with her account, though, so I think she and the store slipped under my radar. Before searching for Sage, I check the little heart icon to get an update on my notifications. There are a dozen new followers and a lot of comments from people asking if I ever got picked up at the airport and saying things like "vacation fail."

Back on task, I look up the name of the store, simply called Little Goods, and add it to my follows. I scroll through a few of the store pictures. There aren't very many, and the ones posted are lackluster to say the least. One of the front of the store. One of a few folded sweaters on a shelf. One of Alana holding a cup of baby food and a spoon.

"Quincy, what is this store?"

"Sage's shop," she answers, like she's already explained this.

"Yeah, but wow. These are the most boring pictures I've ever seen. How can you let her do this? You guys are seriously shitty friends for not helping her to liven things up."

Quincy laughs. "It's not that bad."

"Okay," I scoff. I study the last picture of Alana. She's dressed in the same color palette as Quincy, the earth tones and mustard yellows. When I take in her grid as a whole, I can see the amount of attention she must put into every detail. All her pictures have at least some of the same colors. White, tan, a little yellow, some green. The wide-leg pants, floral print bandannas, and crumpled straw hats like the one on my head. Even Alana's kids dress this way. And they all look adorable doing it. It all paints a picture of comfort and ease, but a very specific, very admirable style. She makes it look so easy to have what she has. Even if it's completely out of your reach. I may have to steal this hat from Quincy.

"So do you want to see the beach next?" my friend asks.

"Actually, I kind of want to shop. You know, support these small local businesses."

"I'm guessing you're not looking for baby clothes?"

"No." I smile. "I want your pants."

She smiles back. "Ah, she's already settling into the ways of the Bay." She nods. "This we can do."

A few hours later, I've unpacked and changed into new green cotton wide-leg pants that have small patch pockets in the front and a high waist that hugs me in but still lets me breathe. I also have another pair of beige linen pants that are so wide they look like I'm wearing a skirt. Plus, a lacy white cotton dress that's smocked at the top and happens to make my boobs look amazing. I probably shouldn't have spent so much with how limited my funds are, but I got a little caught up in the excitement of being here, and I kept picturing Pete's face when he stood next to me overlooking the Cove. Plus, all my New York clothes feel wrong in the small and casual town.

I borrowed one of the bikes available for hotel guests. They're all new but vintage-looking beach cruisers, each with their own woven baskets on the front of the handlebars. Some even have racks on the sides where you can attach your surfboards. I can't wait to pick out a new board and hitch it up to one of these adorable bikes and take myself to the beach for a morning surf.

Between the kids and her husband, there wasn't room for me in their car, so Quincy gave me directions to Alana's so I could get there on my own. She offered up Pete, again, since he'd be leaving work at the hotel and going straight to Alana's, but I feel like I've asked enough of him for one day. I like to tease him and annoy him on my own terms. I don't actually want to be a pest.

It's nearly four thirty when I arrive. Quincy said they were starting at four, but I couldn't get over the idea that it seemed pretty early for dinner.

"Everyone goes to bed really early here. With little kids and morning surf sessions, people appreciate an early night," she explained. "You'll see. People will start leaving by seven, and everyone will be cleared out completely by eight."

This might take some getting used to.

I park my bike against a yellow picket fence. A fence I've seen in pictures online many times. Decorated with pumpkins before Halloween, strung with lights at Christmas... It's a little surreal seeing it in person now. I snap a quick picture of the cute bike I borrowed perched against the fence, then run my fingers through my hair. I hope it has that effortless windswept look, but my fingers get stuck in the tangles and I give up.

Now off I go to meet Alana Tatamo in real life. We've emailed and talked on the phone many times. She's not Oprah, but in the lifestyle influencer world, she's a thing. I let myself be a little more excited than would be cool to admit. I've seen the pictures of her events on her blog and her Instagram, and they look so beautiful. Now I actually get to go to one. Coming here was a great idea. I would never have seen two different beaches, shopped at such a charming store with brands I'd never heard of, and biked to a dinner party (in the afternoon) if I were still on the East Coast. I would have been at work all that time. I'd still be at work, actually.

I feel a twinge of guilt in thinking about my old office and try to shake the feeling of failure bubbling up in my chest. I can't do that again. I never want to be in a position where I'm working so hard just to see it all fall apart.

I open the gate and follow the noise to the backyard. And there's a lot of noise. Like, so much noise. When I turn the corner, I think first how charming and weirdly familiar the backyard looks. Familiar because I've seen this place a dozen times online, and charming because Alana Tatamo knows how to do it. The firepit is burning, smoke curling artfully in the air as if it wouldn't dare do otherwise. The mismatched chairs that surround it look inviting draped with Turkish towels. Beat-up surfboards lean carefully against the wooden fence that lines the yard. Oddly, or maybe it's not that odd, the surfboards coordinate perfectly with the colors in the throw pillows resting on the chairs, making the whole yard a cohesive color palate of light greens and blues. Of course there are string lights. No self-respecting blogger is going to have a backyard party without them. That doesn't stop me from being totally awed by the amount of thought and care that went into choosing everything that set this scene. My admiration for Alana and her carefully attended aesthetic is real.

The second thing I notice about the yard is that it's epic chaos.

Two toddlers are crying. Some older boys are sword fighting with sticks while standing on chairs and shouting at each other. Another boy is crouched in the corner digging with his back to everyone—I recognize him as Quincy's older son, Monrow—and three or four older girls are screaming at each other, half of them nearly in tears. The other two cross their arms over their chests and stomp off toward the adults. I'm guessing to report whatever injustice has taken place. I recognize the girls who stomped off as Alana's oldest two, Lake and Tiegen. It feels weird knowing their names on sight when they have no idea who I am, but I feel like I've watched them grow up over the last few years. Which, truthfully, I have.

I remember when her son, Miles, was born. I sent him a Butterfly Bridge fire truck with his name burned into it like a brand. Now I think he's one of the sword fighters. I remember when one of the girls had to get stitches after a fall and how brave she was. I've seen the girls struggling to learn to knit, but watched as they persisted and finally presented their mom with a pair of adorably lumpy socks.

However, this scene isn't like Alana's Instagram. Her posts are always of the kids embracing each other with big smiles and *reunited* or *lovebirds* written over their heads. By the looks of it, these kids would be grateful for some time apart. Or to never see each other again.

Still, the setting is stunning. I focus on continuing to admire that.

Now that I'm here, I wish I had taken Pete up on that ride. I've never had a problem going to a party alone, but that was when I knew the people who were going to be there. I miss Kate and Bree instantly. I miss the feeling of walking into a party and seeing their familiar faces smile at me. I resist the urge to duck into a corner and text them just to look busy. I wanted to come here and have an adventure, so time to get going. I just assumed Quincy would be one of the first faces I'd see when I arrived, but as of now there's not one face that is familiar to me, unless it's one I know from online stalking. My heart starts beating rapidly as I scan the backyard again, and then I let out a huge sigh in relief as I spot one person I know.

"Amelia, you have no idea how happy I am to see you," I say to Quincy and Pete's older sister as I approach.

"Millie, yay! It's so good to see you. It's been years." She hugs me, then leans down to pick up a small child I didn't notice before. Likely, because it's so quiet, unlike its compatriots.

"I know, not since you visited Quincy our senior year." It's funny how all these memories are coming back now that I'm with these old friends.

"That was a crazy weekend," she says. Her dark eyes shift around. She might not want to get too into the details of that weekend. I think she had a fight with her then boyfriend. Pete was long graduated by then, and without him around, Quincy and I took senior spring to a new level. But it all worked out for Amelia because that boyfriend is now her husband, so clearly running off to party with her sister in college made him realize what a good thing he had. "I don't think I remember that much of it."

"Me either, to tell you the truth," I say, and we laugh.

"That's probably for the best. I wouldn't want Clark to have to hear stories of me on some rebellious, misspent weekend. Not that spending time with you guys was misspent."

"Don't worry about it. Most of my time is college was misspent." I sigh. "Those were good times."

"Dah!" the baby Amelia is holding exclaims and points in my direction. She's one of the cutest things I've ever seen. I turn around to make sure it's me she's talking to, and Amelia laughs.

"Hi!" I respond to the baby, because that seems to be what she wants.

"Dah," the baby says again, looking slightly over my shoulder again.

"I feel like she's trying to hit on the girl just behind me at the bar," I tell Amelia as I glance back again.

"She's just looking for her main squeeze. This is Claire, my youngest and only girl. We went a little rogue on the name, but I always wanted to name a girl after my grandmother."

I shrug. Claire seems like a perfectly nice name to me.

"She's so cute." I'm not even lying. She's a really cute baby. She has a tuft of blond hair that sweeps down over her gray-green eyes, a Santana family trait.

"How did you and Quincy both get these blond children?"

Amelia laughs. "Blond husbands, and I think Mom's Australian roots found their way through."

"Lucky girl." Mrs. Santana is a total babe. I wouldn't mind that lineage for my kids. "How old is she?"

"She just turned thirteen months. And…" Amelia looks over

her shoulder at the pile of boys behind her. "Sorry, would it be totally weird for me to ask you to hold her while I grab Tasher? We have to go pick up my two other boys from school in Vera Lake. They stay for baseball after school, but it'll take forever to get there with the Friday traffic."

"If you're okay leaving your baby with someone who thought taking off her bra for you to puke into was a brilliant idea, then sure." I hold out my arms to the baby with a blink and a grin. "I'm here for you."

"Oh man, you do remember." Amelia grimaces, but still hands over her only daughter to me. "Well, if you were that nurturing back in college, you're probably a wizard now. You had the right instincts."

The baby doesn't seem to mind me holding her. She scans my face, then acknowledges me by playing with my necklace. She seems pretty unconcerned that a near stranger now is responsible for her. Amelia takes off toward the sword-fighting boys and starts making her pleas for one of them to get his things so they can go. He has no shoes or shirt on so, by the looks of things, this might be a while.

I decide to take baby Claire over to the chairs and sit with her. When I sit, I turn her on my lap to face me. She's supercute. And chill. She hasn't made a peep really since I've met her. This is my kind of baby. She even looks a little like me. I realize it's incredibly vain to think this very cute baby and I look alike. It's just that our hair is similar and our eyes match a little bit. I should send a picture of us to my mom and see if she thinks Claire looks like me when I was a baby.

I snap a picture with Claire and text it to my mom. She responds seconds later.

Mom: Whose baby is that? Do they know you took her?

I exhale deeply. I should have known better.

Instead of responding to my mom, I pose with Claire for another picture. I sort of swoop my hair across my forehead to match hers and take a few more photos and send them to my mom. I'll let her think that in addition to becoming a surf bum, I'm also pursuing a career as a professional kidnapper.

"Yeah, hi. Sorry, but this party is embargoed. You can't take any photos," says a voice calmly and sweetly, but also firmly and clearly not messing around. "Also, who the fuck are you?"

I look up and see Alana Tatamo standing above me in all her floral maxi-dress glory. Her black hair is down and straight, with her signature bangs in a perfect neat line just above her eyebrows. She's holding the hand of her miniature self, her daughter Mavis, who I again recognize from the blog. Alana's Hawaiian and Japanese genes are so strong that all of her children are basically her clones. Her husband, another blond California surfer guy, didn't stand a chance this time. Which is another weird thing to know about a person who doesn't know my name.

"Oh, sorry," I say, getting to my feet. "I'm Millie. We talked on the phone when I worked at Butterfly Bridge. Quincy's friend? Sorry about the picture. I had no idea." I still don't, but I don't need to admit that.

"Oh, Millie, of course. I should have realized." Alana reaches out and hugs me. "There usually aren't people I don't know at my event shoots, so I was caught a little off guard. It's really nice to meet you finally."

"You, too, and thanks for inviting me. This is so dreamy. How did you find fall leaves here in August?"

"Oh, they're fake," she scoffs, with a wave like it should have been obvious. "I spray-painted them to get the color right." She says it like it was the simplest thing in the world. Instead of an intensive and messy project I would likely never attempt.

"Well, you fooled me. Everything looks beautiful."

"Oh good. Good." She bites her lower lip and nods a few times. "I'm glad you think so." She keeps her lip between her teeth as she scans the yard, probably checking everything is in order. "I need to get things to the next level with the blog this year. I'm not fucking with little sponcon anymore, you know? Clothing and product lines, it's all possible. More now than ever and shit, well…"

"You wanna get some of that bread," I say, because aside from all the swear words, Alana is speaking my language. It's no surprise she's savvy in this little corner of the internet, and I know I can learn a lot from her.

Alana laughs. "Something like that. You must have seen a lot when you were working at Butterfly Bridge. I'm so sorry that didn't work out, by the way. They were nice toys."

"Yeah, just too expensive to produce and sell for the regular market." I know on some level I didn't cause the company to fail, but I was a big part of the team as they crumbled. It's hard not to feel like maybe if someone else had been in my job, someone who didn't have the problems focusing that I have, things might have turned out differently.

Mavis tugs on Alana's hand. She's wearing a green cotton pinafore in a soft, textured weave with no shirt underneath. Her hair is tied in a loose topknot. She's more stylish at three years old than I might ever be, but most of the kids at this party look like they were styled by their parents, or maybe they just all shop at the same store. It must be Sage's stuff. You'd think with the internet they'd have more options, but everyone in the same color palette does make for a pretty picture. I'm even gladder I wore my new green pants. I want to slide right into my own place in this picture.

"Hold your business, Mav," Alana shoots down to her mini me with a wink. "So what are your plans now?"

I'm a little surprised how quickly Alana went for this question. I figured the casual surfer-village life would be less about the hustle. That's what I get for making assumptions. "Honestly, nothing. I just want to surf and be lazy for a while. I'm posting on Instagram, I guess as something to do. It's called Here to Stay." Why don't I want to act like I care too much about my Instagram account to Alana? Heaven forbid I show I'm putting effort into something, only to watch as it fails like everything else I get involved with.

Alana gives me a tight smile and nods. I can tell she's not impressed with my "just surf" response, but Alana is big time. She didn't create one of the biggest lifestyle blogs by just surfing, and I'm not trying to insult her.

"It would be great if I could get a following going, of course, so if you have any tips…"

"Oh, you know, authenticity is key. Connecting with your followers helps. Respond to comments and DM's at least at first, if you can."

"Okay, sure." Sounds reasonable.

"You can't take any pictures here tonight because I can't have anything go up online before I do my post, but I'll tag you in one of my teaser posts. That might help."

"Really? That would be amazing." It's a really generous offer to include me, especially since we barely know each other.

Alana waves me off. "It's nothing." She puts a hand on her stomach, which I then notice has a slight roundness. "Ugh, I'm so fucking queasy. Again, you can't say anything. My friends all know, but I haven't announced it yet. I'm planning a big baby-reveal thing in a few weeks. That you can post about when the time comes. I'll want a lot of cross-promotion."

"No problem, but could I ask... What's a baby reveal? Doesn't that kind of thing happen, you know, at birth?"

Alana laughs. "Fair, but influencers like us have to plan some-thing to announce to our followers that we're expecting again. It keeps people engaged during the course of the pregnancy. I'm announcing this baby later than usual though. My ad calendar has been packed this year."

My eyes widen. I had no idea how calculated it all was. "I don't know how you keep all of it straight."

"Mostly, I don't." She laughs, but it's strained. She looks around again, and I feel like I've taken up too much of her time. She must have a lot going on with the party. "We're just all trying to do our part to keep the town afloat."

I don't have time to ask what she means because Amelia returns, dragging a shirtless boy by the wrist behind her, his shoes in her hand. She holds out her other arm to Claire, who has been so quiet I hardly noticed I was still holding her.

"This child is angelic," I say to Amelia.

"You're welcome to her anytime." She grins. "Especially when I have to shuttle the boys back and forth to school or practice."

"I wouldn't mind babysitting if you get in a jam sometime. I did a lot of babysitting back home in the summers." One of the only jobs I managed to hold on to was babysitting for tourists in the summers. Plus, it's the least I can do to help her since her family is putting me up at their hotel so affordably.

Amelia starts to back away, still wrestling her shirtless son along with her.

"I may take you up on that." She smiles.

"But I still get first dibs." My body stills at the voice. I turn to see Pete coming toward us, and I'm covered in goose bumps. It might be awhile before the sight of him doesn't completely overwhelm me. He plants a little kiss on Claire's head, then grabs the boy and tosses him over his shoulder like he weighs nothing. This tiny display of familial devotion with sheer masculine strength has me breathing much heavier than I was five minutes ago. "You going to get the big guys, Amelia? I'll help you get this monster in your car." Then he meets my eye and gives me his tiny, tight smile. "Hey, look, Millie's here."

"I know, isn't it fun?" Amelia says, waving goodbye to me and Alana as she tosses a large bag over her shoulder.

"I think it is," Pete says. His eyes are unreadable, but they don't leave mine as he backs away with the squirming boy over his shoulder.

Me too, Pete. Me too.

Chapter
6

A FLASH GOES OFF IN my face, temporarily making stars pop in front of my eyes. It's been happening pretty regularly all evening, but it still catches me off guard. My eyes refocus and I'm able to redirect my attention to my overflowing plate of Thanksgiving food. Which is a little odd in early August, but I'm never going to complain about stuffing and mashed potatoes. Especially when it's made by Alana's husband, who's a chef at his own restaurant in town. The menu reads like a Thanksgiving wet dream. Aside from the roasted pig instead of turkey, it's all pretty traditional. Three-cheese mashed potatoes, butternut squash with sage butter, and to drink, a cranberry and orange bourbon sour. I don't know what to eat first, so I dive into all of it.

"It's a little like being at the world's weirdest wedding, right?" Pete leans in and murmurs.

"A very trippy Thanksgiving-themed wedding. One where the bride and groom don't know it's their wedding and keep posing with the food and decor. In August."

Pete grins and then digs into his plate again. Alana has a

professional photographer here to get the shots she wants for her posts. I'm sure the photographs will be beautiful, but it does make me feel a little like a prop and less like a guest at a party. Which I guess I kind of am. It seems like I'm the only one not used to it, because everyone else around me is chatting and enjoying the food and company while the kids continue to run around playing. How they haven't gotten tired yet is downright fascinating.

"It's too bad Amelia couldn't stay," I say to Pete. I'm trying to embrace the nice night and focus less on feeling like an extra in a movie. "It was fun seeing her again. I guess her kids must keep her pretty busy."

"Yeah, since they started going to school in Vera Lake, we hardly ever see her for more than a minute. She works three mornings a week at the hotel, so I get a glimpse of her more often, but that's about it."

"She didn't want to do the homeschool thing like Alana and Quincy?"

Pete gives me a look. "Is that what Quincy says it is? Homeschooling?" He thinks for a second. "Well, maybe it is. I've never really asked. But I think Amelia and Clark had had enough 'homeschooling' after 2020. They even debated leaving Peacock Bay and moving closer to the boys' school, but I think Amelia wanted to stay close to family and the hotel for now. She's definitely a flight risk though."

"What about you?" I ask him. "Are you a flight risk? Do you ever see yourself living somewhere else?"

"Not really. I tried living 'away from the Bay,' but it didn't really appeal to me. And I always wanted to run the Waveline. You know that."

Pete is the second youngest, but the only boy. I know part of the reason he worked so hard in school was to prove to his parents he was responsible enough to take over. I don't think he had too much competition from his oldest two sisters, but he might have gotten lucky that Amelia got so busy with her kids. Which seems a little unfair if you ask me. I know she still plays a big role with the marketing of the Waveline, but I wonder if she ever wishes she was able to make more of an impact in its ultimate success.

"The Waveline has always been what you wanted?"

"Yep, it's gone through a lot of ups and downs, especially in the last few years. It means a lot to me to be the one to bring it back up. When we were in college, my dad threatened to sell it. I'm not sure if you knew that."

I shake my head. "I didn't."

"Yeah, it wasn't doing that well, and I don't think he thought I could handle it."

"You?" I say, shocked. If anyone is going to put everything he has into something he believes in, it's Pete. I may not have given my parents reasons to believe in me, but Pete always did. "He clearly doesn't realize who he's dealing with then."

He dips his head, but smiles at my compliment. "Thanks. Maybe you can tell him that next time he calls to check our occupancy numbers. But I'm the second youngest. A baby in our family, and that's sort of the way my dad still sees me."

"Man, do I know what it's like for your parents not to trust you to adult on your own." I don't give my parents a lot of reasons to believe I can handle things like an adult, but I'm surprised Pete's dad sees him this way.

Pete's eyes meet mine and he holds my gaze for a brief moment. I can't tell exactly what he's thinking, but it feels so nice just having him look at me after so long. I don't want to lose his attention so I keep talking. "Your grandfather was the one to open the hotel, right?" I know it's been in the family a long time, but I'm a little fuzzy on the details.

"Not quite. My great-grandfather moved from Mexico with my great-grandmother when my grandfather was a little kid. Did you know that part of the story?"

I nod. I'm not an expert on Santana family history, but I know a little from Quincy.

"My great-grandfather worked at the hotel, which was owned back then by a guy named Peter Winslow."

"Peter." I feel my eyes light up in recognition. I turn in my seat and cross my legs, angling slightly toward him.

"You got it," he says with a nod. "Peter Winslow was a great guy, but he wasn't a great businessman. He kept the hotel way over-staffed so that he could give as many people jobs as possible, which was well intentioned, but the hotel couldn't support all the staff and he nearly went bankrupt."

"How did your grandfather come into the picture?"

Pete shifts in his seat so he's facing me better. I reach for my drink to wet my suddenly dry throat. I take a sip and feel Pete's eyes on my throat as I swallow. "He came back from college, the first in the family to go, and Peter sold him what was left of the place for not even close to what it was worth. Helped figure out the loans and everything. My grandfather turned the place around. He made the Waveline into what it is today and taught me everything I know about business."

"And then your dad took over and kept it going?"

Pete makes a face. "Not as much. My dad grew up here. He was a California kid whose parents ran a successful hotel. He wanted to travel the world and surf. He wasn't as interested in running the family business, but he was the only boy and my grandfather was pretty old school." He shrugs. "He did everything a certain way, and it worked for him."

"But your dad wasn't as into it?" I sip my drink again as Pete props his arm on the back of his chair, inching closer so we're nearly knee to knee.

"My grandfather told him that after college he could have two years to do whatever he wanted, which was pretty generous. Then he had to come back and learn how to run the hotel."

I know this part of the story. "That's when your parents met! Your dad was surfing in Australia and met your mom. He convinced her to move back with him, and they ran the hotel together." I've only met them a few times, but Pete's parents are relationship goals, and his mom is a total knockout. I'm pretty sure she was an Australian model when they met, and there might be a story about how she thought Peacock Bay was closer to Hollywood and that she'd be able to still have a career as a model or something. She laughs about it now, but I would have been pretty pissed to find out LA is over six hours away and that I'd have to give up my career chances.

"They did, but my dad never really cared about it. He kept things afloat, but barely. He idolized the way Peter did things and wanted to provide as many jobs as possible for people just starting out, which I want to do, too, but I'm not going to overhire and bankrupt my family's business again. We've almost lost this place a few times, and running it is the only thing I've ever wanted to do. I'm not sure what my life would be like if we lost the hotel." Pete runs a hand over his hair. He's stressed just thinking about this, and I'm a little sorry I dug so deeply into it.

"Does your dad still have a hand in running things?"

"Not really. About a year after Amelia and I got a handle on everything, my parents took off for Australia. My mom always wanted to move back. Her whole family is there, and my dad loves it too. We could never spend much time there before because someone always needed to keep an eye on the Waveline. They check up on us a lot though." He sighs.

He probably could do with less of this. "Is that good?" he asks, pointing at the drink in my hand. Instinctively, I hold it out for him, and to my surprise, he takes it and sips right from my glass. I watch in awe as the cords of muscle in his throat tighten as he swallows. Then I nearly die as he licks his lips and hands the drink we're now sharing back to me.

"So what does the Peter Santana era of the Waveline look like?" It comes out a near whisper while I let my thumb trace the spot on the rim where his mouth was. I'm praying he doesn't notice, but his eyes flick quickly to my fingers and I freeze.

There's a hint of a smile on his face, and I feel like our bodies are having one conversation while our mouths have another one entirely. "I'd like to run a business we can all be proud of. I'm not doing it alone, thank god. I've got Amelia, and even Quincy helps in her way." Why do I find it so sexy that when he acknowledges his sisters' help? "My dad is constantly telling me to add more staff. He always says that if someone hadn't done that for his grandfather, we wouldn't be here, and I get that. But I also have to run things my way. A profitable way. I can't be the one who lets the place fail. I won't."

Something about the set of his jaw and the determination in his eyes stirs something in me. I can relate to this so much.

I sip the drink again and freeze when Pete's eyes flick from the glass to my lips. The corners of his mouth turn up while I swallow, and I almost choke on an ice cube.

When I'm able to speak again, I have a new question in mind. "You never had a backup plan? Never considered doing anything else?"

Pete's eyes meet mine. "Nope," he says with not a hint of doubt. "I have everything I want right here."

I swallow hard, trying to ignore the dull ache between my legs as another bright flash goes off too close to our faces. We blink at each other as stars burst in my eyes, swirling my vision. Pete's lips part, about to add something else, when the guy on his other side taps him on the shoulder with a question about the new cyber-security software they're using at the hotel. Pete's eyes sweep my face one last time before he turns away completely to answer. The photographer's flash has broken the spell.

Quincy arrives halfway through dinner because of car trouble again, and she brings Sage with her, the friend who owns the baby-food store.

Pete gets up from the table around the time people start collecting their kids to take them home. The sun has started to hint at setting, and just as Quincy predicted, the guests take this as their cue to leave. Sage and I are chatting while we watch the adults go into kid-wrangling mode, and I notice she doesn't have any with her. I've seen them on her Instagram, so I know they exist and don't feel too weird asking of their whereabouts.

"They're with my husband," she responds simply, but her eyes shift around. "They went surfing and, uh, out for dinner." She says this like she's ashamed to admit it. Though I would have thought this was a pretty understanding crowd when it came to skipping events for epic waves.

"Do they love surfing too?" I ask.

She nods and shakes her long, stick-straight dark hair over her shoulders. "They do, but just to be difficult, they claim they love skiing and snowboarding even more. I'm originally from Colorado, and we started teaching them when they were little."

"Ha, I like that. They like what's not as readily available. There are probably a bunch of kids freezing in Colorado that would gladly trade places with them. How old are they?"

"Nine and eleven. They're pretty good, actually, which is the problem. They've been pushing us to let them live with their grandparents so they can focus on skiing. Which I think is nuts, but my husband... Never mind, I'm boring you."

"No, not at all. Would your parents mind having your girls stay with them?"

She smiles. "Not at all. They always wanted me to be more focused on skiing, but I wasn't that into it. I was always destined for the sun and surf." She smiles. It seems like she's really found her home here, and I fight off some jealousy. I never thought I'd like a small town after growing up in Nantucket, but even after just one day, I can tell there's something special here.

"You know"—Sage, shakes her glossy black hair over her shoulder again while she changes the subject—"I could really use your advice. Quincy says you worked in marketing and, um, my shop needs help." She tries to form a casual smile, but I can tell she wants me to take her seriously. "I really need to increase my online orders. There are only so many people in town who are going to shop with me. Any chance you want to give me some free advice?"

"I can try. Though you do know I'm here because the company I was doing marketing for laid me off and is likely about to go under, right?" I don't want her to think I can save her business if I can't. It's not as if my track record for pulling business from the brink is that good.

Sage smiles. "I know, but I'm sure you know more than I do."

"I don't know about that. Don't you have something like five thousand followers on Instagram?"

"Not quite," she says, looking down. "Alana has come in and posted about the store a few times, which has given me a little boost, but every time I get another thousand followers, it feels like so much more pressure to produce some exciting content that I freeze. I don't know what anyone wants to see so I don't post anything, and then my follower count drops again."

It's a problem I'd love to have, but it sounds like Sage has stage fright with all those digital eyes on her.

"Would it help if you don't post about yourself or your family? Maybe just focus on posting about the store? New shipments. Do some flat lays of cute products styled together. Or repost anyone's kids who are wearing stuff from your store. People love to be included in those things."

"That's a good idea. Maybe I can do something when I get the new fall collections in. A contest or something." She puts a finger to her mouth and chews a nail, thinking.

I nod. Maybe I *can* help her a little. She seems a little lost, but "a contest or something" is better than nothing. It's a place to start at least. "You're a natural at this stuff. You don't need me." I'm trying to encourage her. "Just don't give away too much for contests if you can't afford it." I don't want Little Goods to be another Butterfly Bridge. Not on my watch. Not again.

"So, I should probably stop giving my friends such big discounts on stuff at the store, huh?"

I fold my arms over my chest and look at her seriously. "Well, let me ask you this: Do you enjoy feeding yourself and your family?"

Sage puts a hand over her face. "I know, it's killing me, but I feel weird asking them to pay full price. Especially if they're going to tag me in posts."

"Sage, don't feel bad. I doubt you opened your store so you could treat your friends to free stuff. Everyone will understand that you need to make a profit. Maybe you can let them shop a sale a few days early. You don't owe them a discount forever." I put my hands on her shoulders. She's petite. A few inches shorter than me and I feel a natural urge to protect her. "You can do this."

"I can do this," she repeats with a nod. But she sounds less than convinced.

"How about I come by tomorrow and we can play around with some product posts? What time do you open?"

"Oh, well, sort of whenever…"

"Right." I narrow my eyes at her. "So I'd think about getting on more of a regular schedule with store hours. As a thought."

Sage laughs. "I know, and we have a sign with hours posted, but sometimes it depends…"

"On…"

Sage looks at me with a look like it should be obvious. "The waves."

With that word, it's as if she's summoned people into our conversation.

Quincy sidles up with Alana not too far behind her. Pete even turns toward us to gather any wave-related information.

"What are the waves doing tomorrow?" Quincy asks. "Has anyone checked the surf report yet?" She pulls out her phone to start her own search when no one answers.

"No pictures," Alana reminds her. Quincy nods with an eye roll, clearly used to this reminder.

"The Cove should be good in the morning," Pete calls out, then slides his phone in his back pocket.

"Not all of us can get to the Cove in the morning. There are small children that need feeding," Quincy fires back without looking up. "There might be some decent waves in the afternoon. We can take shifts."

"We trade off at the beach," Alana explains to me. "Someone watches the kids while they play and a mom gets a little surf session. Then we switch."

"That's so nice." I smile, but then I remember I'm still without a board. "But I need to get a new board before I can join in. Where do you guys like to shop for boards around here?"

Alana waves her hand at me. "Oh, don't buy a board. A company that wants to send me a new board just reached out. I can just give to you."

"Really? That's so nice of you. Is it a longboard?" I don't want to sound ungrateful because a free surfboard is nothing to turn my nose up at, but a lot goes into choosing a surfboard. What's good for Alana might not be right for me, and who knows what size it'll be or what it's made of. Still, it's really nice of her to offer it to me when she doesn't need to.

"I think so?" She shrugs. "I'll check and let you know. It shouldn't be long before it's here."

"You can borrow a board from me in the meantime, Mills," Pete adds. "I have a few longboards. One might work for you."

"Pete has a million boards, Millie," Quincy says. "Just take one from him."

"I have four." Pete rolls his eyes at his sister.

"If that's cool with you," I tell him. "I'd really appreciate it."

"Sure." He shrugs. "So, you coming to the Cove tomorrow morning then?"

"Now, when you say 'morning,'" I start. "What hour specifically are you referring to?"

"Six a.m.," Pete says, flatly.

"Yikes. Better get me to bed then," I say to Pete, and my cheeks instantly heat. "I mean, we better get to bed. Wow. I mean, I should go to sleep, like, now. If I want to get up that early."

Pete's face twists, mocking me. "Better get to bed."

I start backing away because if I stay here any longer, I'm going to continue making accidental sexual innuendos to my good friend's brother in front of said friend and other people who only just met me and may not as easily brush off the things I say.

"I'll see you in the morning," I say.

"Six a.m.," he reminds me, like a stern professor who just gave me a deadline on a paper. I've never had professor-student fantasies until this exact moment.

"Have you heard about the new one? People are calling it seven? I hear it's really deluxe, the new and improved early morning hour."

"Six a.m.," he repeats with a teasing rise in his brows. The memory of the back of his fingers grazing my knees floods my mind and brings a flush to my cheeks.

"I'll be there," I say, sighing. I thank Alana and say goodbye to Quincy. I make plans to meet Sage at her shop around noon to play around with some Instagram posts, and then retreat to my bike.

The air is still warm while I bike along the path that brought me to Alana's and will deliver me past the beach and to the Santana family hotel. When I get to Turtle Beach, I can't help but stop to take a few pictures as the last bit of sun sets. I post those pictures to my main feed. I watch the photos upload, then wait to see any movement in my notifications, but I exhale slowly through puffed cheeks as little comes.

I type out a quick text to Kate and Bree, begging them to like and comment on my posts, and try not to feel like a complete loser while asking for this favor. My finger hovers over the send button, but I can't quite follow through. Hitting Send feels like admitting I don't know what I'm doing. It's putting down in writing that things aren't going well and I should quit before I embarrass myself. I'm not sure I'm ready to have this conversation with my friends, and I'm definitely not ready to admit it to myself.

I delete the text of desperation and slide my phone back into my pocket before getting back on my bike. Just as I'm about to pedal off again, a sensible gray station wagon drives by. The horn honks, and he slows down. I almost think he's going to stop and offer me a ride. My heart starts beating rapidly. Being in the car with Pete in the daylight is one thing, but at dusk on the way to my hotel room…it's too much. It would feel suggestive. I mean, his face would be right there. I'm not sure I could stop myself from dragging my fingers down the stubble on his cheeks if we were alone in near darkness outside a hotel.

It turns out I don't have to worry about it because he doesn't stop. His brake lights release and he continues down the road without stopping. But before he disappears he lifts a hand out of the sunroof. A tiny wave to let me know he's seen me.

Tucked into bed in my hotel room that night, I check my Instagram one last time before going to sleep. I have only one new follower, and the sight of the name makes me sit straight up in the comfortable Waveline bed. One tiny sentence and my entire body feels like it's been struck by lightning.

> **@waveline_pete** is following you.

I squeeze my eyes closed as I smile like a grommet on her first wave and click Follow back. My heart is pounding, and I know it will take me hours to fall asleep now. Worth it.

Chapter 7

COOL WATER CRASHES OVER MY shoulders as I struggle to gather the massive board I borrowed from Pete under my arm and haul it to shore. It's a good thing I didn't sell my wet suits because the water is a little colder than I expected, and since I spent so much of my surfing time falling into said cold water and less time riding actual waves, the full-length suit has proved essential.

My shoulders ache and my legs feel like jelly as I heave the beautiful Robert August board Pete lent me under my arm. I did not do this custom board justice, and to prove my point, another wave crashes onto my back and nearly knocks me over. *You will not win, ocean.* I'm only in waist-high water now, but the current is so strong and the waves won't hit pause for even a second, even when I ask really nicely. I just want out of here. I've already looked like a complete fool for most of this morning. Just let me get out of this water with a tiny sliver of dignity.

Another wave, bigger than the last, slams into me and this time succeeds in toppling me over. I land hard on the sandy ocean floor. The massive board slips out of my arms. I put my arms over my head to protect myself in case the board, still attached to my ankle by the leash, is washed into me. The last thing I need is to end up unconscious in the water. I feel the board being pulled away by the water, and I brace myself for it to come back and bang into my body at some angle that will surely leave me with a painful bruise. I feel another tug on my ankle, but the board doesn't come back.

I manage to get to my feet after a few more seconds and push the tangled mess of my salty hair away from my face. When I'm up, I see Pete standing a few feet away with both boards under his arms. More used to the water temperatures than I am, he wears only a midi suit. Beads of this relentless ocean dot his muscled forearms as he holds two huge surfboards like they're made of air.

"Are you okay?" he asks, his face creased with sincere concern. I must have really looked helpless if he looks that worried. "I would have ditched the boards, but I didn't want you to get pummeled by them. I figured you'd get up easier on your own if I got them out of the way."

"I'd like a refund, sir," I say as another smaller wave crashes into my legs. I reach down and rip off the Velcro around my ankle that's attached to the leash and fling it at Pete's chest. "Whose stupid idea was surfing? Did I really like this once?"

Pete laughs. "You're just out of shape."

"Excuse me?"

"Not like that," he backpedals. "Not your body. That's perfect. I mean, you're fine. In fine shape for life or whatever." I wish I could enjoy seeing him stumble over his words more, but I'm still fighting the current, which is now trying to own my knees. A few more steps and it's like someone has taken the weights off my legs. The ocean has released me. I rush onto shore and collapse facedown on the sand where we left our towels, not caring in the slightest that I'm adding sand to my salty ocean hair. "The current gets really strong at this time of morning. It can make the paddle back to shore really hard. You'll get used to it. You just need a little more practice. You caught some good waves out there, Mills. Next time try to ride one to shore so you don't have to paddle in."

"Are you still talking?" I say into the towel I have pressed against my face. I regret it instantly, especially when I look up and see the hurt in Pete's face. "I'm sorry. Really. I'm just pissed. Or disappointed. I don't know. I know it's been awhile since I've surfed, but I thought it would just come right back to me."

"It did. You looked great out there. I'm not sure you're going pro anytime soon, but you can hang."

"I'm not nearly as good as I was."

"No one is, Mills."

"You are," I grumble. "You're better than you used to be."

Longboarding isn't about flashy tricks and three-sixty spins, so there are not a lot of obvious ways to show off your abilities, but there is a style to it, and Pete has that dripping off him when he's on his board. If I hadn't just gotten completely worked, I would have found it very sexy.

"That's only because we hardly surfed in college." None of us did. The area around the University of North Carolina isn't known for its waves. We made a few overnight trips to Wilmington, but for the most part, the Santanas got their fill at home.

"I bet Quincy is probably pulling all kinds of air and crazy tricks these days."

"Quincy hardly ever gets on a board. Mostly, because she's busy with her kids. It's not because she doesn't want to. Though Ari always makes time for it somehow. I'm not sure why Quincy doesn't too."

"She's always posting pictures from the beach though. I know I've seen tons of pictures of her with boards at the beach and videos of Ari and the kids getting pushed into the whitewater."

"Videos she took sitting on the beach. It's pretty rare she takes an afternoon with no kids and just surfs."

"I think you have to cut her a break. She's got her hands full. Surfing just isn't her priority right now. It's not a crime."

"That's what I mean. With the baby and what they have going on with Monrow… It's all falling down on her, and I think she'd be happier if she took some time for herself once in a while."

"I didn't see you offering to babysit so she can go surfing. And what about Monrow?"

"Nothing. I shouldn't have brought it up. And watching her kids isn't the same as chilling with baby Claire for an hour. Quincy's kids are a different story."

I know these are Pete's nieces and nephews. so he knows them better than I do, but little Clay seemed fine to me. I'm not going to raise my hand to babysit a whole bunch of little kids quite yet, but maybe if I get my feet wet with a Claire, I could volunteer later on. But since he brought up all the kids…

"It's funny how the kids don't seem to get along that well. Last night they seemed like they were going to rip each other's faces off at times."

"Oh yeah, the older ones, right?" Pete says it so casually, like he's seen them like this one hundred times, so I'm guessing it's old news.

"But Alana's posts make it look like they're all so close."

"Come on, Mills. Haven't you figured it out yet? It's a bunch of bullshit."

"What is?"

"Seriously? Do you really still believe everything you see on the internet?"

"Of course not. I worked in PR."

"So…when you see a picture of a bunch of happy, smiling kids, do you think about the yelling and the bribes that it took to get them there, or do you just think about the happy, sweet smiling faces in the picture?"

I guess he has a point. "I usually just think about what they're wearing and wonder how it's possible little kids have better style then me."

"There you go. No one cares how the Instagram sausage gets made, Millie."

"You seem to know a lot about it for a social media ghost." I pick up a handful of sand and let it flow through my fingers to avoid looking him in the eye. Letting him know I've been looking for him online makes me feel like I'm holding out my heart for him to swipe away.

"When you live in a town of influencers, you watch how it all goes down. Whether you want to or not."

I know this isn't Pete's thing; it's more than obvious he sees the influencers in town as necessary but annoying. I'm not trying to do exactly what Alana and Quincy do, but would it be so bad if I had my own little piece of engagement? I'm already in a different spot than those women due to my lack of kids and husband, but I'm here and I'm surfing. I may have spent my morning wiping out and getting stuck in the washing machine, so time will tell if that becomes something anyone would want to follow.

I comb my hair with my fingers and slick on some of the tinted lip balm I stashed in my bag, then grab Pete's enormous board. And yes, I have been wondering all morning if this is a euphemism. How could I not?

"Okay, influencer expert. Will you play Instagram Husband for me and take some photos of me while I paddle out again?" I hand him my phone and give him a pleading grin.

"You're going in again? You just got out of the water." His eyebrows crease in concern, probably because of what he just saw, but if I don't go now, I'll lose my nerve.

"I just need few good shots for my feed. So come on." I wave my phone at him. "Be a pal."

Pete's mouth tightens. He's not meeting my eyes, and I can't believe he is so anti–social media that he won't take my picture. I think I can convince him though.

"Come on, Pete. I'll do whatever you tell me to do." Pete smiles at the idea. It's too tempting to be able to boss me around, as if I'd ever really let that happen. "What do you think? I should ditch the wet suit and pose next to this giant board with my boobs barely covered by my bikini top? Or what if I have my head tipped back, like just standing close to a surfboard is about to get me off? Is that the kind of picture you want?"

Pete's jaw pops open, his mouth moving, but no words find their way out. I can tell I've made my point.

"No, you don't get to tell me what to do." I roll my eyes at the very idea I suggested. Why is it so fun to tease him?

"I'm not sure I could survive trying," he mutters. "You do look great like that though."

I feel my cheeks heat at his compliment. I see Pete being sweet to his family often, but having a small hint of it is confusing the many lines I have drawn where he's concerned. I need to pull myself together. "Well, come on, dude, these pictures aren't going to take themselves."

Pete looks like he's about to say more, but I think he's afraid to dig himself deeper, so instead he wipes his wet and sandy hands on his towel and takes my phone.

Later, after I've showered, I look through the pictures Pete took, and while the ones on dry land are somewhat usable—I especially like the one where I rolled down the top of our magic dress to make it a skirt—the videos of me in the water are a complete embarrassment. Even the times I was able to get on my feet, I look like one of those inflatable stick figures you see at car dealerships, bending and wobbling, trying to hold my balance for longer than three seconds.

Pete did give it his all as Instagram Husband, and there are at least one or two pictures I could use that don't involve any evidence of me actually trying to surf. There's one of me looking back over my shoulder, sticking my tongue out at him before I paddled into the water, that feels cute, and one he took that dare I call a selfie. It's the top half of his face, just a hint of those magnetic gray-green eyes and his thick, dark eyebrows. You can see me in the background straddling the longboard, waiting for my next wave. I tap the few I like and add hashtags to the post that will go on my main feed. When I'm searching the hashtags to see which ones are most popular, I check #InstagramHusband and #InstagramBoyfriend. I won't add the picture with him in it today, but it's a nice idea that one day maybe he could be one of those things.

Chapter 8

"SO, YOU LIKE THE TOWN, but not the surfing?" Bree asks. We're talking on FaceTime, and I'm trying to explain to her my disappointment about my first attempts back in the water while she gives herself a pedicure on her fire escape.

"The surfing is fine. That's not it."

"So, what? Pete's a dick? Quincy's friends suck?"

"That's not it either." Pete is anything but a dick. Which is part of the problem. The more time I spend with him, the more I want to be around him. Which is really not helping me pretend I'm here for some carefree fun in the sun.

"Then what? I'm trying to figure out what's bringing you down so much. Because everything I've seen from your posts so far looks like a dream to me. Maybe you've hit one or two bumps in the road, but it's funny. I think if anything, people would like seeing that."

"I guess. I know I shouldn't expect everything to be perfect right away, but… Back right up. What do you mean it's funny seeing the bumps in the road?"

"What do *you* mean? The videos you posted crashing or what-ever you call it when you were surfing? They're funny. Plus, no one expects you to be a professional—"

"No, no, no. I didn't mean to post those!" I tap into Instagram and look at my last post. With my heart frantically pounding, I scroll through the pictures I posted: one of me posing with the board, the one where I'm wearing the dress as a skirt, and then there at the end not one, but two videos of me looking like a complete ass, flailing around trying to catch waves.

"Bree, what is wrong with me? This isn't what I wanted to post!" Not only are the videos clearly posted by mistake, but they don't exactly ooze the cool confidence of a woman reclaiming her childhood passion. "What's influential about this?"

"Who cares about being influential?" Bree says dismissively. Which is fine for her, but seeing how seriously Alana and Quincy take this stuff is pretty inspiring. Like Alana said, there's a lot of opportunity out there with Instagram, and what would be so wrong with me going after a piece of it? Well, except for the fact that I continue to look like a complete idiot every time I create a new post.

"This is a disaster." I wanted to come to Peacock Bay and move on from being a failure, but I can't even manage a simple Instagram account without showing the world who I am. "I'm not saying I blame the dress, but she is in the first picture, and I need somewhere to shovel my annoyance."

"The dress is a she now?"

"Ugh. You're right. It's obviously a dude trying to derail me at every turn."

"Millie, get ahold of yourself."

"At least I barely have any followers. I can take this down before anyone notices."

"Don't worry, babe. Even the followers you have probably didn't notice either."

～ ∾

That afternoon, I go to help Sage at her shop. When I arrive, I'm pleased to see she actually has a customer at the register. But while I wait for her to finish, I overhear them, and it seems it's not someone buying, but returning.

"I think my son had an allergic reaction to this. He's just not going to eat it," the woman says, placing four jars of baby food on the counter.

"But they're open. I can't resell these," Sage says. I'm proud of her for standing her ground, even if she looks visibly shaken to be dealing with this kind of confrontation.

"But what am I supposed to do? Just be out the money? He's allergic," the customer repeats, dragging out the last word in a clear effort to get her point across.

"Well, no. I guess, maybe I could offer you store credit?" Sage responds. I can see her wavering, and it doesn't seem fair. She's not Whole Foods; she's a tiny local business.

"I really think you should give me a refund, Sage. This is a medical issue."

Okay, now I feel like Sage is just getting bullied. And if this customer knows her well enough to know her name, she has to know that Sage's business can't survive if people are returning used goods and demanding their money back all the time.

"Excuse me?" I jump in. Probably where I'm not wanted, but that doesn't usually stop me. Both Sage and the customer stop their conversation and turn toward me. "Hi, I'm Millie. I'm the new business manager for Little Goods. Did you have a problem with a product you purchased?"

"Yes." The woman looks at me skeptically and then shakes her bangs out of her face. "I need to make a return. My son refused to eat this and then broke out in a rash three days later. He's clearly allergic."

"I see. Do you have a receipt?" I ask.

"Of course." The woman holds out her phone to show me the emailed receipt. I look it over while I form my careful response.

"I see," I say again, handing back the phone. I fold my hands and place them on the counter. I'm trying my best to look like someone in a position of authority. "How do you two know each other?"

"I've known Sage for years. Haven't I? Our husbands put on the Rad Dads Surf Contest together every year."

Sages gives a half-hearted smile.

"And it's so nice that you support her small business."

"Of course I do. But my son wouldn't eat this baby food. I'm sorry to make such a fuss, Sage. If you could just issue a refund…"

"The thing is, you bought this baby food two weeks ago. It's completely homemade and organic. It doesn't have preservatives like other baby food, so it can't just sit on the shelf until you're ready to use it. Now, we've been making some changes to our return policy. I'm sorry if you weren't aware of that, but returns can only made for store credit now. Especially when the product is expired."

The woman shifts her weight. Her cheeks redden a little, but she won't give up that easily. "Well, I wasn't aware of that, so I think you should honor the old policy."

Seriously? Who knew such a bulldog lived in this town of peace, love, and sunshine. If I wasn't so annoyed with her, I'd probably give her the refund just out of pure admiration.

"I know this is an inconvenience, and I'm sorry about that, but Sage is a small-business owner. A *female* small-business owner, and shouldn't we all be doing everything we can to support her?"

"Well, of course, but…"

"I thought so." I nod solemnly. "I know you wouldn't want her to be run out of town by a big-box store that sells baby food full of GMOs and"—I lower my voice to a whisper—"guns."

"I would never want that!" the customer says, aghast.

"Exactly." I take the women across the shoulders and lead her out the door. "I knew we wanted the same thing. Thanks so much for coming in today. I really hope your son's rash clears up. Have you checked your detergent?" I give her a gentle shove through the store door and close it behind me. I turn to face Sage, who is rooted to her spot, blinking into her bangs behind the counter, utterly stunned.

"You really need to have a return policy posted somewhere in the store where customers can see it," I tell her, but I'm smiling, high from my victory.

"On it." She grins. "But explain this to me. Was the big-box store going to be full of guns or baby food?"

"Both?" I shrug with a wide smile.

We spend the rest of the afternoon restyling the store and taking pictures of cute baby outfits for Sage to post every few days. She actually has a decent selection of kids' clothes, and she's a fantastic stylist. She puts things together I never would have thought of. Floral shirts with corduroy overalls. A tulle skirt and turtleneck sweater. I want to wear these outfits. I make sure she includes little hair bows and socks in each pictures in case someone wants a complete look for their family photos or is attending an event that might require small fry to be dressed to the nines.

I can't believe I'm having this much fun putting together baby outfits. I'm trying to get Sage to be more thoughtful about driving sales, but it's being met with some resistance. Sales just doesn't seem to come naturally to her, and it's starting to make me wonder why she opened this store in the first place.

"I feel like doing this kind of thing is like asking people for money," she says.

"You're asking them for money in exchange for goods they want. It's an even exchange. One our capitalist society is accustomed to. Don't worry about it."

Sage chews her lip while she considers this. I think she's a little shy and this kind of thing feels hard for her. But eventually she must accept what I'm saying as true because she keeps right on styling and taking pictures and doesn't bring it up again. We stop when we get hungry, and she runs over to the pizza shop across the street and brings back two small pizzas. One is goat cheese and red peppers and one is meatball and fresh basil. They're both delicious, and we eat happily as we put everything away.

"I really appreciate you helping me today, Millie. But you know I can't actually hire you as my business manager, right?"

I swallow hard. Of course. It's not like I expected her to offer me a job here, but the last few hours have flown by and I thought we made a pretty good team. For the first time, maybe ever, I got a glimpse of what a great working relationship could be like. I remind myself that her store is struggling, and surely this is just a financial thing. Not a you-just-got-laid-off-and-have-obvious-attention-issues thing, but it still stings. I force a smile and wave her off. "Of course not. I just said that to give myself some authority. Don't worry about it."

Sage smiles back at me, and I shift the topic away to hide the twist of surprising disappointment that's stuck in my chest. "How about you just tag me in a post while I fake style these shelves? I can use all the help I can get building my following."

"No problem," Sage responds, and she takes a few photos of me while I pretend she's not there and I just happen to be stocking her shelves with the utmost attention to detail. I do my best to look deep in thought over where to put the hand-carved baby rattles while she clicks around shooting. "I think this one is the best," she says, holding out her phone so I can approve the picture.

"That's perfect. I really look like I know what I'm doing there."

"You do know what you're doing. This is the best the store has looked in weeks. I may actually have a chance of making a living from this place if I can get my online sales going. I always loved clothes and styling, but I'm not exactly a businesswoman. That's more Alana's territory."

"Says who? It's hard to keep a business going in a small town. Don't beat yourself up."

"Hence the need for online sales."

"Is your husband putting a lot of pressure on you for the store to be successful?" I don't know anything about their relationship, but maybe they invested a lot in the store and can't keep it going if it's not turning a profit. Of course, I know she doesn't want her store to fail, but she keeps mentioning how she really needs to make a living from Little Goods.

"No, not my husband." She bites down on her lip. "We're, um, we're actually getting divorced. None of my friends know yet, so please don't say anything. Alana is really protective of the friend group, and I'm not sure I'm ready for her reaction."

"Do you think she'd take sides? Can't she be team both?"

"Sure," she says. "Maybe. Alana just likes everything to be peaceful. Perfect. She thinks it's better for business." Sage glances at the clock on the wall nervously. "She's stopping by today, pretty soon, I think. So, don't mention any of this to her, please."

Alana has always been so supportive of her friends—at least in her blog she has—so it's hard to believe she'd dump Sage when she needs her most.

"I know I don't know her that well, but that doesn't seem like something she'd do." In fact, it seem like the opposite of everything I've learned about her from her blog. All the united forces of mom friendships and whatnot.

"You're probably right. Alana is the best, really. She might seem like…a lot sometimes, but she's the most supportive friend I've ever had. It might seem pushy to other people, the way she gets involved with everyone, but she really just wants the best for her friends." Sage chews her thumbnail nervously.

"Pushy like she helped you open a business you weren't sure you really wanted to run?"

She smiles, but shakes her head. "It's not that I didn't want to. I really did, I was just scared to jump into it with the way the businesses had been suffering here during the pandemic. Alana convinced me it would be the best thing for the town and set things in motion before I could think too hard about it. Next thing I knew, I had my own business with a brick-and-mortar store and a website for online orders." She shrugs nervously, and I get the feeling Sage lacks a little confidence in herself. I can understand that feeling. I can't even post something on Instagram without embarrassing myself. But just because I screw up everything I set my sights on doesn't mean Sage has to. Maybe I can't help myself, but I might be able to help Sage.

"Well, then let's get these online orders happening. Let me show you some accounts that I know of that are doing some cool posts to attract more orders." I pull up the store based in Cincinnati that I want to show her and hand her my phone. I followed a few stores that carried Butterfly Bridge toys, and I hope some might inspire her. We look through the posts together and click around to different stores coming up with ideas for Little Goods. I make her put notes in her calendar to remind her to post new things every day. When she hands my phone back to me, she smiles gratefully.

"I think you have a few new follows," Sage says.

I click the heart icon to see, and when I do, my own heart starts pounding in my throat. Then I check my follower count.

Two hundred new people have started following me.

"That's really strange. I just checked this a few hours ago. You didn't post anything yet, did you?" My heart feels like it's pounding out an extra beat for every new follower. Two hundred new people?

"Not yet. Maybe someone else tagged you?"

And there it is. A picture of me from Alana's stories teasing her upcoming post about her Friendsgiving. I'm leaning forward in my chair at her beautifully set table. I think I was talking to Quincy across from me. My face is aglow from the warm candlelight, but there's something else too. Pete. He has his arm around the back of my chair. He was talking to the person on the other side of where I was sitting. It looks like he was being affectionate, casually draping an arm over me, like it's something he's done a dozen times before. Something tugs inside me when I think that if I had just leaned back a little, it could have been real. Would he have moved his arm if I had leaned against it? Would he have let it linger, or maybe let his thumb brush against my arm?

My throat is thick when I blink my eyes back into focus. I scroll up in my notifications and see that Alana has posted the same picture to her stories, but this time the photo of me and Pete is cropped and written across the top are three simple words: *Cute Couple Alert*.

I go back to the original post and read a few of the comments. It's mostly stuff like *friendship goals* and *relationship goals*. There's a lot to get through and there's nothing directly about me, but there's one that I hover my finger over for an extra beat.

Who's Pete with? A commenter asks.

Could be his wife. Another answers. She's in the Bay too. Check her Insta.

So, it's all very weird. People seem to know Pete at least a little from Alana's other posts, and maybe someone tapped over to my feed and saw my recent pictures. It's bad enough I might have embarrassed myself with those terrible surf videos, but now I'm humiliating Pete by association. He won't be happy about this.

Alana didn't tag him. I haven't, either, but people seem to know him and talk about him. I don't blame them. You can't see that guy's stubble-dusted jawline and not want to talk about him.

I stare at the picture like it's a puzzle I'm trying to solve. Why would she say we're together? It's a cute picture, and it gives off a cozy Friendsgiving feeling, but why make us a couple? I ask this question out loud to Sage, but she's not the one who answers me.

"You're welcome."

Sage and I both turn to see Alana, holding a mason jar filled with a sludge-like green smoothie. She shakes her long, dark hair over her shoulder and starts looking around at the shelves we've reorganized. "This looks great, guys," she says. "Let me get a few pictures for my stories."

"Thanks," I tell her, but I still want an answer to my first question. "And thanks for tagging me in your recent post, but you know, um, Pete and I aren't together. We're just friends. I don't want people to get the wrong idea." Or put myself in any awkward situations with the guy I've been crushing on since college.

Alana picks up a tiny shirt I just folded and holds it up to examine it. "I did you a favor," she says, not even looking at me. "Aren't you here to launch yourself on Insta?"

"I never said that, and Pete definitely isn't along for the ride."

"No. That guy is never leaving this town." She laughs, then finally turns my way and smiles. "Why would he? It's the best place on earth."

I nod in agreement. "I can't argue with that, but what are we going to do about that post? People are already commenting, asking who he's with and what our relationship is."

"Do whatever you want," Alana answers with a tilt of her head. "But you should probably just roll with it."

"But it's a lie." I look to Sage for help, but she's suddenly very busy with something on her computer and cash register.

Alana shrugs. "So make it not a lie."

I stare at her blankly, because if it was that easy to manifest a relationship with the object of my lust, wouldn't I have done something like this a long time ago? "So, I should just ask Pete to marry me?"

"Pete's a businessman. He knows the drill, and he's always looking for ways to bring new eyes to the hotel. So, now that you have a few new followers, just keep hanging out taking pictures. The rest will fall into place."

"Totally, except for all the lying." I'm running out of arguments. I want Alana's help, but bringing Pete into it was never part of the plan. There's no way he's going to want to tie himself to someone who can't even be trusted to post the right pictures.

Alana smiles at me, but it's anything but warm. "Like I said, he's a businessman and you're in PR. I'm sure you can figure out a way to spin this. But I would take down those videos of you falling into the water. We want people to think that the easy surf life happens the second they roll into town. Seeing you show up, landing the perfect guy, and catching great waves will boost tourism, and Peacock Bay desperately needs that. I'll hook you up with a bunch of followers, but you need to do your part too."

I look down at the phone in my hands. I know the town has been struggling these last few years. The hotel and stores like Sage's depend on tourism to survive. If I can help with that even in a small way, I feel like I should. I doubt a few posts from a nobody screwup like me is going to make much of a difference, but if it might help Alana and Pete and the rest, I don't see what harm it could do to go along with this.

Then there are all the comments. I scroll through them again and let the deep burn of jealousy flame into a bonfire in my soul. There they are. Right there, for anyone to see. An endless buffet of heart eye emojis and flirtatious jabs for Pete to feast on. Yes, anyone with eyes and a healthy amount of sexual bravado can see how handsome and charming he is, but so what? What if he really was my husband? Would all these people still be asking if he'd come over and give them back rubs? Or offering to wash his car? What is that even supposed to mean?

Maybe Alana is right and I can convince Pete this could benefit him too. I'll appeal to his ego and say that just by being his extremely hot, sweet self, he made this happen. I might not use such flattering language for fear of blushing so hard I'd look sunburned, but maybe I can find a way for him to feel like he's getting something out of it too. If helping me out isn't reason enough, maybe I could frame the whole thing as a way to help the hotel. A little mutual social media back-scratching perhaps, nothing crazy. Because if he goes along with this, I could actually have a chance at making this work and not being a failure for once. Because these people know Alana and Quincy and Pete. And now they know me.

Chapter 9

THE NEXT MORNING, I DECIDE to go for a walk into town to clear my head and think over what Alana proposed to me yesterday. I plan to grab a coffee at a place near Sage's store to kick my daily extended-release meds into high gear. Since Alana tagged me in the picture with Pete, my follower count has been creeping upward like a turtle bravely taking on Everest. It's not a mad rush, but there is this feeling (at least to me) that something is happening, and I'm not sure I want to stop it, even though I probably should.

The early morning sun warms my shoulders, and I can smell the scent of the ocean curling around me. It's like a siren song pulling me toward the beach, where it will likely swallow me whole on my next attempt on a board. I still haven't taken down the videos. I want to blame my general scatterbrainedness, but I know that's not it. People have only responded to my posts when I'm brandishing my mistakes and missteps. I'm not like Alana and Quincy, with their picture-perfect California surf lives. It's not like I'm proud of how often I find myself failing at life, but there is a little freedom in not having to feel like I have to hide it.

It seems I'm not the only scatterbrain in town, because when I reach the coffee shop I'm greeted with a locked door and a dark interior. I look both ways down the street. What am I missing? Aren't coffee shops always open early? I look down the street to Little Goods, but I don't expect it to be open. I don't get it.

I snap a picture of the dark shop, thinking it could be funny to post yet another example of me striking out.

When you're up before the baristas. I caption the picture.

I add a short video of the charming but empty street and add another caption. When you try to support small businesses and strike out. It's 8 a.m. Where is everyone?

I put my phone back in my pocket and turn to make my way back to the hotel. On my way, I see a blur of dark hair with a stroller barreling toward me.

"Hey, Super Mom," I greet Quincy. She rolls her eyes, but smiles as she parks the stroller and flips the brake.

"Hardly," she says, then adds, "I need Pete. Have you seen him?" My stomach does a small flip as I think, *Join the club*, and I pray nothing shows on my face as I shake my head in response.

"Not today, but I'm heading back to the hotel now. Hey, what's the deal with the coffee shop? It's 8:00 a.m. Prime coffee time and it's closed."

Quincy smiles and shakes her head. "Waves were pumping this morning. Jace and Nora must have paddled out."

"They went surfing instead of going to work?"

Quincy shrugs. "I'm sure they'll open up soon. It's not like business is booming around here. They probably don't think it'll make much of a difference."

"That's sort of sad. Have things really been that bleak?"

"It's been getting better, but if you want the truth, well, yeah. It's been a rough few years."

"But how are things going to get better if the coffee shop owners aren't there to sell coffee?"

Quincy laughs as if she hadn't thought about it this way. "A fair point, but you have to understand how bad things got during the pandemic. While some small towns saw a huge influx of new residents and local support, Peacock Bay was almost completely shut down. We rely on tourism here, and we've barely recovered. I don't think that makes the business owners all that confident."

"I get the lack of confidence thing. You know I do." I'm the queen of crashing and burning, but even *I* know I have to keep trying. "Isn't there something we can do? I mean, if it gets me a cup of coffee before noon, I'll do whatever it takes."

My friend smiles at me as we near the hotel. "Just keep doing what you're doing with your Instagram. Your new followers seem to be into it."

"Yeah, all four of them."

"It's more than that. And in a few months we'll be in our busiest part of the year. A fresh new account like yours could help bring a lot more tourism to the town."

"But I can't stay here that long. You know that. Plus, that stuff Alana said about me and Pete being together. It wasn't the smartest move. I'm surprised anyone believed it in the first place." This is a really embarrassing thing to have to admit to Pete's sister, but here I am.

It's just like Alana said yesterday. I want to be here and do my part, but I don't think putting out false claims on a friend's romantic life is the way to do it. I've had a day to think about Alana's idea and try to invent a better argument for him to go along with being my Instagram Husband, but so far all I have is, *please?* Somehow, that doesn't feel like quite enough.

"Please. People love to believe anything pretty on the internet. And you and Pete together are about as pretty as it comes."

I roll my eyes. "Why were you looking for your brother before?" I would very much like to change the subject now.

"Oh right!" Quincy pulls over to a bench near the sidewalk and parks her stroller. "I need someone to take a picture of me being cool with kombucha for Instagram." She pulls a black-labeled bottle out from the basket under her stroller. "It's my first ad in forever so I need to make sure it's really good. Pete usually does it. He's, oddly, a really good photographer." She's right. All the pictures he's taken of me have been great. My cheeks heat, wondering what else he might secretly be really good at. I need help. At least I can recognize this.

"Oh, got it. I'll help you. How do you want to do this?"

She flips her hair over her head, fluffing it up a bit, and then straightens. She shifts her weight onto her back foot and suddenly her whole posture is different. I would buy anything she's holding right now. "This is fine. I can give you a photo credit in the post, and we can tag the Waveline, too, so everyone wins."

I chew on my cheek, thinking. "Does it make a difference when you tag the Waveline in your posts?"

"It doesn't hurt. Pete and Amelia say the more we can include the hotel in our posts, the better it is for bookings. I don't really get the whole marketing thing. You would know better than I would, I'm sure."

"Yeah, sure," I murmur, but I'm not thinking about marketing. Or I am, in a way. Maybe it isn't such a crazy idea to ask Pete to pretend to shack up with me online if I can get him to see that it's just another way to help the hotel. More eyeballs are more eyeballs, right? It's *marketing*. "So, just standing here? A few yards from your hotel? And how much are they paying you for this very carefully planned ad?" I continue. She won't think it's weird that I asked. Quincy and I are close. Plus, it's important that women are open about how much they're getting paid, especially when they're in the same industry. How else will you know if you're getting paid too little?

"Five grand for three posts," she states simply.

"Wow," I say. *Go, Quincy.* I look at her through the phone's camera. "Okay, for five grand, maybe I'll make sure the light is a little better." I move around, checking for shadows until I'm satisfied. "Much better. Okay, smile. Look cool."

She cocks an eyebrow at me. "'What? Like it's hard?'" she says, quoting *Legally Blonde*. One of the movies we must have watched a hundred times in college.

I snap a few pictures and show them to Quincy for approval. She posts the one she likes best, and then together we watch as the likes roll in. The kombucha brand comments quickly, too, so hopefully they're happy with the picture.

Instinctively, I check my own account. I'm not expecting much more than a few likes from Kate and Bree. To say I'm shocked at what I see is an understatement. Dozens of likes burst onto the screen, looking to me like fireworks on the Fourth of July. I know it's nothing compared to what Quincy and Alana are used to, but it's nothing I've ever experienced before. Plus, there are comments. People I've never met are joking around about how I struck out again at the coffee shop and how "the hits keep coming."

"That's weird." I look up at Quincy and hold the phone out for her to examine.

"I told you. People aren't as put off by you as you think."

I laugh and scroll through the comments again. The funny thing is...she's right.

"I guess people like watching me be a disaster." I try to smile, but it likely looks like I smelled something sour. This is what I wanted, after all. Followers, a piece of what Quincy has, a reason to show I belong here. I'm just not sure this is how I wanted to gain them.

"It's relatable. Who hasn't screwed up in their life? Owning those screwups is probably pretty fun to watch. Be careful though. Alana may not think it's as fun as everyone else."

I scroll through the messages in my DM's and then check my email just for good measure. I understand what my friend is saying, it just might have been nice to start this new path without lying about having a boyfriend and waving my mistakes in the air. "Holy shit," I say. I freeze where I'm standing just outside the hotel lobby. I reread the message in front of me just to make sure this isn't a joke.

"What's up?" Quincy asks and leans over to share the view of the screen with me.

"Someone just bought one of my stickers." I look up at her with wide eyes, but she's waiting for more explanation. "Kate made me, like, two thousand stickers with the Here to Stay logo on them before I left, and Bree helped me put them up for sale and now someone actually bought one!"

"That's so cool. What do they look like? I want one."

I click back to the comments and reply with some heartfelt thanks to the commenter. "I have them up in my room. I'll give you one."

"No way, I'm buying one. I support friends' businesses too."

"They're three dollars. I can swing it."

Quincy reaches into her tote bag and pulls out her wallet. She takes out some bills and waves them in the air. "Nope. I'm paying for it. Now you've made two sales today."

I blink at my computer screen, then back at her in wonder. "Three." I look back at her with a mix of pride and confusion. "Someone else just ordered one. Oh my god. This is so cool." I start looking around. "I need to buy stamps. I need mailing supplies. Where am I going to get that stuff in this tiny town?"

"Relax, we'll steal them from Pete's office. Come on." My friend grins at me, then squeezes my arm and steers me and her stroller into the hotel and toward the back office. I grip my phone to my chest and try to think of a way to stop her that doesn't involve the words *husband* or *need to see him naked*. Nothing is coming to mind.

"Hold on a sec," I say, jumping in front of the stroller as if I'm protecting it from an oncoming bus. "He's not there, is he?"

"Who? Pete? In his office? Probably, why?"

"I just don't want to bother him."

"Since when?" Right, because not wanting to bother him is actually the odd behavior.

"He's working. What if he's on the phone or something?"

"Then we'll leave. What do you think we're going to find him doing? Boning his assistant?" A look of horror must have broken out across my face because Quincy quickly backtracks with a look of barely restrained amusement. "Relax, he doesn't even have an assistant."

I exhale a little too forcefully in relief. Quincy gives me a little wink and steers her stroller to roll around my useless human barricade to her intended destination.

Quincy stops the stroller in front of a solid wooden door and gives it a gentle knock. She doesn't wait for an answer and Pete ends up saying, "Come in," at the same time we're doing just that. His expression goes from surprise to confusion at the sight of us.

"Hi?" he says and, Jesus, he looks so good. He's wearing a washed-out red button-down shirt that looks ridiculously good against his dark hair and light-brown skin. I hate standing here just looking at him like some visitor at a zoo. I want to walk over to him and run my fingers over his hair. I want to wrap my hand around his bicep and squeeze the lean muscle under his shirt. Maybe this is why I never visited Peacock Bay before. The more I'm around Pete, the harder it is to stop myself from jumping on top of him and ripping his clothes off like a wild animal. Maybe Alana is partially to blame for this. Seeing that picture of us looking so *together* and the ideas she put in my head have me charged up and completely out of control.

"We need stamps," Quincy says and starts opening his desk drawers and closing them a little too forcefully with a look on her face that shakes me into the moment and brings me back to our original purpose.

"Go to the front desk," he says as he rolls away from his desk with his hands up in slight surrender. "Or, I don't know, the post office?"

"We don't need that many," his sister answers.

"How many do you need?"

"Three. Aha!" She pulls out a roll of stamps and starts counting them out.

I check my email just to be sure, and I'm delighted to find more orders. "Um, actually four. No three. I'm not mailing yours."

"Four? Yay," Quincy exclaims and shakes her shoulders in celebration as she counts out the extra stamps.

"Maybe I should just go to the post office. I might need to get more for later." I feel bad stealing Pete's office supplies. This is his business after all. Plus, it feels great to think that these sticker orders won't be my last. It's not five thousand dollars for three Instagram posts, but it's something and it's mine.

"What do you need them for?" Pete asks me, and just the blink of contact of his eyes on me sends a shiver down my back. There's no telling how I'd react if there was any actual touching between us. I'd probably murder him with lust. Or he'd kill me. It wouldn't be pretty, that's for sure. I can barely stand in the same room with him as it is. If we were touching each other? Forget it.

I pull myself together enough to respond, but my heart is pounding in my throat. "Sticker sales. Some followers ordered the logo stickers I have for sale. I want to mail them out right away."

"That's great, Mills." Pete's eyebrows pull up when he smiles. "Can I get one?"

I fight the strong urge to squeeze my eyes closed as I try to keep my smile cool. It's so nice that he wants to be supportive. But I know that's all it is.

"You have to buy one," Quincy instructs him. "I'm buying one. So cough it up."

"He could just trade me for the stamps," I suggest. That seems fair.

"Nah, consider those a donation. Or an investment. How much is the sticker?"

"Three dollars." I roll my eyes. "But you really don't have to…" They're already giving me such a discount on the hotel room it's almost criminal. I'm basically paying the price of staying in a hostel and getting a luxury hotel room. It feels like he's doing too much for me already.

"Yes, he does. What is with you?" Quincy shoots to me. She squints her eyes at me and something like realization washes over her face. *Shit. She knows.* How obvious is my face right now? I can't hide this from her. I know she was joking when she said she wouldn't care if we hooked up. I'm an easy target because it would never happen. It's always been like this between the three of us. Teasing, joking, trying to see who we can make squirm. To that point, I'm not one hundred percent sure she's not about to make some joke about me doing something dirty in exchange for the stamps, and I need to get out of here before she does, because with the way I feel about Pete now, I just know I won't be able to handle that with any kind of smoothness.

I shake my head. "I have to go out to get envelopes anyway. I can just get stamps then too." I start backing out of the office. Pete gets to his feet and takes the stamps out of Quincy's hand. He's going to follow me out to give them to me, I'm sure, and for some reason that is just too much. I'm not sure I can physically handle Pete's generosity without pushing him up against a wall and sticking my tongue in his mouth. Which would be a really odd response to someone giving you a few stamps. Seriously, what is going on with me? I am getting way too worked up at the prospect of a conversation with a guy about stamps.

"Millie." I hear Pete call me back, and I stop in the small hall outside his office. I blow air through my lips without actually breathing before turning back to him. I will not smash my mouth against his. I will not trace my fingers over his thick muscular biceps. I will not touch him in any way. These are not options. I repeat these sentences in my head like mantras because that is what crazy people who have had way too many stimulants do when they're spiraling out of control. "It's fine about the stamps. I was just messing around when I said that about the post office." He holds out the little strip and I carefully take them, pinching one end with two fingers, so as to avoid any touching of our hands.

"Thanks, I feel bad though. You guys are already doing a lot for me."

"Hardly," he scoffs.

I bite my lower lip because he doesn't know. He hasn't seen the posts about us, and I know I have to be the one to tell him about them and what I've done.

"Well, you might be doing more for me than you realize."

His throat bobs as he swallows and I realize how suggestive that sounded.

"Here's the thing. Alana did something and it was really dumb, and I didn't stop it so maybe I'm partly to blame, but I need to you to just be a pal and go with it."

Pete shifts his weight to his back foot and crosses his arms over his chest. Narrowing his eyes, he teases me. "What'd you break?"

I squint my eyes and brace myself. "The internet?"

He's not laughing.

"There's a post on Surf Shack Dream House that makes it look like we're together, and Alana told all her followers that you were my husband. It's a little unclear, but the thing is…" I pause, trying to come up with the best way to phrase this. "The thing is…it's going to be good for both of us." I start nodding my head, as if that will convince him.

"Millie." He's rubbing his forehead with his fingertips. "Please, no."

I'm stressing him out. He hates this kind of thing. He's made that very clear, and now I can see his whole body clenching and I'm sure he wishes he'd never encouraged me to come here.

"Hear me out. You don't have to post anything. You can still linger in the social media shadows if that's what you want to do. But for some reason, ever since that picture of us at Alana's Friendsgiving went up, I've finally started to get some followers. There's a chance I could really do something here and I know I didn't plan this, but now it's starting to happen and it's something I'm making on my own." I straighten myself up and look Pete directly in the eye. "They're buying my stickers. I don't want to screw this up too."

Pete's face softens. I can see his resolve loosening. He looks down to the floor and rubs his hand against the back of his neck. I know he wants nothing to do with this—or me, for that matter—but I also know he has an idea of what not looking like a failure means to me. The same way I know what not letting the hotel fail means to him.

"Plus, it could be good for the hotel." Pete looks back up at me. "The more followers I have equals more people reading all the glowing things I have to say about the Waveline."

Pete's eyes search my face, looking for something I'm not sure I'm offering. "So, this is just a business transaction? A marketing strategy." His eyebrows are creased.

"Yes!" I exclaim, because I think he's finally getting it. "But a mutually beneficial one. And nothing would be that different for us in reality. We take some pictures together, hang out, surf. All stuff we'd be doing anyway. I'd just caption the pictures a little more... romantically." My chest flushes at the word and the heat creeps to my cheeks. I'm sure he sees the color spread, but there's nothing I can do about it now.

Pete rubs his fingers across the stubble on his chin, then takes two small steps toward me. He gets so close I have to take a step back so he doesn't feel the heat from my flushed skin that is surely radiating off me. I feel the wall of this small hallway meet my back, but Pete comes even closer. He plants one arm on the wall above my head and dips his head down. His mouth hovers just above my ear, freezing me in place.

"So, we'd go to parties together. Like the one the other night?" he asks, his voice just a murmur, low and so gravelly I can feel it in my core. "I walk in with you on my arm. We stand next to each other all night, my hand on your back. Right...here?" His other hand grazes up the side of my body and finds a place to rest just under my ribs. His thumb strokes once against my shirt, and I have to fight my body so it doesn't arch fully into his. Pete sucks a breath between his teeth when he notices my body respond to his touch, and I lower my eyes so they don't give away what he's doing to me right now.

"Then we leave together and I drop you back at your room at night?" My eyes flick back to his, and I swallow hard at the idea of him taking me back to the hotel at the end of a night out. It would just be a ride, nothing more, but the way he says it makes me lose all ability to speak. I nod, hoping he doesn't catch how affected I am by his words. "We'd hang out on the beach together. You'd lay your head on my chest after a long morning surf."

What is happening? How does he know this is one of my favorite daydreams? "I'd pose for pictures with you pressed up against me. My fingers tangled in your hair?" Oh shit. This is too much. I feel a tingling between my already weak legs. My mouth tips up toward him without permission and I hear him exhale long and slow when I do. "And then nothing changes. We go on with the rest of our lives and everything stays exactly the same? Is that what you had in mind for your Instagram feed?"

What am I supposed to say to this? How am I supposed to respond with his sister ten feet away in his office, while his hand is still tucked into my waist?

I force myself to meet his eye and regain a slice of composure. Those gray-green magnets aren't making it easy. He stares right back and waits for my response, so I nod. The smallest bob of my head.

"It's just a favor," I say. If I gave him anything more, it would unleash years of carefully protected feelings, and I don't think I can handle watching his reaction and the rejection that's sure to follow.

He watches my face for what feels like half my lifetime but reasonably is a few seconds and then pushes himself off the wall.

"No," he says, sharply, then turns away toward his office.

"Pete," I call. I feel so stupid. I shouldn't have even brought it up. I should have just apologized for my posts and left it alone. "I'm sorry. I know this isn't your thing. I just thought... I don't know. It was just an idea."

Pete stops, his back still facing me, and I see his shoulders release slightly. He turns his head and I can see the smallest hint of a smile, but that tiny upward curl of his lips is enough for me to know I haven't completely ruined everything. He might not want to be my fake husband, but at least he's still my friend.

"Yeah, I know. It's no big deal. I was just messing around too."

Of course, he was just screwing with me. "Well, you got me." I try to smile, but who knows what it looks like.

He looks like he's about to say something else, but just before it leaves his lips, he shakes his head, changing his mind. So I add, "I'm really sorry. Forget about it?"

Pete looks up to the ceiling, a small, tight smile on his lips. He doesn't answer me, or not my question anyway. "Are you surfing today?" he asks, one hand on his office door, one foot out of this conversation.

"I don't think so." I rotate my stiff shoulders, trying to loosen the tight muscles that are actively rejecting my reentry into the surf community. "My shoulders are killing me, plus my ego could use a little break after the beating it took. I think I'll just get these stickers out. What about tomorrow?" I'm not exactly inviting him, but I'm not *not* inviting him either.

His face falls. "I can't tomorrow. I have this big call I've been preparing for…"

"Don't worry about it. I'll still be here." I wave it off, hopefully not showing my disappointment.

His lips turn up in a grin so sweet it nearly breaks me open. "Good, be here." He nods and taps his hand against the doorframe before he dips back into his office.

Chapter
10

I SHAKE THE ROPY, WET strands of hair over my shoulders as I pick up the surfboard that keeps knocking into my shins. My back now joins the shoulders that were aching yesterday from hours of paddling into wave after wave, trying to pack a few years of practice into one morning surf session. It didn't go well.

Add it to the list.

"I'm going to blame your board," I shout to Quincy on shore. "I can't ride a shortboard."

"Dude, that's a fun shape. My nephew rides it sometimes," she calls to me over her shoulder while she changes Clay's diaper. "He's nine."

"Not that much fun for me." I trudge out of the whitewater. "The waves are big too. Too big for me, anyway. Why do I like this sport when it's so hard?" I groan and toss the board on the sand, startling Monrow, who's lining up a collection of shells in careful order. He looks up at me and starts to howl like he's come face-to-face with his personal nightmare. Quincy abandons the freshly changed Clay and moves to comfort her other child.

I bury my face in my towel, completely useless. I honestly don't know what I was thinking coming here. That I'd set foot on the sand and instantly have a huge Instagram following that would launch me into a new career? That Pete would see me after all these years and sweep me off to his bed? That my parents would back me jumping onto an unpredictable new career path with no reservations? What a joke. I humiliated myself in front of Pete, I can hardly surf, and now I'm making small children cry.

"Sorry, Monrow," I say toward the small boy who's slowly calming down.

"You're horrible," he shouts.

"Monrow," Quincy scolds. "That's not kind."

"But accurate," I concede.

"Stop. For someone who hasn't surfed in a few years, you're doing fine," my friend says, coming back to sit next to me. Which makes me feel even worse because now she has to take care of me like a third kid. "You need to stop thinking about how good you used to be and start thinking about how much better you've gotten in just a few days." She picks up her phone and unlocks it. "Look at the last few videos I got."

I take the phone from her hand and tap the screen. *Ugh.* I look like such a grommet. I grimace at the screen, watching as a video of me plays where the board slips right out from under me and launches itself into the air and me into the water. I know I'm relearning this skill and that takes time, but I talked such a big game coming here. To my friends, my parents, even Pete. Surfing was supposed to be the place I felt most comfortable and calm. Not the thing that reminds me even more what a screwup I am.

"So, I guess I should post these?" I haven't decided if I'm going to keep up my pattern of posting all my mistakes. I'm not sure I really want to build a brand on how terrible I am at everything, but without the Instagram Husband thing Alana suggested, I don't have much else to work with.

Quincy shrugs. "Up to you. I don't blame you if you'd rather not, but I think what you've been doing is pretty unique. Showing yourself falling and getting back up over and over is pretty inspiring. No matter how much you're getting worked." She nudges me, joking, but I don't respond. I know there's something real and true in what she's saying, and I wouldn't mind if *that's* my identity online. But the problem with that is that's not me. I've got the getting-knocked-on-my-ass part down, but there's a limit to how many times I can force myself to get back up before I stop trying.

I post the videos and caption them, Ever have a day when it seems like even Mother Nature is against you? And after a few minutes, the likes start rolling in. *Great.*

"Why are you being so hard on yourself about this? It's not like you to care so much what other people think."

I shake my head as I watch the waves rolling in. "I care what some people think," I tell Quincy truthfully. My humiliating proposal (for lack of a better word) with Pete replays in my head. "Surfing was the one part of this that I thought I had down. I came here with no job and no real plan and I owned that, but the surfing part…" *And the Pete part.* "I knew nothing would happen overnight, but gaining a following for screwing up wasn't exactly my goal. At the very least, surfing was supposed to be the easy part."

Quincy looks at me with a glint in her eye. "When has easy ever been fun?"

I nod. I know what she means. I know the more I have to work for it, the sweeter it'll be if or when I get it. I'm not even sure what *it* is anymore. I thought it was an escape from the city, making sweeping changes in my life, or the thrill of showing my parents I can still do something with my life even if it looks different than what they'd imagined. But aside from packing up my stuff and finding an old dress in a box, I haven't made that many changes. I'm still me. Still a joke, just now people like it that I am.

Monrow has calmed down and returned to his digging in the sand, so Quincy shifts back to the baby. She really has her hands full. I'm not sure I realized it before. And I definitely haven't lent any support since I've been here. I need to do better in at least this one area.

"Hey, if you ever need a break, I'd be happy to help you out and watch the kids sometime. I may not be a great surfer, but I could be an okay babysitter."

Quincy smiles. "I wouldn't do that to you. Plus, you have enough going on."

I don't, but I'm not going to bring that up and make her explain that she doesn't want to leave her children with me.

"Hey, I know what you could do. Post a question asking people for their favorite beach recs. It would be a good way to engage with your new followers. But fair warning, you'll probably get a million responses from Pete saying something like, 'The waves suck everywhere else. The only place you need to go is the Cove.'"

I shove her gently on the shoulder. She loses her balance, the only time she's done that today, unlike me, and falls to the side.

"He's not wrong. It's pretty great on his little beach." I don't know why I feel the need to defend her brother or her hometown, but this place is so special. I wonder if she's been here too long to see it the way I do. "He barely follows me though."

"Are there degrees of following someone now?"

"You know what I mean. He's not very active online."

"Well, he's following you all right. Just maybe not online." She grins. I know what she's doing. She wants me to admit my brain has turned into a Pete Santana thought factory. Everything I see and do now makes me think of him. I am staying in his hotel, run by his family in his hometown, so that's not making it easier, but with the way I operate, sometimes when I get onto a subject it's hard for me to get off it.

Luckily, I'm able to avoid confessing anything for a little longer because something over my shoulder catches Quincy's eye. I turn to look and see yet another thing connected to Pete—his sister Amelia with little Claire bouncing on her hip, making their way across the sand. I'm sort of disappointed, which is dumb. He wouldn't come out to the beach in the middle of the day. Pete's working, and I know how seriously he takes work and the hotel. But I haven't seen him since the weird moment outside his office yesterday, and I would have really liked an opportunity to smooth over whatever awkwardness is between us now. Plus, I have a really cute yellow bikini on today that I wouldn't have minded him seeing me in, and it's not like I keep thinking about the way his chest looked when he carried his board over his head to the beach. So lean and so strong. Ropes of muscle climbing his back like vines. A real surfer's body if I've ever seen one. Yep, stuck on one subject.

"Hey, guys," Amelia says as she places Claire down on our towels. She reaches to hug Monrow, but he shrugs out of her grasp and yells, "Stop!"

"Okay, Monrow," Quincy says to calm him. I can tell she's running out of energy. I don't know how she's handling all this and balancing the time she has to put in to keep her blog going.

"It's fine," Amelia says, and she gives us a smile to brush it off. "How are the waves?"

"They weren't bad before," I tell her. "Even if I was. But they're getting kind of choppy now." We watch the windy rough waves for a few minutes, the loud rush of the water soothing the group of us. Maybe I am being too hard on myself about surfing. I'm trying and I'll keep trying until I get myself back to the place I want to be. What more can I do? Everyone starts from somewhere. I think about young girls just learning the sport. Maybe if I keep working at it, some little surfers will find my Instagram and get motivated to stick with it even if they have bad days sometimes.

"Did you see Mom and Dad earlier?" Amelia asks her sister.

"No, I'm going see them later. They're coming over for dinner," Quincy answers. "They'd like to see you too," she adds to me.

"I didn't know they were in town. How long are they staying?"

"A week or so? I'm not sure. But they were excited to hear you were visiting. I'm sure they'll be around the hotel a bunch so you can say hi."

"Oh, they'll be around the hotel all right," Amelia says. She doesn't sound that excited about it.

"Are they giving Pete a hard time?" Quincy asks. She leans forward to get a better look at Amelia.

"Kind of, you know how it is. Dad doesn't care much about the business until he's here, and then we're all doing everything wrong. Especially if it's something new that he doesn't understand."

"Like social media?" I ask. I know that's a big part of what Amelia does for the Waveline.

"Yep. He's not that out of touch, but he's never had a good grasp of the importance of marketing. Especially online." Amelia looks at her phone in her hand that has started ringing. "Shit. This is the boys' school. Ugh, I just got here. Watch her?" She points to Claire, and I nod as she gets up to answer it.

Quincy pulls her niece onto her lap and scoots closer to me. "Picture time," she calls, and we pose for selfies with Claire. The baby is, as usual, the most patient participant and goes along with all our requests for photos. My favorite is one Quincy takes of me and Claire back-to-back looking over our shoulders at each other. "You've got to post that one. It's so cute."

"Amelia won't care if I post a picture of her kid?"

"Why would she? I do it all the time."

"I'm going to send it to Kate and Bree first. They'll love it." I open up the group text that also has Pete and Quincy on it. It happens to be the first one I see, but I also wouldn't mind showing Pete what I'm doing and stirring up a little jealousy that I'm hanging with his favorite niece.

Quincy eyes me and looks down at her phone. "You sent it to the group?"

I shrug. "There's no reason not to."

Kate texts back first. Then Bree hops in.

Kate: Is that Amelia's daughter? She's so adorable.

Bree: Looking like flames, Millie. California looks good on you.

I smile at their responses and watch my phone to see if Pete will add anything. He has to have seen it. His phone has buzzed three times from the group text. But nothing comes and my stomach sinks with disappointment.

"So. Tasher is puking. I've got to go get him. Which means I get to drive to Vera Lake three times today and Miss Claire gets dragged around even more," she gripes.

I feel bad. It's not like I have much I have to do today. I could easily help her out.

"I can hang with Claire while you go get Tasher," I offer.

Amelia clutches her phone to her chest. "Really? That would be so nice."

"Sure. Is it okay if we play on the beach for a little bit and then walk around town?"

"Totally. Take her to get shaved ice in town, and you'll be her favorite person ever," Amelia says, reaching for her keys.

My eyes bulge out of my head. "You guys have shaved ice here?" I don't believe it. "Like real shaved ice, like in Hawaii? And no one thought to mention this to me? I've been here for almost a week. What kind of friends are you?"

Quincy laughs. "There's a place near the bookstore in town. It's pretty epic."

"Oh my god, afternoon made. This place really is perfect." I hold up the picture I just sent to the group chat. "Is it okay if I post this photo of Claire?" I ask Amelia.

"Yeah, it's fine. The girl is basically a local celebrity around here anyway," she answers.

Claire and I walk into town and share a rainbow shaved ice as we make our way back to the hotel where we can hang out until Amelia can pick her up. As we're walking back, I see a familiar figure walking toward us on the sidewalk. A figure whose curve of shoulders has been etched in my brain since one very long summer-school class in college.

"I think I see your uncle Pete," I say to Claire. Her big eyes fill with recognition and joy. "I feel you, sister." I smile at him with pins in my stomach as he approaches. I study his face, looking for some clue as to how low I've fallen in his opinion since my proposition yesterday, but he gives nothing away. He sends a quick smile in my direction and then sweeps Claire into his arms in one fluid motion.

"Hey, sweet girl," he says. I actively try not to melt and definitely do not imagine he was talking to me. Claire spares me not even a second glance as she paws happily at Pete's scruffy cheeks.

"Wow, I feel like old news," I say.

"Sorry, not everyone in my family can prefer you over me. My parents say hello, by the way."

"I'm sorry I didn't get a chance to see them today."

"I'm sure you'll see them next time," he grumbles. It sounds like he could use a little less being checked up on.

The three of us walk back to the hotel together. I guess I don't really need to come along anymore. Since I've handed over Claire to her uncle, I could go about my day, but it's nice having an adult to talk to after being with someone with only a handful of words at her disposal. Plus, I should see the rest of my babysitting duties through and make sure Claire gets to Amelia. It has nothing to do with the way Pete's shoulders keep brushing mine as we walk along the narrow sidewalk.

"How did it go with your parents today? Are they happy with how the hotel is doing?"

"They're not unhappy, I guess. The real test comes later on when the colleges have their breaks. Usually the motels are the first choice since they're cheaper, but last year we did pretty well. We're closer to the beach and our rooms make for better vacation pictures than the motels, so people will spend a little more sometimes."

"My room is very photogenic. I can attest to that." I've only seen the motels from the outside, but they're your classic kind with doors to the rooms leading out to the parking lot and a sense of your impending murder kind of place. They can't compare to the Waveline. "Do you offer any kind of special rate to help lure the college kids over?"

"Yeah, but so do the motels. Plus, I don't want to lower the prices too much. We still need to pay our bills. And people don't spend much at the café or our bar. They tend to load up on food and booze before they come to save money."

"I remember it well." My stomach actually rolls as my body has a physical reaction to the memories of my senior-year spring break. I shudder at the amount of cheap alcohol I consumed at room temperature with barely anything to mix it with.

"Well, I'm happy to do my part and post very flattering pictures of the hotel. I doubt it will do much, but I'm happy to try."

"About that." Pete's eyes shift my way, and he pauses on the sidewalk. I can tell there's something he wants to say, so I do the same.

"I'm sorry about how I overreacted the other day," he says, while trying to meet my eyes unsuccessfully. I don't blame his nervousness. I don't want to talk about this much either.

"No, it wasn't a great idea. I shouldn't have suggested it, and I really shouldn't have tried to make you a part of it."

"Have you corrected them? Alana's followers? Do they know we're just friends?"

I bite my lip. "I haven't. I'm really sorry. I don't know why I haven't. I don't even have that many followers yet, and the ones I do have only started following me after Alana posted that picture of us together." Embarrassment creeps into my cheeks as I admit this. Pete probably has the same perspective as Quincy that launching a moneymaking Instagram account is as easy as cruising waves at the Cove. "I was kind of hoping people would forget or move on. But I'll post something soon…today. It seems people love watching me screw up anyway, so I can just add this one to my list of mistakes."

"What if you lose the new followers?"

I shrug. "I'll miss him." Maybe a joke about my lack of followers will disguise how terrible I am at this.

"Millie." Pete tilts his head to the side. "I don't want to be the reason this doesn't work for you."

"That's nice of you, but this isn't your problem. I'm not going to drag you into another one of my screwups."

"Well, that's just it. My dad and I were talking and that got me thinking. I mean, I know you're a lot better at this marketing stuff than I am, and like you said, we're going to be together." He coughs. "I mean, hanging out together anyway while you're here, so I don't see the harm if people think we're together if it could help the hotel."

I blink, trying to make sense of what he's saying. "But you hate social media." It's the only thing I can think to say.

"That's a little dramatic. Anyway, I wouldn't have to post stuff, right?"

"Not if you don't want to." I shake my head. This seemed like such a ridiculous plan when I came up with it before, and it still might not make a difference, but now Pete is suddenly on board and the idea of spending extra time with him is incredibly tempting. It's too hard to pass it up even if it would be just pretend. With all that extra time together, who knows where this might lead. "We would be surfing, hanging out, having dinner, regular stuff, but I'll just post pictures and caption them to seem like we're..."

"Married?"

"And super into each other." At least one of us won't be completely faking it.

Pete nods, seriously thinking this over.

"But our 'relationship' can't look like a screwup," Pete says as he chews his lower lip, considering. "I know you've been building a following that way, but if you make our relationship look like another one of your funny disasters...it's just...it might reflect badly on the, um, hotel."

"So, not only will we have a fake relationship, but it will also be a perfect one?" I swallow hard. Did Pete just rip a page out of my college daydreams? "I'm not sure I can keep that going forever."

Pete winces, so I feel the need to clarify. "I just mean we'll be found out eventually, and I wouldn't want that to impact your business. I can frame it like it was another one of my 'funny disasters' like you said, but we can't let it go on for too long or we might catch some real heat for it."

"How about one month? Then we'll come clean. I'm sure you can figure out a good way to spin it. And a month will put us close to fall, when people are planning their winter travels." Pete runs a hand over his short brown hair in thought. "The timing should work out."

"If you think it will make a difference. A month it is. We'll have a perfect month-long relationship. I will carefully document our breakup, and we'll both be more successful when it's over. But you know I would have done this anyway. Posted about the hotel. That place is basically a thirst trap for anyone with the smallest amount of wanderlust."

I'm not sure if pretending we're together will help the hotel much, but Alana seemed to think partnering up was a good idea. And if the side benefit is extra time with Pete, I'm more than happy to give it a chance.

"Good, I was definitely going for thirst trap when we decorated."

"What about when you picked out that shirt this morning?"

Pete blinks. "What?"

I can't believe I just said that out loud. "Never mind." I shake my head. I really can't help myself with him sometimes.

Chapter 11

I'M DREADING IT, BUT IT'S time to check in with my parents.

I've been here almost a week and I've barely sent them more than a handful of texts. So I take a cup of coffee onto the small patio off my hotel room and have a seat on a reclining chair to make the call.

"Hi, Millie, we're just about to walk onto the ferry," my mom greets me. She's letting me know she can only talk for a few minutes. They must be heading back to Boston now.

"I just wanted to check in and let you know things are going well." I try to sound extra cheerful. I want her to think I have everything under control. No cause for alarm or for me to come home.

"Well, I was wondering when I would hear from you. How is it there? How's Quincy?"

"She's great. It's great," is all I can think to say. "Have you seen any of my posts?"

"No, but we will. I'll pull it up on the ferry. We were just so busy getting the house ready. We are following you now though. Dad figured out the Instagram and we saw your picture on the Surf Shack Dream House with Peter. How is he?"

The way she says his name is the way I picture every commenter saying it when they see a post featuring his gorgeous tan face. I still can't believe that face agreed to pretend to be my husband.

"He's good. The same. Working hard and taking care of everyone." I try not to sigh into the phone when I realize that now includes me. He didn't have to agree to my plan or help me in my attempt to jump on Alana's internet coattails, and I really hope I don't disappoint him. I'm going to really try my best to make him and the hotel look as wonderful as they are in real life so he gets as much from our deal as I do.

"That's nice. I'm glad you've had a chance to spend time with your old friends. Maybe we can have them out to the island this summer when you're back. You father and I were thinking you could stay in the garage apartment. It never really rents, so you can stay there until you find a job. Don't worry."

My molars clench and I have to force my shoulders away from my ears. "I'm not moving into the garage apartment on the island."

"Millie, you have to have a plan. You can't couch surf for too long. You'll wear out your welcome. It's rude to take advantage of your friends this way."

"I'm not couch surfing. And it's not like I'm doing nothing. I've even sold some of the stickers Kate made."

"Well, I'm sure that bought last night's cocktail, but in a few weeks when things go south, just remember you have a place to stay with us."

I shake my head, so frustrated. "I'm not staying with you. I didn't run home during the pandemic, and I'm not doing it now. People are starting to follow me. Alana reposted me. I'm building a following."

"How much money do you get for a repost like that?"

I swallow hard. "Nothing. It doesn't work like that."

"Ah," she answers. "You know, I saw Janet Macado a few days ago, and she mentioned her daughter is starting her real estate course next month. I could sign you up. When people get tired of watching you fall headfirst into the ocean, of course."

So, she is checking my account. "I'm not moving in with you, and I'm not getting my real estate license. I can do this, Mom." The last thing I want is to be working with my parents, letting them monitor my every move and mistake. Nothing would prove I can't function on my own more than that.

"Okay, it was just a thought. One last thing before I go. I saw people saying something about an Instagram Husband. Were they talking about you and Peter? What does that mean?"

I squeeze my eyes shut and try not to shatter my phone with the death grip I'm using on it. "It's just something people say on the internet, Mom."

The next morning, I pull on *the* dress over my favorite red bikini and stuff my wet suit into a mesh string bag to bring to the beach. The conversation with my mom yesterday put me in a weird mood for the rest of the day. I tried writing some new posts, but kept second-guessing every other word I wrote. If I can get one sponsorship or paid ad soon, I know that will change everything. It would show my parents I can make this into a career worth pursuing and that I'm not just chasing the next best wave. I'm not sure who I'd like to prove this to more, my parents or myself, but maybe if I start by trying to show up for myself first, proving that I don't always let things go down without a fight, my parents will see that too. First order of business is getting my surf skills back on track. It's kind of embarrassing trying to be a Peacock Bay influencer when I can hardly surf.

The problem is I still don't have a surfboard. I don't want to ask Alana for an update on that board she was going to give to me because that seems a little like I'm trying to use her for her access to free stuff. Which I'm not. She did offer, but I can't exactly call her up and say, "Hey, did that free surfboard come yet?"

I can't borrow a board from Quincy because she's shortboards forever, and I can't ask Pete to borrow one because he'll come with me. Even though watching his sculpted triceps as he carried two huge surfboards out of the ocean was the highlight of my month, I'd really like it if the next time I surf with him he doesn't look at me with so much pity. There has hardly been a time in my life when I cared about looking stupid, but with surfing and Pete, well, this is one of those times.

After that talk with my mom, I kept thinking about how Pete called my posts "funny disasters." I know they kind of embarrassed my mom, and Pete thinks I'm exaggerating things for comic effect, but I'm not. The reality is that this is just me. I screw up a lot, and maybe owning up to that, making mistakes and not hiding them for once, could help me feel okay about this part of myself that I've never felt comfortable with before.

Failure has never been a happy place for me. It brings up all those memories of struggling through elementary school until my parents had me tested for ADHD. How embarrassed I was thinking there was something wrong with my brain, but then how much easier things became in school when I began taking meds under a doctor's care. So, I threw together a post talking about all this. It felt good to be able to say how grateful I was to my teachers and parents for getting me the aides that I needed and for helping me turn things around and get into a good college.

I also talked a little bit about why it's so important to me to pick up surfing again. Something I'm not sure I had really thought much about until now. The main thing I discovered while I was writing out my thoughts was how much I love the time on the water because it forces me away from technology. I wrote about how I actively missed my phone when I was on the water and how weird that was, but also kind of freeing. There are so many things to think about when you're out there, paddling out until your shoulders burn, watching the waves to find one that will be just right to catch, not to mention keeping your balance once you do finally catch one—there's just a lot going on. The whole exercise forces you to be present. Which, for me, has always been hard, and with the invention of smartphones nearly impossible.

When the post went up on Instagram, after only one hour more than two hundred people had hit Like. That's a huge amount for me, and it's even more encouraging to see the comments people are making. Talking about things they used to do when they were young that they miss doing: horseback riding, painting, and ceramics got a lot of shout-outs. It's really cool to think I might be inspiring people to consider picking up old hobbies they once loved. There are even a few new sticker orders.

So when I go tromping through the hotel to find Amelia to try to borrow a board from her, I'm feeling a little better. The silk of my dress swishes against my legs as I make my way to Amelia's office and adds to my high.

Apparently Amelia keeps a board at the hotel in case she has a few hours after work where she can sneak off while the kids are at school. Once I have the board, it takes a few minutes to figure out the whole bike-rack surfboard situation. This is when I curse myself for choosing to avoid shortboards. Biking to the beach with a five-foot-long shortboard would be tricky but manageable. Balancing on a bike with a nine-foot board attached to it requires an entirely different set of skills.

I nearly have the board secured to the bike when Pete appears with a look on his face that lets me know I'm in trouble, and not the good kind.

"What are you doing?" he asks.

"Picking out our wedding flowers, darling," I joke. Because what does it look like? He sputters, so at least that's fun.

"You're... You... Ugh, Millie." He exhales sharply. "Whose board is that?" I can tell he's trying to hide how annoyed he is, but I can't imagine how any of this offends him.

"It's Amelia's. I didn't steal it. This is all out in the open."

"Why didn't you ask me for a board? I left one in my office for you to use whenever you want it."

He did? That was nice, if a little surprising. I know he agreed to the fake relationship, but I'm not going to pop into his office and start demanding selfies and surfboards. He'd instantly pull out of the deal, and I don't want that.

"I'm only just getting the hang of things again. It's better this way." I only mostly mean surfing.

"You think I'm going to make fun of you? Did I do that the last time? Did Quincy?" He looks so annoyed with me, and I'm not sure why. I didn't come bothering him for this reason. He's off the hook. I'm not sure what the screwup is here.

"No, but I also didn't want to bother you."

"Since when?" It's a good point. Pete looks back at the hotel and shifts his weight as if unsure what to do next. "Never mind. I have some work I need to finish, but if you just wait a few hours, I'll go with you. Did you even check the tides?"

He might have a point there, but I won't let him know it. "Pete, I want to go by myself."

"No, you don't. You're not that stupid."

Okay, nope. No. No way. I narrow my eyes at him. "I think that's a typo."

"You wouldn't go surfing in a place you don't know when you don't know who else is out there, when you're out of practice. You know better than that, Mills."

"Wow. So many insults to unpack here. Just because we're fake married now doesn't mean you get to tell me what to do."

Pete puts his hands on either sides of his head and rub his temples. "You're not going to tease me into dropping this. It's not safe. You don't have to prove anything to me."

Don't I? Don't I need him to see how capable I am of taking care of myself? Don't I need to show that to myself too?

"I don't have to justify myself to you, but since we've been friends for so long, I'll just tell you calmly that I've been surfing my entire life except for a break for the past few years. I've already surfed at both the beaches here, so I know what the currents are like and where the rocks are. And *since* we've been such good friends for so long, you're going to remember that and shut the fuck up before I get really pissed at you for calling me stupid and a terrible surfer."

"I didn't say—"

"Bye, Pete!"

"Millie," he argues, but I'm done talking now.

I mount the bike and wobble annoyingly as I try to speed off. Which I can't do effectively with this massive board attached to my bike. It's the least satisfying dramatic exit as I stand on the pedals and grind my feet down, trying to get some momentum to move me away from Pete and his condescending tone. I've looked smoother in my life, that is for sure, but I push against the pedals of this beach cruiser with the strength of every girl surfer that has ever been mansplained to about surfing alone or how girls don't belong on big waves without a big-brother figure to look out for them. Pete really should have known better. At the last second, I arch my back slightly, sticking my ass out, because if he's still watching I want there to be something for him to really see.

I surf at Turtle Beach for I don't know how long. The waves are pumping. A little too big for a longboard, but I don't care. I paddle into huge waves, turtle rolling my board to let them crash over me. My shoulders burn with exhaustion and then go numb. There are few other surfers out. All of them guys, but I don't let that slow me down. It makes me work even harder to keep up. I'm not going to look like a grommet in front of guys I don't know and prove Pete right.

I follow the universal surfing rules of the lineup. I don't steal waves. I wait my turn. I want to show the guys out here that I know what I'm doing and that I belong on these waves just as much as they do. But it really sucks that I feel like I have something to prove at all. Why can't a girl just surf on her own and be respected for her skills the same way guys are? Why should I have to be extra careful about following the rules when the guys out here today probably aren't even thinking about them?

Logically, I know Pete was just trying to look out for me. It's dangerous to surf alone no matter your gender. But I really didn't need another person telling me I couldn't do something, and when it was a guy telling a girl what to do related to surfing, I don't know, it just hit an already raw nerve.

I'm forming a post about all of this in my head while I sit on my board, feet circling in the water beneath me, and I feel filled with a new determination. It's also the moment I spot the most perfect wave of the day coming right to me. The swell is high as I paddle hard. I feel the pull of the wave as my board and I meet it, and then magic happens. My board feels solid, steady as the earth, instead of rushing water. I pop up to my feet easily and bend my legs, keeping even pressure on both feet. I'm riding right into the pocket. Not a hint of wobble from me.

I hear the strangers I was surfing with, the ones Pete was sure would offend or attack me in some way, hoot and cheer in celebration of this perfect wave after I pop up. Encouraged, I take a tiny step, bringing my back right foot over my front left, then I step again to uncross them. I inch like this toward the nose, but I'm not ready to go all the way yet, so I cross step back to the center. It was still pretty sweet. A perfect wave to end the day on. I ride almost into the shore and then hop off into the whitewater. Behind me, a few of the guys give me wolf whistles to cheer my wave as much as me. I turn and give them a wave in thanks.

"Yeah, way to ride," one guy calls.

"Come back and ride me," another guy shouts.

Okay, that's the end of that. I roll my eyes and hold up a middle finger. The guys moan their disappointment, but I'm sure they were expecting a response like that. If that line has ever been successful, I've got my work cut out for me with the younger surfer-girl generations.

I dunk under the water to smooth my hair back and then reemerge to gather the board and climb out of the ocean. When I do, it's like another guy has teleported here to annoy me.

Pete is sitting on the shore on a large woven blanket. He hasn't changed since I saw him at the Waveline, not a wet suit or swimsuit in sight, so I know he didn't come to surf. Which means he came to chaperone. And, holy hell, that will not stand.

I stomp my way to the shore. He doesn't get up to help me. I think he knows better at this moment. I'm getting ready to lay into him; it's all right there on the tip of my tongue. When I look up at him, shaking my wet ropes of hair over my shoulder, I see he's not alone. In fact, he is actually babysitting.

The adorably tiny Claire sits beside him, attempting to dig in the sand with a tiny shovel.

"I brought the baby so you couldn't yell at me."

"A sound strategy," I tell him.

"Plus, I know you like her better than me so she was likely to improve your general feelings about my being here."

"I don't need you to supervise me while I surf. Did you see me out there? I fucking crushed it." I clap a hand over my mouth when I realize I just dropped an f-bomb in front of the world's sweetest child.

"Don't worry, she can't repeat anything yet. And yes, I saw you crush it. It doesn't look like I'm the only one either." He narrows his eyes at the guys in the water briefly, then returns his focus to me. "That was some pretty fancy footwork out there."

I grin a gloating smile and then cancel it because I don't need his praise.

"And I didn't come here to supervise or anything like that. I haven't even been here that long. I just came to apologize and bring you hot chocolate." He reaches into a reusable canvas tote, pulls out an insulated travel mug, and holds it out to me. I really want to huff and puff my indignation a little bit longer, but this combination of sexy apologetic man holding eco-friendly goods is weirdly doing it for me.

I dump my board on the ground, but don't reach for the mug right away. I don't want it to be too obvious how much this thoughtful apology means to me.

"Just so we're clear, I am an only child, Peter Santana. Which means I do not have a big brother and I have never felt the need for one. Those guys out there were celebrating me." Pete makes a sound like "fuckers," but I can't be sure. "They weren't giving me any trouble until the very end, but I handled it. Did you see me handle it?"

"Yeah, you handled it all right," Pete says with a look of stone as he looks around me again at the other surfers in the lineup. He probably knows a few of them, and he doesn't look pleased at their presence. "Listen, this is a small town, which means an even smaller dating pool. A hot girl with skills like yours shows up in the water, and the guys are going think they've seen a unicorn." I swallow hard because I think there was a *hot girl* in there. "I don't want them hunting you down."

Pete looks at me, his eyes blazing, and I'm trying to parse out what he just said. Not just the *hot girl*, but the thing about a *unicorn*, and I'm now having visions of him dressed in a fur loincloth hunting me like a caveman, and I'm squeezing my legs together to fight the deep pull of my body toward his.

"That actually doesn't sound like the worst thing," I manage. Compared to my dating life in New York, being a unicorn would be a major improvement. Why is he bothered by this anyway? Even if we're going to post like we're together, that doesn't mean I can't keep my eyes open for a real relationship, does it? A girl has needs, and I'm sure he does too. We might have to talk about this sometime. Being married online is going to be a problem for him if he's looking to hook up with someone else.

"Come on, Mills. I even brought you one of these giant handmade marshmallows that cost as much as that surfboard over there." He pulls out a small cellophane package and sets it on top of the mug.

I twist my mouth up as if I'm thinking this over. Like there's a chance I'm not going to accept his apology now that there's extra sugar involved.

"One?" I ask, crossing my arms over my chest. Well, might as well make him work for it a tiny bit more.

"Fine, you can have mine too," he says, sighing.

I break into a grin and take the mug out of his hands. I make him scoot over so I can sit between him and Claire. When I run my pruny fingers through her soft baby curls, she looks up and gives me the most adorable toothless grin, then returns to her shoveling.

"You know, you actually gave me a good idea for some posts, about how women surfers are still treated like second-class citizens in this sport. How we're constantly underestimated and pushed out of the best surf spots by overbearing alpha males."

"Okay, okay. I'm sorry. I get it. I swear to never again question your surf skills."

"No… I mean yes, don't. But I think there's something there. I don't want to always have to post about my mistakes and failures. Wouldn't it be better for everyone to find a way to build a community around my platform? Not just another girl standing around posing in different wet suits and bikinis?"

Pete's eyes flick to my wet-suit-covered frame, and the corners of his lips turn up just slightly. A chill rips through me, but I shove it. I can't let him see how a look like that makes me feel. Like I'm hot and cold and wearing way too many clothes.

Speaking of wearing too many clothes, I start to unwrap the marshmallow to add it to my mug, but realize my mobility is very much compromised by the thick wet suit I'm wearing.

"Unzip me," I order my friend's brother.

"W-what?" Pete asks.

"Unzip my wet suit please, fake husband. My hands are full." I try to sound like this request is nothing unusual, when really I want to make it clear to Pete in no uncertain terms that I am very much not his little sister. I know exactly what bikini I have underneath my suit. It's bright red and mostly strings. It's unicorn-hunter bait if it's anything.

When Pete takes hold of the long zipper pull, he doesn't just hold it between his fingers. He twists it around his hand as if he's about to start a tug-of-war with my wet suit, even though I've never known a wet suit to tug back. He gives one big pull, but when he reaches the middle of my back, slows it down to a crawl. The zipper creeps down the remaining length of my spine, and you could say it's because of the awkwardness of the angle, but also maybe, just maybe all my bare skin is causing his brain to forget how to make his hands operate a zipper.

I wish I could say it wasn't having any effect on me, but holy shit, the slow click of the zipper is making the goose bumps on my already cold skin pinch even harder.

Pete's hands reach up and tug at the openings of my wet suit. One on each side of my shoulders. Inside my suit. Touching my skin.

I have to put the mug down.

"Do you…do you need more help?" His voice is rough, but I can feel the heat from his hands burning on my icy, wet shoulders. I nod. I don't want this skin-to-skin contact to be over just yet.

He tugs gently on the top of my suit as my arms go limp at my sides. He coaxes my shoulders free and then pulls down hard so I can get my arms out. He can't go any further after that without laying me down and stripping me completely. There's no reasonable way to explain that so I murmur my thanks over my shoulder. But just as I'm about to rise to my feet, I feel his fingertips graze my spine.

My entire body freezes. That was no accident. It was a full-length appreciative stroke, and my body is reacting. I let out a shaky breath and close my eyes, trying to collect myself.

I can't look at Pete now while I pull the rest of the wet suit down and slowly step out. I'm trying hard not to ruin whatever just happened with that last little touch by getting twisted up in the legs of my wet suit and falling over. The sun warms my skin and I know I'll dry quickly, but Pete hands me a towel anyway. He's not even looking at my face, and I think maybe I hallucinated his fingers tracing the length of my back.

It's only after I've wrapped the towel around my torso and gathered my composure enough that I can look at Pete again. But he's still not looking at me. He's looking right past me out to the water where the three guys from the lineup are bobbing on their boards close together. But they're not watching the waves. They're watching me. When they see me turn, they give a few hoots in appreciation. I shake my head, dismissing them, but when I look back at Pete, he is not amused.

"I'm a unicorn," I say, popping a hand to my hip.

He stands up to his full height and brushes off his hands. He stares down at me with dark eyes, but keeps casting glances back to the water. He looks ready to pounce, and I'm not sure whether it's at the guys or at me. "Can you just sit down so I don't do something stupid?"

My cheeks heat up as I try to imagine what kind of stupid thing Pete would do if my new surf buddies got any braver. Or if I just stood here and dared him. Is this new protectiveness because we're supposed to be married? I could understand his annoyance if guys were catcalling his wife, and I guess it kind of looks like we're together since he came to meet me at the beach. Maybe that's it.

I'm not going poke the subject anymore, so I sit back down and bring the hot chocolate to my lap. Then I plop the two marshmallows I was promised into the mug and take a sip. It's so good. Thick and rich, and if Pete says he made this from some secret family recipe, my bikini may fall to ground. So I don't ask.

"I got a video of that last wave, by the way," Pete says. "For your 'Gram."

"Thank you, can you send it to me now?"

"Sure, instant-gratification girl."

I shrug and sip my hot chocolate. "Who likes waiting for something good?"

"Come on, even you can admit that sometimes the delay makes the thing you want even better."

"Why *even me?*" I ask. It feels like a dig at my ADHD, but I'm pretty sure Pete isn't starting another fight with me after he put in all this effort to make peace from the last one.

"Nothing. I meant nothing by it. Just you know, the internet and social media. Everything happens instantly now. It's nice when some things take a little longer, don't you think?"

If this has anything to do with his hands nearly inside my wet suit, then my answer is simple. "No, I don't think so at all."

Chapter
12

THAT AFTERNOON, I WRITE UP a short post to go along with the video of me on my one perfect wave. In my stories, I post the same video, but call out the guys who harassed me in the water. Their faces are obscured in the video, so I'm not worried about it getting back to them. I am worried about their reactions after they saw me surf. The realization that they thought it was okay to ask for sexual favors points to how different a day in the water can be for a woman versus a guy.

After the post goes up, I start digging a little deeper into the subject online. It doesn't take much time reading articles about women surfers to find something that shocks me. I learn that women only started being invited to the most famous of big wave contests, like the one at Jaws in Hawaii, in 2016. And even when Maya Gabeira surfed the biggest wave of the year in 2020, every article mentions how in her early career she was criticized for putting herself and others in danger by attempting these big waves. However, never once do I find an article that references something similar about a guy.

I'm sitting on the front porch of the hotel, letting that knowledge sink in, when the responses to my post start rolling in. My DM's are from women with stories about the times they were harassed in parking lots or told to get out of the water and "leave it for the boys." Stories about guys trying to pull off girls' bikini tops in lineups so they feel they always have to wear surf shirts, or how it took them years to try surfing because they didn't feel they had the ideal body type a girl surfer was supposed to have. I ask if I can repost several of the DM's, and with permission, I add these messages to my stories.

Other women are chiming in with agreement. My email pings with sticker orders. For a split second I wonder if I might actually sell out of them. "Relax, Millie," I mutter to myself. I started with two thousand. I don't think selling out is even a possibility, but the idea is thrilling as I watch a few more orders land in my inbox.

I text Kate and Bree.

Millie: People are buying the stickers!

Bree: What are you wearing?

I'm shaking my head, not because she sounds like a horny long-distance boyfriend, but because I know exactly why she's asking. I almost don't want to admit it. Why should a dress get credit for my post and the attention it's stirring up? Then again, it kind of feels smart not to make it mad.

Millie: I'm wearing our dress. Fine.
Maybe there is something lucky about it after all.

Bree: Tell me more about how you're getting lucky in it?

I think I'm just going to leave that one there. There may be a little bit of good luck around me, but it definitely hasn't extended *that* far. Though I'm not sure how it could now that I've effectively been taken off the market by my new deal with Pete. I might need to bring that up to him. A month is a long time, after all.

Luckily, that's when Quincy pulls up and hops out of her mint-green Bronco.

"Do my eyes deceive me? Is that my friend Quincy Santana, the supercool mom and influencer of Peacock Bay?"

"That's me." She grins up at me as she climbs the steps to the porch. "The least influential influencer in town."

"Did you see my post? I actually got a lot of DM's on that one. A few followers are popping up too." I smile at her.

"That's awesome. Getting the followers is half the battle." She looks down at her hands and picks at her pinkie nail.

"What's the other half?"

"Keeping them." She sighs. I nod. Makes sense, but I need to get the followers first. "And the sponsors."

"Whatever, kombucha queen. I wish I had your sponsors."

Quincy picks at her thumbnail. "Yeah, well, let's just hope they feel as warmly about me as you do."

I wait for her to continue, but she doesn't offer more, so I change the subject instead of pressing her. "Hey, wait a second? You're alone," I say.

"I am." She smiles. "My parents were with the kids this morning while I ran to Vera Lake, and they said the kids could stay until dinner. I wasn't going to turn that down."

"That's great. I'd suggest we go surf, but I went this morning and I'm kind of beat."

"That's cool. I'd rather just chill with you anyway."

"What was in Vera Lake?" I glance down at my computer and check the stats on my blog post again. My eyes go wide at the numbers. People are actually responding.

"Vera Lake Academy," Quincy states simply but chews the inside of her cheek. I close my computer, determined to focus on my friend. This isn't a conversation I should have with my computer open.

"Is that where Amelia's boys go?"

"Yeah, her boys have been really happy there and…I don't know. Ari and I think we need a better plan for Monrow. He's not… exactly thriving in the homeschool. And next year is kindergarten. I don't want him to get behind."

"Well, I think that's great that you're checking out different options then."

She nods. "Alana doesn't think we should move him. She's so into the idea of the kids growing up together and going to school all as one big happy group, which would be great if it worked. But it might not for Monrow. Vera Lake has a lot of really good special ed programs. If we need them," she adds quickly.

"You're the mom, Quincy. You know what's best for your kid."

"Yeah." She sighs. "I do. I think we have to have him evaluated, Millie," she says softly. I wonder how many times she's said this out loud.

"For school?" I hope she feels like she can talk to me about this. She knows enough about my struggles with school that I hope she knows I'd support her.

"For autism spectrum disorder. Ari has wanted to do it for a year now, and Monrow might not be able to start at Vera Lake unless we have an evaluation done. They said if we're thinking of having the evaluation, it would 'benefit everyone' to have it done before so they can meet his needs when he starts."

"You know what a difference it made for me once my parents finally got me tested for my ADHD. I wish they hadn't waited so long, but that was me. What do you think?"

Quincy turns her head and looks out to the ocean in the distance. The breeze catches her wavy brown hair. "I think it's too soon, but what do I know? Part of me thinks he's still just a little baby. I mean, he's only four. But the bigger part of me watches him with the other kids and compares him to Amelia's boys, how they were when they were his age, and I know he's not like them. I hate the idea that things are going to be harder for him than other kids, and I'm not sure I'm ready to face it yet."

I put my computer on the side table and go over to my friend and wrap her in a tight hug. She rests her chin on the bend in my elbow.

"You're a really good mom. I know you'll figure out the best thing for him." When I let her out of my hug, I have a thought.

"You know, you should write a post about what you're going through with Monrow. I think a lot of moms would relate to that feeling of trying to do the best thing for your kid even when you're not sure what they need."

"Oh, no way. I wouldn't even know where to start. Plus, there's a part of me that feels weird sharing so much personal stuff about my kids. Like, how are they going to feel when they grow up and go out into the world knowing I've laid out the toughest stuff they've gone through to total strangers? It's not like I have a million followers or anything. I wouldn't even want that, but still stuff lives on the internet forever. Imagine Monrow in college and his roommate looks up stories about him clinging to his mom at birthday parties when he was four and throwing epic tantrums when he didn't like the seam on his socks."

I hadn't thought about this. I guess there is a line somewhere. Something each person who chooses to live their lives this way has to figure out for themselves and their family. How do you know how your kids will feel about having so many eyes on them? I think there's a lot of good that can come of this, and I still think it might be cathartic for Quincy to share what she's going through with Monrow, but I can understand that as a mom she wants to protect him from people's judgment online.

"Not to mention, Alana would kill me," she continues.

I tilt my head to the side. "Remind me how Alana is related to your kids?"

"No, I know, it's just that all of our careers revolve around this idea that Peacock Bay is some kind of mom-life utopia. Our A-plus marriages, happy and thriving kids, and that look that's just inches from being attainable if you have the right pants." She gives me a look because, yeah, it happened to me.

"I'm too deep in this to rock the boat. I felt like my sponsors were going to pop up out of nowhere and drop me the entire time

I was touring Vera Lake, which is nuts, I know, but still. And you're part of that now, so you should keep that in mind. Alana created this as the brand and it's not for me, or you, to poke holes in it."

I'm grateful Alana tagged me in her post, and I know it gave me a huge bump in followers, but I'm not sure her brand is my brand and I try to say as much to Quincy. "I'm not trying to poke holes in anything, but I'm not even a mom. Which isn't something Alana can change anytime soon."

"I just think you can post all you want about you and Pete together, but Alana may not like you calling out the rude surfers on the beach or making fun of the hours our stores keep."

"That's not what I was saying about the coffee shop and you know it. And I like how you're throwing your own brother in the mix for me to use as I see fit," I tell Quincy.

"Please, it's, like, Pete's dream to be used by you," she says with a grin.

"He knows it could be good for business, that's all," I counter.

"So, you got him on board after all? Do I get a fake invitation to your fake wedding?"

I make a face at her teasing. "It's just for a month, then I'm going to explain it away as another one of my funny screwups. I know that basically goes against your entire brand, but hey, any publicity is good publicity right?" I think Pete sees it that way. Plus, it's likely only going to be me that faces the backlash. I won't let Pete or the hotel look bad. He's not as used to messing up as I am, and as long as it doesn't go on for too long I think I can play it off like I was just joking. A sort of dream-it-into-existence kind of joke. Which is partially true.

"Just as long as you can handle the fallout."

"I appreciate you being concerned, but I'm the internet's lovable surfing buffoon. I'll be fine."

"That's not exactly what I meant, but sure. Let's go with that." Quincy laughs. When she does, the sound takes me back to late nights on our dorm room floor eating s'mores we made in her microwave. Kate and Bree already passed out in their rooms. I know who that person with that laugh is—she's wild and carefree and a badass surfer. And I know it's not for me to decide what she shares of herself online, but I can't help but think she's missing a chance to really help someone who's going through the same things she is and might not have anyone to talk to about it. But maybe Quincy feels like she doesn't have someone to talk to about what's happening with Monrow.

I wonder if my mom wrestled with the same kind of feelings when she was dealing with my attention issues. I've never thought about how it affected her when I was growing up, but now that I see Quincy's concern over Monrow, I can see it was probably hard for my mom to watch me struggle as well. Maybe it still is.

"Hey, Quincy," I say. "You know you can talk to me about anything, right? If you want to vent to me about Monrow or kids' stuff, I will totally be that person for you. I might not have the same problems as you…"

"But on the internet you do?" she jokes.

"You know what I mean."

She doesn't say anything. She nods, then looks out to the water, and I know her mind is on other things. But that changes again when I see her spot something coming toward us.

"Hey, would you look at that. It's your husband." She grins at me. This is about to be awkward. How I know this I'm not sure, but I can feel it like I can feel the breeze on my face.

Pete jogs up the steps of the porch and stops when he gets to where Quincy is perched against the railing. He greets his sister with a low five, but then promptly asks her to leave.

"Are you kicking me out of my own hotel?" she asks, laughing.

"It's only one-fifth yours and you know it. I just have to talk to Millie for a second."

"Am I in trouble?" I ask. My heart starts pounding. He's changed his mind already? We've been fake married for what? Three minutes?

"No, nothing like that," he says, but I can't get a read on him. How can someone this good looking seem so uncomfortable in his own skin? If I had that skin, I would be walking around showing it off any chance I got. And I mean that in the least serial-killer way possible.

"Come on," Quincy says, poking at his side. "I can stay, can't I? Millie doesn't care, right?" She's just messing with him like we always do. Teasing Pete is a place of joy for us.

"I don't care," I say, but regret it right away when I see Pete's face. His jaw gets tight and he shakes his head.

"Never mind. I'll just talk to you later," Pete says and then starts down the steps again.

"Aw, now I feel kind of bad," Quincy says with an exaggerated frown.

"Yeah, poor Petesy." I frown back at her. "Hold on," I call to Pete and get up from my chair. I catch him in a few steps, but he doesn't stop until I tug his sweatshirt sleeve at the bottom of the porch steps. "What's up with you? Why didn't you wait?"

Pete takes another step away, but I'm still holding onto his sleeve and he almost pulls me in to him. Our chests nearly touch, and there is no way he can't hear my heart thumping against my ribs.

"Because I'd rather not ask you out on our first date in front of my sister."

My jaw goes slack. A date? With Pete? But then I remember… "Oh right. Our first fake date. May it be the first of many," I tease, then regret it. I don't want this guy to rethink fake dating me.

Pete's shoulders sag, and I think he's thinking the same thing. He gives his head a tiny shake, and then his mouth forms a tiny smile. "Sure, Mills. We need to create some content, right? If this is going to have any impact for us both."

"Look at you talking about content. So you want to go out tonight? With me?" Even if it's a fake date, I still like the way it sounds.

"No, with my sister," he shoots back with a look, but there's something softer in it than I've seen before.

I break into a grin and grab onto his forearm without thinking. I let go quickly because he's not really asking me out. I shake my head, embarrassed. Pete laughs and his smile zaps me low in my belly. I don't know how I'm going to do this. Putting myself in romantic scenarios with Pete knowing they're all pretend might be a special kind of torture. But Quincy said it's just as hard to keep the followers once you have them, and there's no denying my posts featuring Pete have gathered the biggest number of likes. Plus, this was my idea.

I glance up at Quincy still on the porch.

She smiles down at us. "What's he saying, Millie?" she calls, delighting in poking around between us.

"We're just planning our first Instagram date," I shout back. Pete puts a hand over his face and drags it down slowly. "Is that okay?" I say to her, smiling back at Pete. He's probably regretting this idea now. "I wouldn't want things to be awkward or anything." This is killing Pete, and that only makes me happier about the entire situation.

"Of course it's okay. My brother is your brother, right?" It's what she used to always say whenever I needed Pete to help me move something heavy or drive me somewhere. So, that's the way I need to think of this. He's just helping me out. Nothing more.

"Yep, but let's keep this between us. I wouldn't want to embarrass him or anything." I grin at Pete, who's now rubbing his eyes and shaking his head. He hates every second of this.

"Gotcha, wouldn't want things to get weird." She shouts even louder.

"Okay, thanks Quincy," Pete calls to his sister. "Is it cool if I talk to Millie now?"

"Yep, but pics or it didn't happen, Millie. I mean it. I want to feel like I'm there," she calls. "But not for the late-night stuff." She drops her voice low. "You keep that stuff to yourself." She fakes a stern look our way before tromping off into the hotel.

"She's not actually going to be there though, right?" Pete asks.

"Not if I document it really carefully," I tease him.

Chapter
13

I HAD ONLY ONE CHOICE when it came to what to wear tonight. If I had worn anything other than my black slip dress, I'm pretty sure my friends would have flown out here and stuffed me in it themselves. I guess it's time to really put this thing to the test. I hold my phone up to frame a decent selfie while I wait for Pete to pick me up outside of the Waveline and send the photo to my friends. Pete's car pulls up just as I get a response from Bree.

> **Bree**: Like Kamala said, It might be the first, but it's not the last. She wasn't talking about your date with Pete at the time, but I think it applies.

I snicker at her text, but I'm filled with a burst of confidence. I wonder if it's really the dress that brings us these little boosts or if it's the way we're able to connect with each other when in it that makes me feel this way. Sure, I think I look good wearing this dress, but knowing my friends are rooting for me even harder when I wear it makes me feel even more capable of handling whatever I'm facing.

I mean business when I'm wearing this dress. Do I believe the dress knows that? Of course not. But my friends know it, and that's all I need.

I'm still thinking this over when I climb into Pete's car, and the extra bravado of the dress makes me say, "I can't believe you asked me out. Who even does that anymore?"

You'd think I would quell my teasing on a date, even if it's fake and arranged purely for social media purposes, but old habits die hard. Pete doesn't seem to mind. I think he might actually think it was weird if I wasn't making fun of him. That would make the whole fake-date thing even more awkward than it is. I want to keep things relaxed and normal. Just two friends hanging out, helping each other raise their social media platforms. Still, I can't remember the last time someone actually asked me on a date. Every other hookup or relationship I've had just sort of happened. Often ill-advised and hormonally charged. It's possible I'm not great at dating.

"Someone who wants to have dinner with you? Don't make me regret it. Or you'll have to convince one of those dirtbag surfers from the beach to be your Instagram Husband."

"First of all, why would I be interested in dirtbags? Second of all, that was your beach where I was surfing. You could have just as easily been one of those dirtbags in the water with me."

"First of all," he needles me. "That's not *my* beach. The Cove is my beach. Second of all, I wasn't invited. Remember?"

"Details." I wave him off, but I feel way more relaxed now that we're bantering back and forth again. We get out of the station wagon and approach what looks like, what else, a run-down beach shack. But the small front porch is covered with string lights so I know they at least have electricity.

"So, this is my favorite restaurant in town. It's not fancy. I don't know what you had in mind, um, for the pictures. But it's tacos, and we can take them and sit on little benches they've set up on the beach. Is that okay?" His eyebrows pinch together, and I wonder if maybe I should cool it on the teasing.

"How could tacos ever not be okay?" I say, my throat suddenly very dry.

Pete places just his fingertips on the middle of my back and opens the faded-blue screen door to the restaurant. I flash back to earlier on the beach when his fingers where nearly in this exact spot, but I doubt he's thinking the same thing.

I didn't change. I was wearing our dress when Pete suggested dinner, and I figured this could be a good test. Maybe it is a little lucky. I've certainly had some unusual experiences since I came here. Kate said the dress isn't about luck really, it's more about confidence, and I get that now. Since I got here, I have felt a little different. More in control. Maybe it has something to do with broadcasting my mistakes for all to see, or maybe it's just that I feel good in this dress.

Pete and I discuss our order. He has some strong opinions on what should be included in my first experience here at what he says is simply called the Taco Shack or sometimes just the Shack. There's a carne asada that is crucial to my life's happiness, apparently, and a fish taco that he orders four of with extra green sauce.

"How's the pulled pork?" I ask timidly. I'm worried if he says it's not good, I may not be allowed to have it.

"It's excellent," he says and then orders two of those. He throws in two more tacos that might have been shrimp and then deliberates with the person behind the counter on whether or not to get queso with chorizo or not. "No, no, let's go plain. We can always order more if we need to, right, Mills?"

"Yeah, sure." I say because if I need more food after what he just ordered, I think I will also need a second stomach.

Then I watch as Pete produces two large travel cups and hands them over to be filled. He sees my expression and fills me in.

"They don't have cups here. Well, they do for water, but if you want a margarita or a beer you have to bring your own. But it's worth it."

One thing very real about Peacock Bay: it's an eco-friendly paradise. My mind instantly wanders to how much Sage is spending on her shop's reusable tote bags. I should check and make sure they aren't too expensive. It's good marketing for the store if her bags are the ones people choose to bring with them around town. So maybe hers should be better quality than others, and the logo needs to be—

"Ready?" Pete asks, breaking into my marketing daydreams. Old habits, again. He's holding the two travel cups, looking very pleased with himself, or me, or maybe just the promise that tacos are on the way.

I take a picture of the big menu board behind the counter and one where I'm holding the big reusable cup full of spicy margarita with the menu in the background. I write *date night* across the photo and post it to my stories. And we're off. It feels nice spending time just the two of us. We never really did this before. Even in college, we were always in some configuration of our group of friends.

I decide to try my best to relax and enjoy tonight, even if it's just a way to gain more followers.

When we get outside the sound of the ocean hits me first.

When Pete said we'd be eating on benches on the beach I'm not sure what I was expecting, but I know I wasn't expecting it to be this…romantic.

There are some benches in groups around large tree stumps for tables, but some are off on their own. The high-backed benches look private and cozy. They all face the water, with torches and lanterns scattered nearby providing just enough light so you can find your way to your seat, but not so much that it kills the natural mood of the scene. There's only one other group of taco eaters. A couple of guys, all with shaggy surfer hair and sun-faded T-shirts. They look up as we get closer and stop talking. I get the feeling they're more interested in me than Pete. When we pass them, I think I recognize one of them from the beach the other day, and he smiles at me in a way that doesn't feel very friendly.

"'Sup, girl," he begins. "I remember you. You got any more moves you want to show me?"

"Oh yeah, this one's my favorite," I say, giving the guy my middle finger while my heart pounds in my chest. How dare he? It's been hard enough regaining my confidence in my surf skills, I don't need to be harassed out in public.

I feel Pete's hand on my back a little more firmly as he guides me to a place to sit. I know I'm supposed to be all girl-power surfers and such, but it does help knowing Pete is right behind me. But just because he's my friend. I'm sure if Quincy were here, I'd feel the same way.

"This really is a small town, huh?" I grumble, as we sit together on a high-backed bench.

"A small town full of dudes." He sighs when he looks at me, then takes a sip of his drink.

"Are there really so many more guys than girls here?"

"Yeah. It's a small surf town in the middle of nowhere. Not many people move here in general, and if they do, they're usually surf bums looking for easy day jobs they can ditch if the waves are good. Which most often tend to be single guys."

"So, there aren't a lot of single women in town that you don't know," I guess.

"There aren't a lot of single women here, period. Ever wonder why Quincy and her friends wound up married so young? Any quality woman gets locked down early around here. That may have something to do with why I overreacted when you went out surfing by yourself. Who knows how long it's been since some of these guys have seen a gorgeous woman who's not wearing a ring." He nods his head at the guys at the other table. "We may have a lot of waves here, but we don't have a lot of women."

Where did the breeze go? I'm suddenly very warm. "You should really put that on the Waveline website. I think single women from all over the world would flock here if they heard that. At least for a vacation."

Pete's eyebrows pinch together, but then he rethinks it and laughs, though it's not completely sincere. "You can take the girl out of her marketing job, huh?"

I guess my marketing brain is still humming after I was think-ing about the shop bags for Sage. I do have a tendency to jump around to different topics because of my ADHD, and my mouth just follows along for the ride. "So, if this place is a single lady's paradise, our new deal really cockblocks me, huh?" I'm trying to lighten the mood a little. I don't want to drag up our fight again.

Pete grins down at the travel cup in his hands, then back at me. "It was your idea, remember? But yeah, news travels fast, so after being seen out with me tonight, I don't think you're going to be getting much attention from the other locals."

"I did not think this through." I grin.

"Do you ever?" I can't return his smile because comments like that feel like a dig at my attention span, though I know I'm overly sensitive about it sometimes. When I don't say anything, he adds, "Sometimes the best plans are the ones you don't fully think through. I'm probably guilty of overthinking things most of the time."

"Is that why you agreed to *this*"—I wave a hand between us— "whole thing?"

"Not exactly." He grins and looks down at the drink in his hands before returning my smile. "But it is probably good for me to do something that's just fun with a good friend once in a while."

I'm not sure if he means going out tonight or the whole deal, but I'm glad at least he finds my company fun.

"Not that I'm interested in those guys over there, but if you think cockblocking me is fun, I'm not sure how good of a friend you are. You know, a girl has needs."

The way Pete's eyes lock onto mine makes my whole body heat like a dozen different suns are shining on me. I watch as his throat constricts when he says, "Maybe we can figure out a work-around to this problem." He takes a sip of his drink while I'm left to figure out what he means. "Hey, you haven't even tried your drink yet. I went with the medium spicy margarita. And that wasn't some comment on your ability to handle spice. It comes in a range of heat, and the medium still packs a hefty punch."

He might be changing the subject, or he might actually care if the heat level of my drink is satisfactory. I take a sip anyway. It's perfect. The right combination of tart and sweet with a heat that hits the back of my throat and warms me all the way down into my stomach. Pete is watching me carefully for my reaction, so I know it's important to him that I like this drink, which is nice, but how can I resist my favorite sport?

I cough and sputter into the sand at my feet. I put a hand to my throat and cough harder. My eyes start to tear from coughing, which may smear my mascara, but I'm committed to this now. I grab at the arm of the chair, steadying myself while I cough harder still and gasp dramatically for air.

"Shit, Mills. Are you okay?" He puts a hand on my back while I clear my throat a few more times just for good measure, then wipe my eyes and right myself, a giant grin across my face.

"Best margarita I've ever had." I smile at Pete.

His face relaxes and he shakes his head. "You are truly the worst."

"You asked for this. Literally. You asked me out, so this is what you get. Not sure what you were expecting, Santana."

His hand hasn't moved from my back. I'm not sure if he has forgotten about it, but it feels warm and comforting, and I wouldn't mind if he left it there all night.

"I thought you were dying. I thought I had killed the only available woman in Peacock Bay."

"All those surfer guys over there would have been so pissed at you." I smile at him, but being the only available woman in town doesn't exactly make me feel special.

"On the bright side, I don't think they're going to be bothering you anymore."

I peer over Pete's shoulder at the surfers. The one guy from earlier meets my eye and nods his head. I shoot him a glare before turning to look at Pete's gorgeous face.

"I don't know. They might appreciate a lady whose comedic skills are only outmatched by her skills on the board." Why did that seem kind of dirty? I can feel the heat of Pete's hand through the thin cotton of my dress. Maybe that has something to do with it.

"That might be true. If you were funny." He grins.

I slap my hand on his chest. Or at least I meant too. I can't seem to let go once my hand lands on his shirt. I tilt my body forward, closing the gap between our chests. His eyes sparkle and welcome me a little closer. It might be his hand still lingering on me, the way I can feel his fingers pressing gently against my back, a subtle curl and release that isn't accidental, but I'm suddenly understanding his earlier suggestion. "You know the problem you mentioned before? How our new arrangement takes me off the market? This could be a work-around I'm okay with."

Pete's eyes widen and his hand pulls me just a little closer as a devilish grin takes over his face. "Can we start now?"

My heart leaps into my chest. It has to be because of the low supply of women here that Pete is open to adding sex to our deal, but right now, with our bodies so close together, I don't really care what the reason is. I know this would just be two friends messing around. There's no way Pete would ever take someone like me seriously, but if this is my chance to get in bed with Pete, I'm taking it.

My hand is still on his chest. I need to have my hands on him. Need to feel what's underneath his clothes. The curve of his chest, his stomach. It takes all of what's left of my self-control not to root around under his T-shirt and dig my fingers into his skin. He wraps his arm around my waist and pulls me in too. Thank god, because if he pushed me away right now I might scream. Our foreheads are nearly touching. There's a puff of warm breath between us filled with the tart sweetness from our drinks. His lips are right there, so close.

"Order for Pete."

I will murder someone.

We sit up and straighten our shirts like teenagers caught in one of our parents' basement. We weren't even doing anything, I want to say—and we really weren't, which is disappointing to say the least. But at least there are tacos now. I snap a few pictures before we tear into them, making sure the hem of my dress is in each picture. Pete's hand is in one because he was being too greedy. That one is unsurprisingly the best shot, or at least my favorite. I show the pictures to Pete, who barely glances at them before diving in for more food, then upload them to my stories.

These tacos are fantastic, but there's no way they're as good as making out with Pete was going to be. I wonder if that's something actually available to me now. Did we really just negotiate some new terms to our deal? I'm not sure if bringing it up again will increase my chances of some action with Pete, but I would really like to know if this night is going to have a more exciting ending than I had originally thought.

After my third taco, I glance over Pete's shoulder and notice the guys are gone. We're the only ones here. It's only eight o'clock and it doesn't look like people are coming in.

"People really don't stay out late here, huh?"

"Not usually. The lure of dawn patrol." Pete leans back against the bench and shifts so he's facing me, which causes our sides to be touching. I'm not complaining, but I'm also unsure of what it means. "A few times a year, when the spring breakers come or around New Year's Eve, things are a little rowdier, but mostly we're a sleepy little surfers' village."

"Balls deep in dudes," I tease. Pete nudges me playfully, unconcerned.

I wonder how long it's been since Pete has been on a date. It's been a while for me, too, but at least in New York I had some options. Nothing of quality, but still, there were options. I get that Pete's interest in my work-around suggestion might be simply because of a total lack of available women. I think I can be okay with that. I've had casual flings before—not with someone I've had a crush on for years, but as long as I know that this is going to be just a temporary fun-between-friends kind of thing, I think I can keep my feelings in check.

When the tacos have been reduced to crumpled (recyclable) paper containers and we've polished off the last sips of our margaritas, there's not much left for us to do. I can't really suggest we go out for another drink. I'm not sure there's a bar in town that's open. Or if there is a bar in town at all. Plus, I'm not sure how one ends a fake date night planned for social media purposes, especially after you've suggested adding a little not-so-fake hooking up.

"I'm going to go refill our drinks, and then do you want to get going?" Pete asks, answering my mental questions.

I nod. "Sure, where are we going? Is there a bar still open?"

"Nah, I'm gonna take you home," he says simply, and then he's gone with the travel cups and my hopes for a glimpse of Pete without clothes on tonight.

Maybe that whole work-around idea was just a moment and it's over now. Maybe this whole pretend-husband thing was a bad idea. A little fun together while we're linked up online seems like a great way to make the most of things to me. But only if he's actually going to go through with it. I'm not going to stand for him making everyone in town believe I'm not ripe for the plucking. I'm not interested in those dirtbags from tonight, but what if I want to be plucked by someone else? I'm an adult woman who enjoys a healthy amount of consensual sex. Let me pluck and be plucked, damn it.

I don't say much to Pete on the ride back. I'm waiting for him to explain himself. I can't just ask him why he's not going to throw me down in his bed tonight. I guess I could, but I'm not sure I want to hear the answer. I'm gearing up to let him know that if he's not interested in getting down between the sheets with me, that's fine, but he can't actively prevent it from happening with someone else. I'm not going to stand in his way of hooking up either. I know his options around here are limited, but I thought that could work in my favor. Still, if he finds someone he wants, I'm not going to stand in his way. We'll have to figure out how that fits in with our marketing plan, but I can be mature about things and... Wait, we just passed the hotel.

"Hi, that was the Waveline," I say, one thumb pointing over my shoulder.

Pete cocks his head to the side. "Do you think I don't know where my hotel is?"

"You said you were taking me home."

"Yeah, my home."

My arms are instantly covered in goose bumps, and I'm fighting with a smile that refuses to stay off my face. "Are you kidnapping me?" *Please say yes. Please say yes.*

He laughs. "I think when you see the view from my place you'll agree to stay willingly."

I turn my face away, chin lifted, grinning out the window so he can't read the honest thrill on my face. "Well, I do like a nice view."

Chapter 14

WE WIND UP THE TWISTY streets near the Cove until we reach Pete's little cottage. It's not exactly pretty (I won't be taking any pictures for my grid in front of this place), but I know that's not what drew him to this location.

"So, if you go that way"—Pete tells me, pointing to some trim bushes that I can just barely make out in the growing darkness— "there's a path that leads you right to the beach. Only the houses on this street are allowed to use that path. It makes it really tough to get a place here."

"Is that supposed to impress me?" I tease him nervously. Now that we're here, standing at the cusp of some very uncharted territory, I have no idea how to act or what's about to happen.

"Not exactly. It's more to explain why a grown man would live in the world's tiniest one-bedroom house." He looks a little nervous too. Maybe he's a self-conscious that his place isn't nicer, but I'm surprised he'd think I'd care.

"Pete, I've lived in a fourth-floor walk-up studio with mice for roommates like the freaking Cinderella of Bed-Stuy for the last three years."

He smiles and lets his hand brush my waist. A chill runs right over me.

"Want to take our drinks down there? The moon is pretty bright. You might be able to get a few pictures to add to our date-night story."

My throat tightens, but I force a smile and push away the reminder that everything tonight has been fake. I know getting further involved with Pete could be a mistake, and while that is sort of my thing, having my heart broken isn't going to be part of the deal. Pete is an incredibly serious guy, and I know hooking up with someone who posts her every screwup online isn't something he would do for the long term. I need to set some boundaries so I don't end up in tatters when this "relationship" comes to its end.

"Pete, here's the deal. I'm glad you brought me here, believe me. But if we're about to get down and dirty, let's just call it what it is. Two friends helping each other out. It doesn't have to mean anything or be some big event. We have a deal helping each other with the Instagram stuff. This is just, I don't know, an addendum to that deal."

"An addendum?"

"Don't make fun of me."

"Oh, I would never."

"We can be adult friends who bang and stay friends after, can't we?" I don't know if I'm asking him or myself.

Pete's eyes narrow and I can see his jaw tightening. I know what I said was blunt, but as much as I want this to happen, I can't dive in with no self-preservation. I may be impulsive, but I'm not completely reckless. At least, not all the time.

"Whatever you say, Mills." He sighs. "Now do you want to see the beach at night?"

Pete doesn't give me a chance to answer. He turns away sharply and grabs a lantern that he keeps by his front door. His mood is a little harder to read as I follow him down the steep path toward the beach. As we walk, I try to ignore the change in Pete's body language. Maybe I was too blunt. Maybe I shouldn't have used the word *bang* when talking about what might happen tonight. But I never said I was good at this dating thing. Even fake dating seems to be a hurdle I'm tripping over.

"Why didn't we come this way when surfed here the other day?" I ask, because I have other thoughts too. I'm not only thinking about ripping his clothes off or overthinking what got us here.

Pete laughs. "Yeah, right. No way was I letting you near my house on your first day here. I had to let the Cove win you over before that."

"Quincy says you're a snob because you think the Cove is the best place to surf and won't consider living anywhere else."

"She's right. I won't consider it. I don't know if that makes me a snob, but come on, Mills, would you want to be somewhere else when this exists?" We've reached the end of the path, and we stand together looking out over the dark waters. The moon is nearly full, high in the sky and reflected by the ocean, doubling its light for us. The water is quiet, but moving. Small rolling waves dance toward the shore, making a sound I can only imagine must feel like the sweetest lullaby at night.

I take my sandals off and let my toes sink into the soft sand. He's right. There's nowhere else in the world I would rather be tonight than right here. "I don't know," I say, because obviously I'm not going to agree with him so easily. "I hear Paris is nice."

Pete takes my cup from my hand and puts it down with his, then looks at me with a glint in his eyes that makes me think I'm in big trouble in the best way.

"You better run," he says, and I don't wait to find out why. I drop my shoes and take off down the beach, which I know from the other day isn't long so I'm going to run out of distance after a few more seconds. It doesn't matter because Pete's arms are around my waist now, and we're toppling over into the sand. My hands are gripping his shirt and I pull him on top of me. He goes willingly and then, after what feels like years (and really, it has been), he crushes my mouth with his.

I feel like I'm going to devour his mouth. I won't hold back, and he doesn't seem like he wants me to. His lips are so smooth and soft, and I don't care if most of tonight has been fake because there is nothing fake about the way he's kissing me now. I move my hands into his hair and rub them over the short strands. He lifts his head and pushes it harder into my hand. He must like the way that feels.

"No one has done that since I cut my hair," he murmurs. A chill creeps up my back at knowing I'm the only one who's touched him like this. Knowing I'm the one making him feel this good and no one else. I kind of get that possessive instinct now.

"I kind of miss your long hair," I tell him. "But I like this too."

"Good, keep liking things," he says, then kisses me more deeply.

"You're going to like so many things. So, so many things. If I get to keep trying."

Holy shit. "Okay, keep trying." I can barely squeak out the words. I feel like if we keep kissing like this, I'm either going to swallow him whole or be buried alive in this sand. Both would be hard to explain tomorrow—probably a lot of this will be hard to explain tomorrow—but I'm not willing to stop. I will memorize his mouth before the morning. I want to abandon all my goals and zero in on just kissing. Except there is a lot more I can do besides kiss. His hand slides roughly up my side, his fingers brushing over my nipples. He cups one of my breasts and my body bucks against him. I need more. I grip the hem of his shirt, twisting the soft linen in my hand. I let my fingers slide onto his smooth skin and dig my fingers into the well of his spine, holding him closer. But the more I feel of him, the hungrier I become. I want his shirt off. Hell, I want all of his clothes off, and mine too for that matter. "Let's go inside," I manage.

Pete kisses me once more, deeply, like he hasn't had his fill and won't for some time, then sits up. He takes my hand and helps me get to my feet. We're both so sandy. I start to brush some off myself and then start on the sand I can reach on Pete's back. He turns at my touch, then brushes a little off my back, too, his mouth curling in that wicked smile. Then he lets his hand drift down to my ass, pulling our hips together. Something hard meets my stomach and it's just too much. I launch myself at his face again. I feel his tongue warm against my lips and I part my own and oh my god. I think my clothes are going to revolt and fall off if we don't get somewhere indoors soon.

I gently push him off me, and he instantly drops his hand and looks at me, full of concern.

"No. I mean, yes. Really, really yes, but dude, we've got to get naked."

Pete laughs. "Bossy, bossy." He takes my hand and leads me back to the path.

"A deal is a deal, my friend."

Pete pauses on the path and tugs at my hand. "Right." He nods. "A deal is a deal."

I nod back to let him know I understand. This is just fun. We're not getting into anything serious. This whole thing started out as two friends helping each other, and that's how it will stay. No matter what level of nakedness follows. Which I hope is a high level.

We keep walking toward his house, but there's no way this is the same path. It feels like it takes twice as long to get back to Pete's house as the walk down to the beach. But that might be because that was a different era. The time before I felt the weight of Pete on top of me. Before I knew how soft and smooth his lips felt against mine. And seriously, are we still walking?

"Have you always walked this slow?"

"Nearly there, Mills." He squeezes my hand and I think I'm melting. I know there aren't many single women around, but it still seems impossible that Pete is still on the market. You'd think word of his attractiveness, his dedication and kindness would have traveled for miles. The legend of this god among men would draw women from towns hours away. I can only thank the internet mystics for leaving Pete untouched, therefore limiting his reach.

Finally, we're at the cottage door. Pete unlocks it, but before he opens the door to let me in, he looks at me with his calm, serious face again. I think he's going to ask me why I didn't take any pictures, and I don't want to tell him it was because I was too focused on how soft his lips feel.

"Listen, Millie," he begins. "I know you like to skip steps. You like things to happen fast. But I'm going to tell you right now this is not going to be fast. I'm not skipping anything."

I decide right here and now not to worry anymore about how much of this hookup is just because we've found ourselves in a highly unusual situation. I don't really care how we got here tonight. Something is finally happening between us, and I'm going to enjoy it.

So, I nod at Pete, then reach up for his face and rake my fingers down his scratchy, stubbly face. He closes his eyes and leans into my fingers. "Fuck, Mills." He nudges the door open with his toe. "Get inside."

"Now who's bossy?" But he doesn't have to ask me twice.

Once inside, Pete flicks on the kitchen light, giving just enough light so that I can get a look around his place, but not so much that I'm blinded after being cloaked in darkness outside.

"It doesn't feel that small," I say, looking around. It's a narrow room with a couch, a TV, a big wall of bookshelves, and a door I assume leads to a bedroom.

"Hopefully, that's the last time you say that tonight," Pete says. My eyes widen at him.

"Hey, Pete Santana. Did you just make a dirty joke?" I love that I'm drawing this out of him. Serious, stone-faced Pete is the regular, but this new version is just for me. I seriously might eat him alive.

He grins sheepishly. "It's the high ceilings." He points up to the double-height vaulted ceilings. The walls are white from the floor to the ceiling. "Okay, no more tour. This is basically the place. Come with me." He reaches out for my hand and it takes all my restraint not to jump into his arms and let him carry me to bed. Which he doesn't do. Instead, he pulls me to the set of sliding glass doors at the other end of the room, pushes them open, and leads me through.

Outside, I find a starlit paradise. A huge deck that doesn't just overlook the ocean, it *overhangs* it. I feel like we're basically floating over the beach. If the waves were at high tide, it would be almost like they're right underneath us. The night sky seems to stretch over us forever, and the clear sky is littered with stars.

Pete turns on a lantern that sits on a tiny bistro table with two light-blue folding chairs beside it, and then another one on a side table next to a large daybed that looks like it's attached to the ceiling by large metal links. Is it a freaking couch swing? Seriously? How dare he. I wonder if he spends almost all his time out here. I know I would if this were my house. Shit, if I wasn't turned on before…

I turn back to look at Pete, who's been quietly watching me while I take in every inch of this outdoor paradise. "So, this is why you live here, huh?"

"There isn't a better place to be in all of the Bay. I've wanted this cottage since I was a little kid. It became available three years ago, and that was it for me." He joins me by the rail, settling one hand on my side and bringing my hips to meet his. That something stiff I felt on the beach is between us, and I seriously need to get better acquainted with it.

"Are you always that patient?" There were probably lots of other places for sale and rent during the time he moved home after college. How did he even know that this cottage would ever become available? And what if it wasn't as great as he thought it was going to be after all this time? That's a big risk to take, but clearly it paid off this time.

"Only when I have to be." He grins and pulls me even closer.

"And does it always work out for you?" His other hand comes up, and his thumb brushes the base of my throat. I swallow hard.

"It has so far."

And that's enough of that.

When we kiss now, it's not as hurried. I wanted a chance to learn every corner of his mouth, and this is it. He's giving me all the time in the world and I will take it. His arms wrap around me as he pulls me tight against his body. He's so warm, and I think I can make out the rapid beat of his heart. Or maybe that's mine. Who's to say?

I drop a kiss on his throat just below his jaw, and his voice is barely a whisper when he says, "Couch, please."

His hands guide me over, and we collapse onto the daybed which starts to swing when it takes our weight. I laugh at the motion and Pete smiles down at me, then dives into my neck and starts landing tiny nips on my skin.

His shirt is coming off and my mouth is all over him. My magical dress is now a crumpled heap, and I vow to show the proper respect to it later for its good work tonight. Right now there is no square inch of Pete I will leave unkissed. Try and stop me. I cannot believe I am getting free rein to touch and lick and kiss Pete wherever I want. Each time my hands reach a new part of him, it's like a tiny explosion goes off in my chest. It makes me hungry for more, and Pete seems equally ravenous for me.

"We can stop whenever you want," Pete murmurs against my chest.

"I have never wanted anything less."

"Thank fucking god," he answers.

If I didn't know how few women were available in town, I would definitely be thinking about how many others have been right here on this daybed taking in the perfect view of the stars from this angle. Praise be to this small secluded town. As it happens, Pete is devouring me like a man who's spent a year at sea, and it could possibly have been longer. He has been starving, and I am his first meal back on dry land. It's a beautiful thing.

His fingers hook on the waistband of my underwear, and when he looks at me for confirmation, I feel like I might nod my head right off my body. I release a small shiver as the cool night air drifts over my bare skin. I'm not cold for long. He kisses his way down my body, and when he finds what he's looking for, my head rolls back against the cushions. My heart pounds as his tongue licks and presses deeply into me. His tongue is relentless as my back arches and heat builds in my body. It feels like every nerve has zipped down to the one spot between my legs where Pete's tongue licks and swirls with no sign of stopping. The sky above me is becoming a blur. The stars start to swirl like an oil painting, and I think I know how van Gogh got inspired for *Starry Night* now. It wasn't drugs. It was this. Lucky bastard.

My entire body is about to explode. I have never gotten so close to an orgasm so fast, and I don't want to unravel quite yet. I need to feel him inside me. I want every piece of him, every way. I grip a pillow next to my arm and summon the strength to whack Pete over the head with it.

He sits up, startled. "Are you okay? Is it too much?"

I pant, trying to catch my breath. It takes me a second before I can answer. "You're still not naked," I manage finally. Then I push him on his back and start unbuttoning his pants.

Here's the thing. I've seen Pete on the beach. I've seen him in a wet suit, I've seen him in just swim trunks. I know he looks insanely good nearly naked. It still does not prepare me for seeing him like this. Completely bare, with only my hands on him. He's so beautiful, I don't think I can stop looking. He's all smooth and dark tanned. His muscled chest and torso are firm, with just a sprinkling on hair leading the way to where my hands are joyfully stroking him. I think I could take this in for hours. Netflix will ask me if I'm still there, if I'd like to keep watching, and I will click continue... Thanks for asking, you perverts.

"Millie," Pete says to make me take a pause. I watch him as he rolls over to grab a condom from his jeans pocket. My body is on fire. Every inch is filled with heat and lust, and I'm slick with anticipation while I watch Pete roll on the condom. I lean back again to lie beneath him. He puts one hand underneath my hip to guide me to him, but I don't need any help. My hands grab at his hips, fingers sinking into the curve of his ass, and I pull him to me. But he pulls back just as I am about to push him into me and let my body consume every beautiful inch of him.

"What? You okay? I'm not skipping steps. I just literally can't hold on much longer."

A grin smirks on the corner of his mouth. I want to eat it. "Tell me why you're here," he says huskily. Pete shifts his weight so his legs are now between mine, what I want from him out of reach. He bends one leg, his hand still holding my raised hips, and slides his lightly hair-covered thigh slowly up against my hot, wet clit. *Oh dear god.*

I shake my head, trying to remember the answer he's looking for. We've had this conversation, and I'm not going to let him tease me anymore. I reposition myself under him and wrap my hand around his dick. He makes a sound like he's choking on a breath and resettles over me. He bends his head near my ear, his voice a whisper. "So fucking beautiful." Then finally he pushes into me just the tiniest bit. "Tell me why you're here."

"You know why," I say. He curves his face under my jaw and kisses me, hot and wet.

"Tell me," he says, nudging me with his nose. He pushes in a bit more, then pulls back again. I let my head falls back against the bed with a groan. Encouraged, he pushes in again harder, and I am so ready.

"My blog, the beach, you know." Why are we talking about blogging right now? I push against him and he matches me. I'm getting greedy, but he seems to like it. We thrust against each other, fighting to get closer, to feel each other more deeply. I have never felt anything like this before.

He lets out a gratifying noise. "Tell me why you came here."

I push against him again, harder still. I want to watch him come undone. He bucks his hips against me until he's filling me completely. I kiss him again. I know what he means now. I know he doesn't need me to say it, just by asking means he knows why, but I know what it will do to him if I say it. And watching my words unravel him is too tempting.

"Because you told me to."

"Fuck," he breathes. "I did." He's almost out of breath. He brings his hand up to my face and kisses me deeply. "And you're here."

He wanted me here. He wanted this. Maybe he was lonely. Maybe there weren't many other options in town for dates, but he told me to come and I did.

And not long after that, we both do.

We lie together after, our bodies still tangled. Pete lets one leg fall off the daybed to the deck to gently push the swing so that we sway underneath the stars. He does it almost without thinking, and I can picture him doing this while he reads a book or answers emails. Thinking of him in these relaxed private moments while I was back in New York trying to keep my head above water makes my heart hurt.

"I really like this deck," I tell him, lifting my head to rest my chin on his chest.

"That's good news. Since there's not much else I can impress you with." He smiles down at me. Was he trying to impress me? "I've got surfing at the Cove, tacos from the Shack, and my deck."

"And your dick," I add.

Pete laughs with his head back. I feel the rise and fall of his chest against my arms that are draped over him. My heart pounds while I watch him. The thrill of being the one who made him laugh so easily builds in me until I can't take it any longer. I lift my head to look down at him, letting my hair fall to one side and brushing the side of his face. He tucks my hair back with one hand and looks deeply into my eyes.

"Hey, Mills," he says, with the hint of a smile still reverberating through his face. The same way he said it when he'd swing by our dorm room or pass me on the way to class. But now we're horizontal, naked, with a very new and interesting knowledge of how our bodies fit perfectly together.

I think I'm in really big trouble.

Chapter

15

BREE SENDS A TEXT THE next afternoon.

> **Bree**: If we were to FaceTime with you right now, what state of nakedness would you be in?

> **Kate**: Inappropriate!

I call them with FaceTime, and when they answer, Kate is moving around an apartment I don't recognize, likely a client's place. Bree is wearing wireless headphones, and the background looks like a coffee shop. She has her hand dramatically covering her eyes.

"I'm not naked," I say to Bree. "You should be so lucky."

"The credenza goes on the far wall. Facing the sofa," Kate says. "Sorry, it's install day on my Williamsburg project," she explains.

"The one for the Korean actor? How's that going?" I ask. This is one of the first projects Kate has been the lead designer for, and I know it's really important to her to do a great job.

"First of all he's a Korean drama *star*. Educate yourself, Millie."

Kate smiles. "I'm just teasing. It's been going really well. He's been really happy with what we've done. Which means Andres is happy with me. Hopefully, if things stay this way, he'll be giving me the lead on more big projects like this. Plus, Sun Woo says he might buy the apartment upstairs and combine them, which would be really fun. He's been great to work with."

"Wow, that's amazing," I tell her, but I feel a tiny pang of regret for not being there while Kate celebrates this big career accomplishment. "You should take it as a big compliment that he likes what you've done so much that he's considering expanding his apartment."

Kate grins and shrugs her shoulders. "Let's just hope everything stays this picture-perfect."

"And now, on to the matter at hand. Do you still believe our dress doesn't work for you? Because the sun-streaked early morning picture I saw of you with obviously just-fucked hair seems to indicate otherwise."

"Bree! You're in public!" Kate scolds. She's probably worried her delivery crew will hear. Even though she's also wearing headphones.

I did post a photo Pete took of me on his deck this morning. It felt right at the time, but now that I know my friends have seen it and that it looks like some morning-after love-fest declaration, I feel a little sick.

"The picture was Pete's idea," I try to explain to my friends and to myself, though it's not making me feel better.

"Awww," Kate coos.

"No, it's just part of our deal. We want it to look like we're together, after all. That coming to Peacock Bay can instantly change your life for the better." That's what he and Alana want it to look like, anyway. The strange thing is that picture hasn't gotten that many likes. Maybe it's the algorithm or maybe people don't care that much if things look like they're going well for me.

"Well, that's true for you," Bree teases. "A hot new man all over you and a popular new Instagram account."

"Well, the hot man is temporary, and I'm getting the feeling people care more when it looks like I'm screwing up."

If I don't keep posting my mistakes, am I going to lose followers? I liked that I could be uncensored before, but what if I don't want to keep that up forever? I don't want it to affect the hotel or Pete, but it's not like I agreed to be the neighborhood clown for the rest of eternity. Of course, I do have the whole I've-been-faking-a-relationship thing in my back pocket. I wish that felt more reassuring.

I need coffee. I need to get out of this hotel room. If I don't, I'm just going to go in circles thinking of all the ways things could turn out terribly. I say goodbye to my friends with a promise to post more details as I have them. I'm glad things are going well for Kate, and Bree is always rock solid. I know both my friends are doing well without me there, which gives me reassurance that getting out of New York was still the right thing for me. Things never went that well for me there. I'm surprised I lasted as long as I did.

After I'm showered and dressed, I decide to go visit Sage at Little Goods and see how things are coming along at the shop. Quincy said her online orders were up. Maybe I can help her get them out more quickly. I'm pretty friendly with the guy at the post office now from my visits sending out stickers.

Just as I'm crossing the lobby, I see Pete emerge from behind the front desk. He's holding a few pieces of paper and stops in his tracks when he sees me. A chill sweeps over me as his eyes drink me in. He looks behind him and then around the lobby before he takes long strides to reach me by the door.

"What is the meaning of this?" he says with a grin. His tone is hushed as he looks me up and down.

I smile at him. "I'm going to bike into town. I thought I'd go check in on Sage at the shop."

Pete's face changes from his coy smile to something more serious. "That's good. I don't know what's been up with Sage and Breck lately, but my guess is whatever it is, she could use a friend like you."

I bite on the corner of my lower lip. I don't like knowing about Sage's divorce when Pete doesn't, but I also know it's not my place to tell him.

"I'm not sure what I can do beyond helping her style her merchandise for photos or trying to improve her online orders, but I like Sage and I like helping her out." In fact I realize that other than surfing, there hasn't been something that's felt like such a natural fit for me in a really long time. Being with my friends, lying quietly with Pete on his deck listening to the waves, and puttering around Sage's shop have all felt so right. But two of those three things aren't up for grabs, and I have to be okay with that.

"Then Sage is a very lucky friend. When you like someone or something, you get a little more...glowy?" Pete squints. "I'm not sure if that's the right word to describe it, but you get sort of... turned on..." He must see the look on my face at this word choice, and he laughs. "Not like that. You get sort of energized, and it rubs off on other people." Pete scratches at the back of his neck, still not satisfied with his explanation. "What I mean to say is you have this way of making people be the best versions of themselves, and we're luckier for it."

My jaw falls open slightly. That may be the nicest thing anyone's ever said about me. I do get a little overly energetic when I like someone. I'm outgoing and I have ADHD, so when I'm enthusiastic about someone or something, I have a hard time corralling that energy. I never thought it could have any kind of positive effect on anyone.

"Do you think you could call my mom and tell her this sometime?" Maybe if Pete told her this, she wouldn't feel like she needs to plan out my life for me so much.

Pete smiles at me and takes a small step closer. "Is there anything else you need me to tell her?"

My mind goes fuzzy, and all I can see are those dark lashes and his full lips. "I can't think of anything at the moment."

"Well, if you do, you know where to find me." He glances over his shoulder, then dips his head down so his mouth nearly brushes my ear. "In fact, I'd be happy to discuss this further in my office."

The roughness in his voice makes all the air empty out of my chest. "Sage can wait."

Pete takes my hand and leads me into his office. He quickly closes the door behind us. and a second later, my back is against the door, my arms wrapped around his neck, and my mouth on his. *God, yes.*

Everything about Pete feels so good, but I know this is going nowhere, and if there's going to be any chance of me retaining a piece of my dignity when this inevitably comes to a close, I need to let Pete know that I understand.

"I'm going to go into withdrawal when I leave," I say against his neck.

I feel Pete freeze briefly. "Right, and when will that be?"

"A couple weeks?" I offer. "After I announce the relationship was a joke. I think it will make sense for me to exit stage right, you know?"

Pete lifts his head and narrows his eyes as they look into mine. "Always on the move, little Mills. Hard to nail down."

"Well, you didn't have such a hard time last night." I grin. I want to lighten things up and get back to the very important business of making Pete moan. If my time is limited with this activity, I'm going to really give it my all.

"Lucky break."

I rub my hand against the grain of the short hair on the back of his neck, and Pete's mouth presses against mine. I'm still not over how short it is and how doing this makes him groan into my mouth. I love this reaction. He kisses my neck and then down to my chest, enjoying the deep V of my dress. His fingers find the delicate straps and hook them so they fall off my shoulders.

"Do you have more dresses like this?" he asks between mouthfuls of me. I can barely answer. I nod. I don't know. I shake my head. What's happening?

"Why? Do you like it?" I manage.

"You have no idea." He kisses me again, wet and hot. "All your little dresses." His hand slides up my leg and finds its way under my dress. I wish I wasn't wearing underwear. I would love to have seen his face if he went searching under my dress to find out I was strolling through his hotel bare bummed, but that might have been problematic for my bike ride.

Pete is pushing my underwear to the side to slide a finger inside me, and my head tips back against his office door. I dig my fingers into his shoulder, and I must say something encouraging because he answers simply, "Yes, Mills."

Thank god there's only one small window at the back of his office that faces what look like some trees. I doubt any of this would be happening otherwise. Pete wouldn't risk being seen doing wonderfully dirty things to a guest of his hotel by anyone.

I need to touch him like I did last night. I want to feel him in my hand. I want to know if I'm making him ache the way he's making me. I pop the top button of his jeans and tug the zipper down. I slide my hand in, gripping him just hard enough to hear an encouraging moan. We stroke and slide and grab and kiss until I think I won't hold on much longer. Does he keep condoms at work? What if he has an appointment or a conference call that I'm keeping him from? These distracting thoughts are good. They're making me slow down.

"Millie, please." Those might be the best words I've heard in my life.

I let him go and then try to add a sway to my hips as I walk over to his desk. I reach under my skirt and slide down my underwear, letting them drop to the floor. Then I lift the skirt of my yellow dress and sit my bare ass on his desk.

"Time to get to work, Petesy." I grin.

Pete rubs a hand over his face and then does a scrub motion into his hair. "The thing is…"

My chest tightens. "Oh no, there's a thing?"

"I don't actually keep condoms in my desk."

"Ah," I say. Now what do I do? Should I put my underwear back on? How did this go from being super-sexy to super-awkward so fast?

"I'm not actively having sexual encounters in my office," he explains sheepishly. That's actually a good thing. He's run this hotel awhile now. There has to have been at least one woman who's come through here that he's been attracted to. I'm glad to hear that bringing someone back to his office isn't a regular move. It's so adorable, even if my entire body is powering down while I sit here.

I can't help but laugh. "Right, so should I..." If this were happening with anyone other than Pete, it might be really embarrassing. Here I am, leaving the mark of my bare butt on his desk, and he's just called the whole thing off. But it's Pete. I've seen him throw up after chugging beers. He's seen *me* throw up after taking too many shots, and then again with the stomach flu. And then again when I took too many shots while I had the stomach flu. Look, it was college; let's not make a thing of it. He also sat with me while I cried after my parents called me when they had to put our family dog down. He's been there. He knows me in the realest way.

"Hold on, I can't just let you leave like that."

Pete walks over and stands between my legs with a hand on each knee. He slides his hands up my thighs and gently spreads my legs wider. I tilt my head to the side in question. Then bring my arms up to rest them on his strong and lean shoulders.

"Like what?"

"Frustrated. Annoyed? You'll go on with your day, and every

time you think about me, you'll think about how I left you unhappy and less than content. That's the very last thing I want."

"Or maybe it's all part of a plan to get me to throw myself at you later because I've been thinking about the unfinished business you left me with?"

"Interesting, but no." Pete tucks a piece of my hair behind my ear and brushes my cheek with his thumb. He looks at me with that sweet, but serious face. "Now that I officially know you're not going to be here for very long, I think it's my duty as your fake husband to make sure you never walk away from me anything less than completely happy."

"That's a pretty big thing to promise," I say, my voice at a whisper. I would love to challenge him on this just to see him prove me wrong. "You might not want to make such a bold guarantee."

Pete just smiles at me, then reaches around my back and pulls me closer in a kiss. I scoot forward and wrap my arms around his neck as we let our tongues lazily explore each other's mouths. So that's cleared up. Even with this new development to the world's worst marketing plan, we are still keeping one rule intact. I'm going to publicly blow the lid on our fake relationship, face the music on the fallout, and then take off to absorb the impact.

At least I'm the one setting the terms. I'm the one calling the shots here even if I know I'll be wrecked when it ends. There's also the fact that he's not asking me to stay. More than that, he's expecting me to leave. He made no argument against it, that's for sure, but what else was I expecting? I have to just enjoy the time while I have it. At least now I can guard myself for what's coming.

Pete pulls me even closer so I'm sitting at the very edge of his desk. He breaks away from our kiss to grin at me as he pushes the skirt of my dress up over my thighs. With just a twitch of his eyebrows, he sinks down to his knees and gently starts to lick me right where I'm aching for him. My mind clears, and every nerve in my body begins to focus on a single point.

The last coherent thought I have before I become completely useless is that maybe it doesn't matter how long I'm here if this is the kind of thing that happens regularly while I am. But if Pete isn't expecting me to stick around, he needs to stop making everything single minute I spend here absolute bliss.

Chapter 16

I EVENTUALLY MAKE IT TO town on my bike. It's about an hour after I'd planned, and my entire lower body—okay, fine, my entire body—feels like it's returning from a liquid state. I was planning to return the favor before leaving Pete, but his phone started ringing and I could tell he actually had to get back to work. I made a big show of pulling my underwear back on slowly and carefully while he was on the phone, which made his face twist like he was physically in pain. Then I kissed him before I left, and he murmured, "Later?" into my hair. All in all, it was a pretty good afternoon.

When I finally get to Little Goods, it's nearly four, but I'm surprised to find the store pretty busy. Sage is at the register ringing someone up, and another customer waits with a few items in her arms. A candle that smells like sweet citrus is burning on the table I helped arrange with new products the other day. I smile, looking around at the bustling business and knowing I might have had the tiniest hand in helping make it happen. I love the energy of the busy store, and I have to remind myself that even though Sage valued my help, she still isn't asking for more of it. That's fine. Really. The store is barely surviving as it is. Sage not hiring me has nothing to do with my employment history or lack of experience. No matter what it feels like to me.

At the back of the store is Quincy. She's sitting on the floor of the shop surrounded by boxes and paper stickers.

"Hey, Millie," Sage says with a big smile. She hands her customer a large tote full of her new purchases, and Quincy looks up at my name. She tosses her long, messy sun-streaked brown braid over her shoulder and sighs with relief.

"Oh, thank god, come help me," she says. I do what I'm told.

"What are we doing?" I ask when I pop down next her on the floor.

"We're putting price stickers on these tinctures. I just started, but my fingers are already going numb, along with my brain. Now you can help me while you tell me about your date last night."

I take a sheet of the price stickers and look for the corresponding box of CBD oil tinctures to label. "It was really fun." I'm not sure what else to say to the sister of the guy I just slept with.

"It looked like it. Pete was really pulling out all the stops for you. Not that you don't deserve it. But that view from his place, huh?"

"It's really something."

"Especially in the morning." She smirks at me and nudges my elbow.

"Quincy, I can't talk to you about hooking up with your brother. Plus, it's not that simple."

"I just wanted to hear you admit that you slept with him. It's about fucking time with you two. Ugh, if I had to spend one more minute in that freaking group chat listening to you flirt and pre-tending not to notice, I was going to kill one of you."

"Jesus, okay. It happened. But it's nothing serious. The whole married online thing was going to be a huge cockblock for both of us, so we just decided to have some fun with it. The end."

"More like the beginning."

"Yeah, of a mess," I tell her. I can handle it, I remind myself. Whatever happens I can deal with it. "Anyway, what up with you? How's Monrow?"

"He's fine, I guess. We decided to have an evaluation done for him. Even if we don't send him to Vera Lake Academy, any school will need to know the best way to support him. It's just scary, you know? The first scary step in a long scary parade. I hate the idea of putting labels on him, but then I'm also so grateful that I can pos-sibly help him find the best possible learning environment. It's just kind of lot for a kid who's only starting kindergarten."

"It is a lot. But you're doing a great job," I tell her. One, because I believe it, and two, because I want her to hear it.

"Alana is pretty pissed about it. She thinks I'm overreacting by doing the evaluation. I told her I was thinking about writing a post about the process, and she kind of lost it on me."

"What? That's messed up."

"She's just stressed. And pregnant. She's not totally wrong either. I can't afford Vera Lake if I lose all my sponsors, so it's kind of rough."

"She can be pretty convincing," I add. "But I don't like that she's making this harder on you than it needs to be." Why should Alana get a say in what Quincy does for her kid? What she's going through with Monrow is hard enough without anyone making her feel guilty about her decisions.

"This is going to be hard whether I write about it or not. I was never certain I wanted to go that route anyway."

I hope being a person for Quincy to vent to is enough. I'd like to have a better way to support her, but for now I can just be the sounding board.

After we finish the last box of tinctures, Quincy and I make a little display of them by the register when it gets quiet in the shop. Sage wanted to have a few impulse-friendly purchases to help drive up her sales numbers and thought these would appeal to stressed parents.

Speaking of stressed parents, Alana Tatamo bursts through the door of the shop, arms full of string shopping bags. She's wearing a stretchy gray cotton dress that hugs the curve of her pregnant belly and a denim shirt with the collar magically standing half-up and half-down in a way I could never emulate and a pair of high-end white sneakers on her feet. She looks just the tiniest hint more fashionable than, well, anyone else.

"I cannot carry these bags one step farther," she huffs and then slumps down on the floor of the store.

"Uh, can I give you a hand?" I offer. "Is your car nearby? I could load these in your trunk for you." I feel bad with her being pregnant and lugging all these heavy bags.

"I didn't drive down here. I thought I'd just walk in and grab a few things I needed for our baby-reveal bonfire. Shit, you guys are coming to that, right?" She looks up and points at each of us. "Then I realized I needed some food for the weekend and I thought I could carry it all back, but oh my god, I hate being pregnant so much." She heaves a huge sigh and rests a hand under her belly, trying to take some of the pressure off whatever is aching.

"When is this happening?" Quincy asks.

Alana's eyebrows pinch together. "Next Friday night?" She covers her eyes with her hand in shame. "I didn't tell you? Fuck. I can't keep this shit together with this pregnancy brain. I spent all morning on calls with potential partners, half of which have clearly never looked at my blog because they want me to do things I literally would never do."

"Like what?" Sage asks.

"Like do a lingerie shoot…with my big-ass belly…and ass, out there for them to tweet and post to every fucking weirdo with an internet connection to jerk off to. How do they think that's even close to my brand? I'm fucking natural. Letting kids be little while they're little and all that shit. Peace and tranquility in the home and fucking essential oils and home births. Fuck off with your thongs and underwire and fucking lace underwire bullshit."

"You said 'underwire' twice," Sage says.

"Fuck underwire. I'm fucking pregnant," she shouts back. Sage really wasn't helping, but still we trade a look and I'm glad the store is empty for this scene.

"Okay, okay," I say, sliding down to sit next to her. "Clearly, you've had a day."

"Yeah, I fucking have. It's been four months long. Plus, the seven years before that. Parenting is no joke." She sniffles.

"Alana still isn't over parenting during the pandemic," Quincy explains.

"Don't even say the words," Alana warns. I don't think she's crying, but she's on the verge. I don't blame her. She's got a lot on her plate. She's also got a mouth on her. Which is slightly off brand, but entertaining, to say the least.

"I don't know if it helps, but I can come to the baby-reveal thing Friday. I don't have any plans." And at least I know I'll be staying here through the week.

"Oh thank fucking god, and then Pete will come so that's something."

"I can ask him, I guess."

"Aren't you guys fucking?" She turns to me, face neutral. As if this isn't anything outside the lines of casual conversation. "He'll be there," she confirms.

"How is that knowledge you have?"

"One, it's a small town. Some of the guys who work in Jeff's kitchen saw you at the Shack last night. Plus, we all saw your posts. If it was supposed to be a secret, it was a terrible one."

"No, it's not a secret. It's just a little weird to find out your personal life has become local news in less than twenty-four hours."

Alana looks around, gesturing at Quincy and Sage. "We've all seen him on your Insta. You've been putting it out there yourself. You can't get mad when people talk about it."

"I'm not mad. I'm just surprised." I don't care if people are talking about me and Pete. I can understand the fascination when some random lady sweeps into town and snaps up a very eligible man. If I weren't doing the snapping, I'm sure I'd be gossiping about it too. "Plus, you put him there," I decide to remind her.

"And you're welcome. Again." She shakes her head.

"We'll be there too," Quincy says, redirecting the conversation. "Ari's mom is usually available on Fridays. I can ask her to watch the kids."

"You can bring them, of course. It works with the aesthetic."

"No, it's okay. It's probably easier."

"Well, bring the baby at least. We need some fucking kids there."

"Okay, sure," Quincy says softly. It must hurt to have Monrow excluded from things like this.

Alana sighs with relief. "And Sage, you'll come, right? Even if Breck is working late?"

Sage chews the inside of her cheek. "Um, I'm not sure. I'd have to try to get a sitter for Sunny and Starling." I'm not sure what the arrangement is with her soon-to-be ex, but I know attending these group functions must be getting more and more awkward for her. I'm sure she doesn't want to go to things with him, but she must know she can't keep showing up to stuff alone. Alana is smart. She's going to notice something is up.

"She'll try," I answer for her.

We're all quiet for a minute, trading looks back and forth. Quincy and I both know Alana doesn't know and that Sage is still figuring out her way around that one. She needs to tell Alana, but even in the short time I've known her, I can tell she has a hard time standing up for herself.

"Oh, Jesus fucking Christ, Sage! Just spit it out," Alana yells. Sage takes a step farther behind her cash desk.

"Alana…" Quincy tries.

Sage is trembling, and I can tell she's fighting back tears. She looks heartbroken to have to admit to her friends what she's been keeping to herself for who knows how long. I can't watch her go through this by herself. She's probably been feeling buried by the weight of all this, the divorce, her store, staying in Alana's good graces. She needs to just get it out in the open. I know it's her news. I know I should stay out of it, but enough is enough.

"She's getting a divorce," I blurt out. I instantly regret it. Not my news, I know, and that's exactly what the look on Quincy's face says. "I'm sorry," I add quickly and sincerely. "I'm really sorry, Sage. But how long could you keep this going?"

Alana rises to her feet. "Sage," she says in a steady but slightly terrifying voice.

Sage says nothing. Quincy and I trade a look, but neither of us says anything.

"Sage?" Alana asks again. "Who knows about this?"

"No one," she says. "I mean, you guys, Breck, obviously, my kids, but it's not like I'm going around shouting about it. It's private."

Alana sighs with one hand on her belly. "Fine, but nothing about this goes online." She looks sternly at us all. "We live in motherfucking utopia, right? The store, the Waveline"—she looks at Quincy and then the rest of us individually—"and all of our livelihoods depend on that ideal. Millie, I know you don't have much stake in the game here, but if you want any piece of this and you don't want your new dude's family business to crash and burn, you won't build your platform on tearing ours down. I know you think it's funny posting all your mini breakdowns, but the implosion of Sage's marriage is off-limits. Got it?"

"I would never do that," I say quietly. Hearing her call my posts "mini breakdowns" and so easily dismissing me doesn't feel great, and I'm hurt she would think I would do that to Sage. I would never throw the destruction of Sage's marriage into the ether like digital confetti.

"Sure, but just so we're clear, don't. I'm too pregnant and too tired to care that much right now about anything, but if you get on your feed and start revealing the secrets of the Bay, I will burn you to the fucking ground."

"Noted," I tell her with respect. This is her town and her life. I won't mess with it. We have the same goal. We want to promote tourism to the town. We just have different ways of going about it.

Alana exhales like she's letting her moment of rage pass. "Sage, I'm sorry to hear about you and Breck. I hope your kids are doing okay with all of it." She says these things like she knows she's supposed to, but at least she's saying them at all. "But let's keep this topic off-line, 'kay?"

We all nod.

"Now look cute and let me snap a pic," she says and digs her phone out of one of her bags. I shuffle over to the counter, and Quincy and I share a look while we pretend to be arranging the tinctures again. "Cool," she says when she's satisfied with our faces on her phone. "Okay, here I go, up the hill." She starts gathering up her bags. "I'll see you guys next Friday, please? Yes?"

Quincy and I agree, Sage says she'll try, which makes Alana sigh, but that also might be because of all the crap she's loading into her arms.

"I can't watch this," I say and start taking bags out of her hands. "I'll help you carry this stuff home."

"Ugh, thank you. I was wondering how much longer I was going to have to huff and puff before one of you got the hint." She smiles as I take a bag full of oranges out of her hands. I take a few more bags and then open the door for us. Alana seems to remember something when we're halfway onto the sidewalk. "Quincy, can you text Amelia about the party? Tell her I need Claire's cute-ass face for some reaction shots when we make the announcement."

Chapter
17

"I KNOW WHAT I SOUNDED like at the shop," Alana says as we're hauling her bags up the hill to her house. "I wasn't trying to be an insensitive bitch. Whatever it looked like, that wasn't my actual goal."

"Okay, sure. And I'm not trying to tell you what to do, but Sage is having a tough time. So is Quincy. They're not trying to mess anything up for you or anyone else. You know the last thing Sage needs with her divorce and the store is to lose her followers. She knows she needs them to support the business."

"I know that, but you've got to understand, we made this town out of nothing. In the last ten years that I've been blogging, we turned this corner of the coastline into a coveted destination. It used to be just hostels and spring breakers with a Domino's Pizza and a tiny grocery store. Then a few people moved here to open organic coffee shops and restaurants and real businesses that support a lot of people around here. I'm not just thinking about myself when I remind people to stay on-brand. I think about the guy who works behind the counter at the juice bar or the people on Ari's landscaping crew who moved here for a better life. And I don't mean the moved-from-a-big-city-to escape-the-grind kind of better life." She looks at me pointedly. "I mean, escaped poverty and violence to find a place to make a living and safely raise their family."

"Right," I say. Because, wow, I am an asshole. "I get it now. I'm not going to expose the secrets of Peacock Bay if that's what you're worried about."

Alana huffs a breath and shakes her jet-black bangs out of her eyes. She's getting tired. So, I take the bags she's carrying out her hands and carry them all. "There's no darker side. We have problems, obviously. We're people, and I doubt our followers expect us to have perfect lives all the time, but that's not what people come to our platforms to see. They want to escape their own problems for a little while, not take on ours. They want to see happy, beautiful kids and moms enjoying the shit out of their place in the world. So that's what we do."

"That's fine for you guys. But I don't have any of that. And I don't know if you've picked up on the fact that I'm kind of a mess. I have no job, a fake boyfriend, and nowhere to live. Not exactly aspirational. I can't post what you do."

"I don't actually give a shit what you do, personally. But professionally, keep it light. Keep it positive and don't mess with the machine we've made. Think about Chip and Joanna Gaines."

"Who?"

"The Magnolia people, with all the shiplap? They used to have a show on HGTV?"

"Oh yeah: *It's demo day!*"

"Right, demo day. They were bloggers. I mean, they had the

construction company, they flipped houses, but she had a store and blog and they built houses in Waco, and who would really give a shit about that, but we did. Didn't we?"

"I still do. I want to shiplap anything that's not moving. How good would Pete's cottage look with shiplap all over it?"

"Exactly, but now, eleven million followers later, they have a bakery, a furniture line, and a million other businesses. They've made Waco into a fucking vacation destination. *Waco.*" She looks at me seriously. "Waco, Millie. Waco."

I laugh. "Okay, I get it."

"Do you? Do you think their brand could have grown that big if they'd gotten divorced during the filming of their show? It happened to the *Flip or Flop* couple, and who gives a shit about them anymore?"

"In fairness, no one really gave a shit about them before their divorce."

"Even so, people still want the pretty picture. The happy family, making it look easy to have a million kids and run a business or twelve."

I see the point. More than I did before, at least. People don't want see all the same problems they have glaring back at them from the people they follow online. They want to be transported to a better life, to be entertained by a husband who's maybe a little bit funnier than their own, to look at kids who might be the tiniest bit cuter, and maybe, just maybe, if we watch all these people and places we can make our own lives a little better too. Sure, that makes a lot of pressure to present a perfect image online and maybe there is something false about it, but no one is doing it maliciously.

Alana isn't trying to trick anyone into thinking her life is perfect because she's a terrible person. She's just showing the most perfect parts, and she's doing it for the good of the community. It's not just for the blog or the 'Gram, all the content Alana creates. It's for the town too. The hotel needs people to keep coming, and the businesses in town do too. I believe in transparency, but that doesn't mean ruining what everyone else is trying to make for themselves. Plus, I'm doing the same thing in a way, but maybe what I'm doing is even worse. I created a fake relationship with the full intention to implode it in real time for the sake of creating content. If I felt weird about this before, now I feel even worse. Maybe Pete and I should call things off before they get more complicated. I thought I was helping him, but now I'm worried it could be more damaging, and if that's the case, I'm not helping him at all.

We finally reach Alana's house, and I drop the bags on the sidewalk with a groan. There are red marks on my arms from where the bags were cutting into my skin.

"There has to be a better way. This is why people like cars. Because you don't have to carry anything."

"I have a little wooden wagon I use for big grocery hauls. The kids decorate it depending on the season, for Halloween and Christmas. It's really cute. I think one of the wheels is broken though." She drifts off in thought, probably thinking about how she needs to get that wheel fixed before her belly gets any bigger. "Hey, do you want to borrow some wheels to get back? A skate company just sent me a board to try, but they didn't know I was pregnant. I need to shoot it, though, because they mentioned maybe doing a sponsored post later in the year."

I haven't been on a skateboard in years, but I used to ride one a little in college to get from building to building between classes. It sounds fun to carve around town on a skateboard, but I might be a little shaky getting back on.

"You want to shoot me on a skateboard?"

"That's how it works." Alana places an absentminded hand on her belly and looks at me with a tiny glint in her eye. "People send me stuff, I shoot it. They send me more stuff and sometimes actual dollars. Which is helpful because god knows I can't pay my mortgage in skateboards."

It's funny. I can't tell if I actually like Alana or not. She's a savvy businesswoman—I have to admit that—but she's not what I was expecting. Online and even on the phone when we talked before, she was always so positive and mellow. Professional, but just oozing that natural organic vibe. I do respect her, though, even if she scares me a little bit.

"Fine, but you better make me look like a badass."

"Well, don't ask for the moon or anything." She tosses me a look over her shoulder before she pops open the gate in front of her house.

Alana goes to grab the board, and while she does, I stand back to admire her house and the others on her street. The light-green picket fence that borders her quaint little house is still as adorable as when I was last here. The flowering bushes and other greenery growing against the fence look well maintained. I know she has an eye for this kind of thing, but her house is by far the most manicured on the block. In fact, when I look a little closer at her neighbors' homes, the differences become more apparent. No one has anything growing. No one has a freshly painted fence. There are cinder blocks lazily piled in one neighbor's yard and a broken-down lawnmower in another.

I know the Hill is a less expensive neighborhood because it's farther from the water, which is why Alana chose it for her large family. It reminds me a little of how I grew up on Nantucket. My parents' modest mid-island home is just a few streets away from colossal mansions that sit empty for more months of the year than they're used.

A lot of things in life are done just for show, and that's nothing new. Instagram just lets you show more people. Still, it would make a funny picture. Zoom in, the perfect family home. Zoom out, reality. But I won't do it. Alana has made herself clear. If I want to build my following here in Peacock Bay, I'm going to do it within the parameters that have already been set. This isn't my world to wreck. I'm just a very lucky visitor, and I'm going to respect that.

Alana returns with the skateboard and, thoughtfully, a pair of sneakers. Riding in my sandals would have been a disaster, but I think it's more about the optics. Sneakers will look slightly cooler on the board.

"Ready to be a badass?"

"Aren't I always?" I answer, but really I'm kind of nervous, and now I wish I had the dress on. That usually makes me feel more confident. I may have been able to carve my way around campus when I was nineteen and twenty, but that was many, many years ago. It's not like I spent a lot of time powersliding down the streets of Midtown Manhattan, and judging by the way getting reacquainted with a surfboard went, I might not escape this without a few embarrassing (not to mention painful) wipeouts.

Alana drops the board on the street, the wheels making a

familiar clatter that transports me to all those years before when I was actually kind of a badass skateboard-riding, surfing college girl. But I'm still that girl. Didn't I pack up my apartment and ship myself to California to chase waves? Didn't I just finally hook up with the guy I've been lusting over for most of my adult life? I can do this. I *am* this. Okay, good pep talk. Now I just need to make it happen.

"I hope these go with my 'fit," I joke, pulling on the sneakers.

"It's fine. You look cool," Alana tells me, then looks up the street, planning the shot. "It's flatter up that way. Why don't you take the board there, and then I'll record you coming at me."

"Great, I'll try not to run you over." I take the board and push it slowly with my foot up the "flatter part" of the hill. Which is still, by the way, a hill. I bring my back foot up and try to get the feel of trucks under my feet. I feel really wobbly, but not terribly off-balance.

"Please don't. I don't need to start bleeding from my vagina in front of my neighbors."

"That would make an interesting Insta story though."

"Ha," she laughs. "I bet we'd each go up fifty thousand followers."

I pause and hop off the board. "Fifty thousand?"

"Oh yeah. Once Tiegen, my second oldest, fell climbing on some rocks at the beach and got a huge gash on her forehead. I storied the whole thing, the stitches and everything. I went up forty thousand that day and another twenty the next. I think it's one of the things that launched me."

"Oh my god, I remember that. I had no idea."

"Yeah, I think people were really captivated because we took her to our friend's house to get sewn up. But he's an ER doctor in Vera Lake. It wasn't like I took her to get sewn up by my local medicine man."

"But that's kind of how it looked." I'm mystified. Forty thousand followers because of a little kid getting stitches.

Alana smiles and shakes her head. "I guess so." She's not guessing. She knows exactly how it looked. I remember Tiegen being so brave. She must have been only about four then, and all the other parents and kids gathered around her and sang her silly songs and danced around in what I know now was the doctor's kitchen to distract her. Someone made her a huge ice cream sundae toward the end to get her through the last part when she started getting antsy. It was a perfect encapsulation of a village of moms and friends coming together to raise a kid. Quincy was there, I remember. She posted her version of it too. I wonder how many followers she gained that day.

"So, if I wipe out, maybe don't delete it right away," I joke. At least I think I'm joking. Maybe if it's a funny wipeout I would post it. I feel like I would have to. A video of me eating pavement might be too useful to pass up. This is my thing now, after all. I crash and burn for all to see. I just hope that after the smoke clears, something strong, something worth having will grow in its place.

"You ready, Freddy?" Alana calls to me.

"Hit it," I call back.

She holds a thumbs-up over her head to signal that she's started recording, and I push my left foot against the pavement a few times to get a little speed. I have trouble deciding how much speed to go for. This is a hill, after all. But fuck it, I'm doing this, aren't I? I'm not here to take pictures of latte art and sunsets. I'm here to make something for myself. Something real. Even if I have to keep creating mistakes and failures to post. Even if I have to screw up the one relationship I've dreamed of for years.

I push once more off the ground, and when I have what I think is the right amount of speed, I do my best to carve like I mean it down the street. I have control of my speed. I feel the wind lift my hair off my shoulders. It whips behind me and hopefully makes me look like the Queen of Dogtown. It feels great, but I know if Alana is going to post it, it's going to have to *really* look great.

I stop a few feet past Alana with one foot on the ground. I turn back to see her reaction. She's making a face at the camera.

"Was that cool?"

"It was good," she says, not looking up from the screen. "I mean, I could use it. I guess."

That means it was just okay. It means I looked like any chick on a skateboard. I can't let Alana post a video of me that's not amazing.

"I can do better. Let me go again," I say and push off to ride back.

Alana gives me the thumbs-up again, and this time I go for a little more speed. One extra push should do it, and then I really push hard, rocking from my toes to my heels to carve the width of the street. I feel the prick of sweat on my skin, wind whipping around my hair. This has to look better, but if it doesn't...

I don't think I can do a grab. Maybe I can if I just move my feet. *Okay, I can. Yes.*

Wait, no.

I feel the board hit a crack in the pavement, and then in a blink I'm going over. It's not like slow motion. It's not like I can see it as if I'm outside my body watching it from above. Nope. It's just me and the street meeting in the middle. My shoulder hits hard and then I feel it on my back.

"Oh fuck, Millie. Are you okay?" Alana calls as she runs over to me, the phone at her side. I don't even know if she got it.

I sit up and move my shoulder and back. I'm okay. My skin feels like it's on fire, but that's probably just road rash. Nothing's broken. Not even my pride. I might be down and ground up, but at least I went for it.

"Just tell me you got it." It's hard to catch my breath. Partly from the fall, partly because the adrenaline is kicking in and everything is a little funnier when you're covered in gravel, I guess.

She throws her head back, joining me laughing. "Oh, I got it, you crazy bitch. But I don't think the skate company is going to want that as the post. You nut."

I laugh, but when I do, my ribs kind of hurt, which isn't that funny. "Use the other one then. I'm not doing that again."

"Yeah, I don't need to clean your brains off my street. My kids will be home soon. They don't need to see that shit."

"Will you text me both though?"

Alana looks up from her phone and shakes her dark bangs out of her eyes. "Sure, but you can't do anything with them until after I post the good one. It's business." I can tell by her face she's not messing around about that. Not that I would mess with another woman's work, but anyway, the point has been made. "And I'll tag you in it so you'll probably gain a few followers. People will be used to seeing you on my feed now, and if they aren't already following you…they will now. I'll make the post cute. Don't worry."

"I'm less worried than you think."

In fact, I'm not worried at all. Go big, or go home, right?

Chapter
18

IF HISTORY AND YOUTUBE HAVE taught us anything, it's that people love to see other people make complete assholes of themselves. With permission, I posted my own version of the skate videos two hours after Alana's went up. Hers was of me looking moderately competent on the new skateboard, complete with the caption: Check out my girl @heretostay and her skills on this bananas Ursula longboard! It's a new skate company designing boards just for women for the first time ever. Millie loves it and I love her! Can't wait to ride it myself post-baby!

There're about a million hashtags underneath, and by the time I post mine, she has over four thousand views on the video.

I posted my version to my stories with *Instagram vs. Reality* written across it. After an hour of getting tons of DM's and laughing-face emojis, I posted it to my grid too. I know I should be pleased with the reactions I'm getting, but there's a strange twist in my stomach with every comment that appears.

How can you look that good falling on your ass?

Oh no! It was all going so well!

You can't have that man and such good balance. Sorry, it's not fair.

You. Are. Everything.

Most of the comments are funny and supportive, but not everyone is rooting for me. I get the sense that some people feel like they're a part of my quest to find my way here. Others possibly are rooting for me to fall and tumble on the pavement because it makes them feel better about the areas in their life where they might have crashed and burned that day. My scrapes and bruises, the ones they can see or not, might allow those watching to laugh for a second at their own mistakes, and that's something I can get behind.

I'm not sure that's exactly how Pete see things though. A little while after I posted the video, I got a text from him.

Pete: Everything okay? Looks like you took a nasty spill.

Millie: I'm fine. Just getting a little more closely acquainted with the neighborhood.

Pete: I got a funny call today.

> **Millie:** It wasn't from my Kate or Bree, was it?

I wouldn't put it past my friends to call and check up on me via Pete. Bree might even try her best to threaten him into making things more than just Instagram official.

> **Pete:** No, should I be expecting a call from one of them?

> **Millie:** Let's hope not.

> **Pete:** It was a woman who runs a surf camp. She said she wants to hold her next camp at the Waveline. She mentioned my "wife's" Instagram.

> **Millie:** Really? I wonder what sold her—me eating pavement or me getting worked by waves?

I'm not trying to be self-deprecating, but I actually don't know what about the stories I post would make someone want to hold their surf camp in the Bay. I definitely don't make things look seamless and smooth the way Alana wants me to, but if it helps the hotel, who am I to argue.

> **Pete:** Does it matter? It's working. Anyway, let's have a drink tonight and toast to surf camps and train wrecks. I'll give your road rash a careful inspection too.

My skin prickles with goose bumps, but there's that nagging feeling keeping me from celebrating what I know is a big win for the hotel. *Train wreck.* One short phrase. Just an expression, a joke, and one that I'm in on, that I started. But even though I'm the conductor of this train wreck and Pete is along for the ride, I feel like a part of him is standing to the side watching it happen and cheering as wreckage piles up.

So that night when I'm responding to comments and DM's from my new favorite spot on earth, Pete's deck swing, I'm trying to think of a way to show more of the things I actually like about myself instead of just my mistakes to make people laugh. Like my loyalty to my friends or my determination to help people when I can. If Pete can see that about me, maybe it's possible for other people to see it too. I'm also trying to come up with a way to reframe what's happening with Pete so that I can help bring business to the town and hotel, while not stomping on my self-worth and dignity.

I didn't think things would get so blurred when we started this. But with every night we're together, I'm losing sight of the strange circumstances in which we started. I'm not sure it's the same for him. He seems very aware of the deal we struck. He hasn't mentioned anything that would make me believe he wants to turn this into an actual relationship—just the opposite. He asks about my follower count and brings up how limited my time is here. Which is fine. I didn't come here to make a permanent move. This is a launching place. A place to breathe and figure out what's next for me. The problem I keep returning to is that "what's next" isn't likely to have Pete in it.

Pete turns me gently to inspect the road rash on my shoulder. His lips brush the scratches so tenderly my chest tightens.

"Did it hurt?"

"If you say 'falling from heaven,' I will filet you."

Pete nudges me. "It looked like a rough fall, that's all. You good?"

"I'm fine. I'm glad it looked real. If I had tossed myself onto the road and it looked fake, that would have been a serious waste."

Pete cocks his head. "You did this on purpose?"

"Not exactly, but I didn't *not* do it on purpose? Isn't that what I'm supposed to do? You know… Alana was telling me about the time one of her kids needed stitches and she posted the whole thing. This is the kind of thing people expect from me now. I'm going to have to create some moments that look worse than they are sometimes if I want to keep this going."

"You're going to have to fake screwing up now?"

"Not faking anything. Just emphasizing it." Though in a way, maybe he's right. At least I have the most epic one coming when Pete and I post our big breakup. I wonder if he's thinking the same thing. By the look on his face, I get the sense that he is.

"You know what we should do?" Pete asks after giving his head a shake.

He's trying to change the subject and I am all for that, so I slide my hand up his thigh and squeeze near his hip. "Why, yes, Pete. I think I do."

He drops a kiss on my head. "Yes, that too." He shifts slightly, trying to hide the stiffness pressing against my back. I can tell he has an actual idea, but doesn't want to change my line of thinking either. "We should go to Mavericks."

My creeping hand stills. "So we can both die? Well, you might not die, but I definitely would. I know I need to create some fails for my feed, but actual deaths aren't exactly what I had in mind."

"Quincy went before she had kids. Did you know that? She and Ari surfed there once. I think Ari's been a few times. It's only a few hours from here." As if the distance is the thing that's been stopping me all this time.

Mavericks is a legendary surf spot in Northern California. The waves there are regularly ten to fifteen feet but have been known to reach forty or even fifty feet high. I have no business going out there ever, and it would terrify me to watch Pete try. I'm not going to hold him back if it's something he's always wanted to do though. Surfers are risk-takers. They're independent and they can get bored easily. You're never going to win if you try to hold someone down when they are really focused on a goal, but especially not someone who regularly paddles into the ocean alone with nothing but a piece of foam and epoxy to keep them from drowning.

I sit up and turn to face him. "If it's something you really want to do, I guess I'll come along and watch." I hate the thought of watching Pete dive under waves as tall as buildings, and I'm surprised he'd even want to. It's not like him. People die at Mavericks. It's not something you just do on a whim.

"We don't have to surf there, but I was thinking about the post you wrote after I was kind of a dick to you about surfing alone, and I started thinking about Mavericks. Did you know the first contest there was called Men Who Ride Mountains?"

"No, I didn't." Though I shouldn't be surprised. Big-wave surfing, to my limited knowledge, has never been that welcoming to women.

"There wasn't even a contest there for women to compete in until a few years ago, but it wasn't until much later that the prize money was the same. Mavericks is kind of the epicenter for women's equality in surfing right now, and it's not too far from here. You should check out the contest this year. I bet a story like that could bring in big numbers." Pete grins at me expectantly while I run over what he's suggesting.

He could be right that a post and some photos from Mavericks would be good content. It's something to consider. "Do you know when the contest is?"

"December," he answers, planting a kiss on the side of my head, as if that settles that.

"December?" I pull back to search his face. "That's kind of awhile from now."

Pete runs his fingers over my forearm, while goose bumps pebble my skin. He laces our fingers together and looks down at them before he looks back up at me. "It's only a few months away."

I search his face, wondering if he's suggesting this because he wants me around that long. Could that be possible?

"Yeah, but I'll be gone by then." I'm presenting a challenge. I want him to admit that he wants me here with him.

"Where are you going?"

"I'm not exactly sure, but I told you I'm going to leave when we post our breakup. I can't stay after that."

"So, you're just going to take off with no plan? Come on, Millie, you can do better than that."

Can I though? I shake my head and look out over the deep, dark ocean for the answers Pete isn't giving me. The stars and moon dance across the lazy waves but, regrettably, give me about as many answers as the man next to me. He didn't say he wants me here. He didn't say he wants me to leave, but I need more than that. As tempting as it is to keep pretending I'm fine just cruising along, sleeping with Pete with no mention of how deep my feelings really are, pretty soon my overactive brain is going to catch up with my mouth and that's not going to be pretty. I can picture the moment and the look on Pete's face when I blurt something out like, 'But what about your feelings for me? And where do you see this whole trapeze act going?'

"I need to think about it," I say quietly, biting back a thousand questions that are banging against my head trying to get out. *Not yet, little fools.* "But it's a cool idea."

"Sorry if I'm overstepping. It was just an idea I had." Pete looks down, and I wonder if he's actually disappointed I'm not more excited.

"Hey, I'd love to check out Mavericks some time. I'm just not sure when that'll be and if my plans will line up with the contest. But I really am happy you were thinking of ideas for me. Shit, that you were thinking about me at all." It's a challenge. A dare. The tiniest push toward finding out what he thinks about me lurking around his deck all the time.

"Seriously?" Pete's eyes bore into mine, and he runs his hand up my side and pulls me close so my chest meets his. My whole body tightens to a pinpoint. "Mills, you're basically all I think about. This is all I think about."

My heart swells. He may have only meant sex, but the tiniest twinge of hope sparks in my chest. He thinks about me. About going to Mavericks and watching massive waves roll in…together.

And he's talking about me still being here in December. Months from now, and well after we agreed to disclose our fake relationship. What if we never have to say it was fake? What if we really were together after all this?

I'm not sure he's willing to give up the attention our little stunt would bring to the hotel, but for the first time, I'm starting to think it's a possibility. The thought of this has me launching myself at his mouth. I suck on the edge of his ear and bite down where his neck meets his shoulder. I'm not sure where things are headed with us, and I don't know how long I have left to be with him. I do know I'm going to destroy him while I can.

Pete is matching me with equal intensity. His hands grip my waist, and he's pulling my tank top over my head before I can even remember what we were talking about. He starts trailing kisses across my chest, cupping one of my breasts in his hand. His fingers push aside the thin material of my bra so he can make my nipple available for his mouth to consume. I can't get enough of it. Of him. I want him everywhere. I want to be everywhere on him and my body agrees.

Except my stomach. There's a loud growl that's not the sexy kind from my throat, and Pete lifts his head to look at me and laughs.

"I guess you can't actually be my snack," I say with a grin.

"Let me go throw together dinner." Pete kisses me once more and I hold his face on mine for an extra few seconds, savoring the taste of his sweet mouth. This is crazy. He will literally be gone for seconds, and I'm preparing myself to miss him.

"What's for dinner?" I ask as he untangles himself from my limbs and heads for the kitchen.

"Panini," he answers. "I wouldn't say I'm a great cook, but I can assemble the hell out a sandwich and then warm it up." He winks at me. A tiny flick on his face, but the motion completely melts me.

I lie back against the pillows on the daybed and let a leg drop to the deck. I push myself into a gentle sway as I listen to the ocean and take in the cloudless night sky. I can't believe this is my reality. For right now, at least.

"It'll only be a few more minutes," Pete says when he returns.

I can deal with a few more minutes. I sit up and wedge myself in the corner of the couch to make more room for Pete. He doesn't need it, though, because he slides down right next to me with an arm across the back of the couch and me. It's just like the picture at Alana's party, except this time I'm leaning right into him.

"Well, then you're going to have to distract me for those few minutes because I'm starving." I look up at his handsome face and run a finger across his sharp jaw. His eyes grow heavy.

"For me or for dinner?" Pete grins. Our noses brush once but I keep them from touching. I want to tease him for a minute more.

"Whatever I can get my mouth on first," I answer and then take what is offered to me. I kiss Pete deeply and let myself get lost in the feel of his lips and tongue. I want to pull him closer, but there isn't any more space between us even though he still feels too far away. I swing a leg around him to straddle his lap. His hands slide down to get a grip on my ass. I tilt forward and grind against him, the pressure zipping a heady feeling into my core. I get a thrill when I hear a groan come from his mouth. I can't get enough of the noises this man makes, and it drives me crazy that I didn't know about them for years. We keep kissing like this, with our hands nearly tearing at each other. I hear him say things like "more" and "burning" until I realize he means something different than I do.

He jumps up suddenly after who knows how long, the daybed swinging wildly. "Paninis are burning," he says on the way to the kitchen. I let my head fall back and cover my face with a pillow, laughing. Then I think what good content this would make and grab my phone and follow Pete to the kitchen.

I shoot a short video while he's fanning the panini press, laughing.

A man of many talents, I write and post. Then I film him again.

"You better stop." He grins at me. I know he hates having the phone in his face, and my time is running out on how long he'll humor me.

"I will as soon as you tell me what we're going to have for dinner now. Huh, Pete?" I laugh. "I was told a man was making me dinner, and there seems to be a small delay here. Can we call it a delay? What would you call it?" I laugh.

He shakes his head as he tries to pull the burnt sandwiches off the press with metal tongs. The cheese is completely blackened and has locked onto the metal grooves like cement.

"I call it being distracted." He grimaces at the sandwiches, but laughs at his efforts when a chunk of panini becomes dislodged and goes flying toward the ceiling.

I completely lose it at this, the phone shaking in my hand while I try to steady myself with a hand on the counter.

"That's it." Pete tosses the tongs on the counter. He gives me a fake scowl, then unplugs the panini press and turns to me with a hungry look in his eyes. I think we all know what's for dinner now.

Chapter
19

"YOU KNOW, YOUR BEDROOM IS nice and everything," I say, pulling the soft cotton sheet up to our shoulders.

"But not as nice as the deck?" Pete finishes for me.

"I can see why you spend so much time out there." His bedroom is small but cozy, with barely enough room for his bed and a small dresser against the other wall. There's only one tiny window that is oddly positioned above the bed. And in the corner is something even odder.

"But there's something else we need to talk about." I lift my head and look at him seriously. "That." I point to the other corner of the room, which contains what can only be called a crib. "Explain please."

"Stop it. I babysit my nieces and nephews sometimes. Once in a while someone has to sleep over."

"So basically it's for Claire," I say.

"Yes, but don't tell anyone. And if you make fun of my bedroom, I'm not going to let you come back to the cottage anymore. You have to take all the parts. The ones with the deck and the view…"

"And the burnt panini?"

"Yep, and the tiny bedroom with one scary prison window."

"It *is* like a prison window," I exclaim. I was trying to think of the right word for it. Clearly, Pete has had longer to think about this. I lay my head back on his chest and breathe in the scent of him. It's an impossible scent. One that's so new yet familiar at the same time. Slightly salty but soapy clean, and something that's just so Pete it makes my eyes sting in a good way. I feel Pete's hand trail up my back and then find its way under the sheet and onto my skin.

Everything is so good when we're like this, and I'm not thinking about all the rest of it. Like how Pete's feelings for me could never be as genuine as mine when I'm constantly showing him what a disaster of an adult I can be online. If I could prove to myself that I am a *capable* adult, then maybe I would be more confident approaching the topic of a real relationship with Pete.

I stare at the ceiling of Pete's bedroom while he slips away to order us a pizza to replace the burnt sandwiches. The ceiling, frustratingly, isn't giving me any answers to my problems, so I reach over and pick up my phone to lose myself in a soothing scroll. But when I click into my email, I'm jolted upright and soothed I am not.

There is an answer to one of my problems though. It's an email from a women's surf apparel brand I've followed for years called Covast. They're writing to say they've been following my Instagram account over the past few weeks and would like me to interview for a job in their marketing department. I read the email three times, forcing my mind to gather every last detail and not simply skim like it wants to.

An actual job, with benefits and a 401(k) and all the things I had before when I was working for Butterfly Bridge. The answer to one huge question that's been hanging over my head. A real-deal grown-up job. One that will prevent me from living in my parents' garage apartment and working with them on their listings. One that would show everyone, Pete included, I'm not always a screwup.

One that will take me far away from Peacock Bay.

Chapter
20

THE NEXT MORNING, PETE AND I tromp down to the Cove for a morning surf. He makes fun of me for still not having a board, which is completely fair, but I still call him a dick for it.

"Admit it, you just like mine better," he says.

I roll my eyes, but he has a point. The board he loans me is his custom-made Robert August longboard. I hate to sound like a board snob, but it's like the Range Rover of surfboards, and I really love it. It's huge and hard to manage out of the water, but I can catch anything on it. It's also gorgeous.

"You could just buy a board," he points out.

"No," I say, laughing. "I've dug myself in this hole and now I just have to keep digging, Pete." I should have mentioned the surfboard Alana said was coming to her last week. She gave me that skateboard, which would have been the perfect time to bring it up, but honestly, it just slipped my mind. "Plus, I just know the second I buy a board, Alana is going to text me and tell me the free board is ready for me to pick up." That's always the way it happens.

Though I'm not sure it matters much anymore. I doubt I'll

have much time for surfing if I get the job with Covast. Even if the company is in LA, a job like that would mean giving up a lot of the things that are in my life now. But I know I can't stay here. When things are revealed about our fake relationship and Pete and I part ways, there's no way I can hang around this tiny town. Just like with the surfboard, I've dug myself into this hole and the only way to get out is to keep digging.

"Who cares? You would have a board then," Pete continues. "Is it really a money thing? I know you want to save cash, but it seems like a surfboard is a pretty important part of life for a surf influencer. Maybe you could even write it off on your taxes," he says as we start to paddle out into the waves. They're small this morning, but clean and long. We should have some nice rides for at least a few hours, until the tide starts to change. Which should be long enough to distract me from making a decision about the interview. Even if the way I present myself looks like I don't take myself seriously, I always hoped a path to self-sufficiency would develop from what I've been doing online. Kind of like pretending Pete was my husband online to gain some followers and hoping a real relationship would develop too.

Hopefully, my potential employers will see my online tomfoolery as the gutsy move of a creative thinker, not a foolish shot in the dark by a horny twentysomething. If I get flak from my tiny internet community, well, I'll have shifted gears into a new job by then and I can try to ignore the criticism. Pete, on the other hand… Well, I've been so worried about disappointing him or being rejected. If I take this job, maybe I can stop that from happening. I wouldn't be an online joke anymore. I also wouldn't be in Peacock Bay, but as much as I want to believe I'll be fine when this all falls apart, I know losing Pete will devastate me. Even if he's had fun with our deal and he cares about me as a friend, it won't be enough to make things okay for me to stay.

"By the way, you might want to look into forming an LLC. I've been meaning to mention that to you, but somehow keep getting distracted." He shoots a coy look to me over a wave as we continue to paddle. "It will make things simpler for you at tax time with the gifts you're going to get and all those sponsorships and ads." He smiles.

"Right," I say and then focus on paddling a little harder to get over the next wave coming toward us. I press up against the board as I float over its crest, then slice my arms through the cool water to gain some distance between us. I need to explain things to Pete. I need to tell him about the interview. It may seem a little impulsive, but hopefully he'll understand that it's actually the responsible choice for me.

We get past the break and straddle our boards, watching the incoming waves while we catch our breath. Pete is a few feet away with his head turned over his shoulder to keep an eye on what's coming. Never turn your back on the ocean. It's one of the first things you learn when surfing. You don't want to be caught off guard. I've spent too much time with my back against the waves, letting the events of my life continuously wipe me out. It's time to turn around and face what's coming next once and for all.

I can feel the pull of the water letting me know a wave is coming. It brings me back to the moment just as the ocean has always done for me. The coming wave looks like it's going to break closer to me, and Pete meets my eye and gives me a nod. He's giving me the first good wave. I'm not sure if it's this act of generosity or the incoming wave, but both make my heart pound and ache in equal measure. As good as this wave is, as good as the opportunity is with Covast, it will take me away from Pete, and the heartache of realizing this is unbearable.

"Come with me," I call to him. It's lame and way cheesier than I would ever admit to him, but I don't want to be apart from him even for the distance of this ride. I'm going to hate myself for ruining this, but with the way things started, we never had a chance anyway. Which is probably why I concocted the plan in the first place. You can't screw up something that was fake to begin with.

He breaks out into a huge grin and starts to paddle hard toward me. I do the same. We keep a safe distance, and when I feel the wave pulling me back, I lose all sense of everything for the next few seconds. The pull of the wave, then the push as my board is propelled forward. I feel the catch and can hop up to my feet.

"Party wave," Pete calls, and I have to laugh. Pete pumps his feet on his board to gain speed so we stay together on the face of the wave. Without thinking, I reach an arm out to him. We're not that far apart; I can almost touch him. He glances back and reaches his arm out to me. Our fingertips, pruny and damp with salt water, barely brush. We're not close enough to lock them together. He drops his arm, so I do the same and it fills me with warmth and longing.

We ride the wave as long as we can, and when we run out of whitewater, I hop off my borrowed board and rip the Velcro on the ankle strap off. I grab the board and use all my strength to shove it to shore. I see it land on the sand and pray it will stay put while I do something sort of stupid. I take three huge high steps through the water and launch myself at this short-haired, scruffy-faced surf god. My arms go around his neck, and he laughs in surprise as our lips meet. The warmth of his lips floods through my body until we fall back into the water and are covered in cold again.

Pete puts his arm gently over my head to protect us in case his board is washed our way, but his other arm is around my back, holding us together. It only lasts a few seconds, but when we come up, it's like my entire world has changed. Yes, I'm the least influential of the Peacock Bay influencers. Yes, I'm about to face some serious internet flogging when I admit to having faked a relationship for Instagram. But even so, there is something real that came out of this little social media masquerade.

I am truly and authentically in love with Pete Santana.

Our morning surf is going to be cut short by, well, hormones, I guess.

"That it for the day?" Pete asks with a grin when we come up from the water.

"I don't want you to be late for work," I say coyly.

He tilts his head. "It's still early. There's plenty of time."

"Not with what I plan to do to you." I raise my eyebrows. "Plus, a shower."

"Well, we better get you home then." Pete grins and quickly

grabs my hand. We stomp out of the water like that. Hand in hand, Pete carrying his board under the other arm.

I gather the other board and try to ignore the tightness in my stomach. I know he just means the place where we can get down and dirty, but still. How does he think this ends? How can he not see that no matter how good the sex is or how much chemistry is between us, there's no way this ends well.

It's fine. Really. I've lusted after Pete for years; this new development of being in love with him isn't really that big of a change for me. I might be more in love than I've ever been in my life, but I can handle it. He wants me now and that's what matters. And I mean right now, because his hand, rough and dusted with sand, keeps finding its way to my ass as we walk up the path to his house. With everything else I've screwed up, at least I'm the only one who will get crushed when this ends. If I thought his feelings went farther than just lust, that he would be hurt when I left, well, that would be just another failure and that would be too much to take.

Pete leads me under the deck to where he stores his boards. He leans his board upright against its rack and then holds his arms out for the next one. Watching him do this, I can't help but notice the vacant space on the rack and think about how easily whatever board I acquire could fit right in with his collection. There are only four boards on this rack. There's plenty of space left over, another would hardly make a difference. I shake my head because I can't think like that. There's nothing here for me other than swooning for Pete, and as much as anyone could understand making a career out of that, it's not the offer on the table.

Once the boards are away, Pete peels his wet suit off, then

collects mine and takes both to run a hose over them to wash the sand off. I wrap myself in a towel and watch as he carefully cleans both of our suits.

"A girl could get used to this kind of treatment," I say, then regret it. Getting used to this isn't an option.

Pete turns off the hose with a half smile and a look in his eye that's nothing but trouble. He crosses over to me and grabs the towel at the place where I've tucked it neatly around me and pulls me against his chest. "Nothing less than completely happy every time you walk away," he says softly, leaving me struggling for a comeback. His head dips to my neck, and when his lips meet my skin, my head tips back. His hand is there to catch it, but I right myself quickly. I need my mouth on his, like, now. I reach up, and when my fingers touch his face, there's the sweetest sound from his throat. Pete loosens my towel and lets it fall to the ground. He kisses me like we're on borrowed time. Maybe it's because he thinks he has to get to work or maybe it's something else, but his hands grip me across my back, and if I could bribe those hands to never let me go, I would.

I have to get it together. I have to tell him about my interview. I'll start there and ease into the rest.

"So, I have something to—" I begin.

"Oh, that reminds me," he breaks in. I nod for him to continue because I'd love to not talk about my stuff anyway. "We need your room. Labor Day weekend is coming up, and the college kids start trekking down here during the break. Since you're planning on staying with me for the rest of the nights you're here anyway, can we just get your stuff and bring it back here? It would save you the trouble of running back to the Waveline every time you need a new bathing suit or sexy little dress to torture me with."

"Was I planning on staying with you the rest of my nights here?" I tilt my head to the side, pretending to remember this.

"Yes, you were. Did I forget to mention that? Maybe I was just going on the fact you spend all your time here anyway." He kisses my neck and lights my skin on fire. This might actually kill me. But with the interview coming up, it's only a few more days anyway.

"I guess, if you need the room," I say, pulling back from his kiss.

I push him back gently so I have him up against the side of the surf rack. My fingers find the ties on his swim trunks.

"It's a very popular hotel," Pete says huskily. "Due to its excellent online presence. Influencers seem to love it. I'm not sure why." He coughs the last word. I think it's because I've reached into his swim shorts and am now holding him in my hand, stroking the length of him.

"Well, one of the hotel owners is really fucking hot," I say. I start kissing and sucking my way down his body. His bathing suit has fallen to the ground and I wonder if he's thanking the former owner of his house for planting such thick shrubs around the house to give it privacy.

"God, that's fucking lucky," he murmurs nearly breathless.

I take him in my mouth, sucking slowly up his length, then stop. "I meant Quincy."

His laugh is strangled, but I feel the surf rack shaking as I brace my arm on it. His hand twists a thick strand of my salty hair and his thumb traces my jawline. He stops laughing when I take him in my mouth again.

Chapter
21

PETE AND I RIDE TO the hotel together. My finger hovers over the reply button on the email from Covast. I spent the second half of yesterday trying to decide about the interview. One second I'd be completely sure it was the right thing to do; my parents would get off my back, I'd have job stability again. The next second (one in which I could feel Pete's skin against mine) I'd convince myself I was just using this interview as a way to shirk the messiness of my current situation.

I can't think about this anymore. I switch to my Instagram for a distraction and start scrolling the comments.

"Hey, look. Baby's first dick pic." I hold up my phone.

Pete's eyes flash as he glances at my phone and then back to the road, the fury never leaving his face.

"What the hell? What asshole sent this to you?"

"A stupid one? Which are always the best kinds of asshole, aren't they?"

"I can't believe guys get off on that kind of shit. Can you block him?" He pulls around to the back of the hotel and into a parking spot.

"Already done. Though a part of me would love to repost it

with his user name loud and proud, but I'm guessing that wouldn't be good for the Peacock Bay brand Alana has carefully created."

"Are there more? Why would people do that?"

"There's always an asshole somewhere, but for the most part it's fine. It's not forever anyway," I say, and my eyes dart to read Pete's face. "Just another week, right?"

"Another week until what?"

"Until I spill about our fake relationship. It was only going to be for a month. I'll probably have to take a step back from Instagram after that, but I think I'm ready for it. I'm not sure I was ever cut out for this kind of thing. I mean, the best I could come up with was posting about what a disaster I am. That's not exactly sustainable in the long term." At least I hope it's not. At some point I have to learn to get things together and be a responsible adult, or at least find my version of that.

Pete clears his throat. "So what does this mean?"

I shrug. It's now or never. "I got an email a few days ago about interviewing for a job in LA. I think it's probably time for me to get a real job again."

"So you're just going to take off for LA?" Pete asks. "Why do you have to go and look for a new job now?"

I want to say, *Because you're not in love with me, and it's going to hurt too much when you let me know it.*

"It's not like there are that many opportunities for me here," I say quietly. I know it sounds like I mean career-wise, and that's what I'd prefer Pete to believe so I leave it there.

"What a bunch of bullshit," Pete murmurs. He may not have meant for me to hear it, but it cuts through me like a knife.

"You're speaking in typos again."

"I don't know what you thought was going to happen in just a few weeks, Millie. You can't skip steps. Things take time to develop, and if you could just calm down and focus for three seconds—"

"Hold it right there." His words knock the air right out of me. He's never said anything like that to me before, and I feel the tears welling in my eyes. "I'm trying to be responsible for a change, but what am I supposed to do? Hang out on your deck and keep pretending with you until another job comes my way? Who knows when that would be."

Telling me to focus was a gut punch. A kick to where I'm most sensitive when I'm already down. I'm not sure I can be responsible for what comes next. "Because it's all been fake anyway, hasn't it? I mean, the sex was real. We had a good time in a weird situation, but that's *it*."

I'm not going to cry in front of him, but I scan his face for any sign we can turn this around and save what was happening between us. Even as angry as I am, I can still see how handsome he is. He shaved today. Not really shaved, but trimmed the overgrown stubble with a beard trimmer. I sat on the sink and watched him the entire time, like a creepy little fangirl. I want to run my fingertips over the freshly trimmed prickles of hair, but I know that I can't anymore. I'm slamming shut the door I had cracked open, but maybe it's better this way. I can't keep pretending I'm not in love with him when he's just been having fun.

I don't want to get out of the car like this. I don't want him to go on with his day and me with mine when my whole world has turned upside down. How is it that a few hours ago he was asking me to spend more time with him and now I'm leaving him for a job in LA? I don't even like living in cities! Something I didn't realize until this exact moment.

"We agreed it was just for a month. Our time is almost up anyway. Like you said, it's time for me to *focus*." There's a sneer in my voice that hurts me as much as I hope it hurts him.

Pete rubs his fingers across his forehead and looks straight ahead out the window. Not even a glance in my direction. "No, you're right. We said it was for a month. I lost track of things."

I wish he would look at me. Try to change my mind or show me anything that would make me think we can be okay when this is all over, but there's nothing. I can't think of a way to fix this either. All I can think of is a change of subject.

"You know about Alana's thing tonight, right? The baby reveal?" I say, partly to have something new to say, but also because I promised Alana I would get him there and I don't want to screw up that too.

"That's tonight, huh? Shit." He looks at me like the last place he'd ever want to be is at a party for Alana's yet-to-be-born fifth child, which will definitely be cross-posted on every local influencer's feed for the next few days.

"You don't have to go. She wants you there, but I get it if you don't want to be there."

"No, no. I'm going." He sighs, heavy with the burden of it. "Alana does a lot for the hotel. She even had her last baby reveal here, and it gave us a major boost after a storm had come through and slowed our reservations down almost to nothing. I'll be there."

Just like Alana said, the blogs support not just the people who created them, but all the business owners in the Bay. Pete knows he can't turn away from these things. I've always known that was the first reason Pete started things up with me, but I guess I always hoped there was something deeper that would make what was fake online close to true. Pete seems to have no trouble reminding me that's wishful thinking.

"So, we better go. You're already late for work and I have a lot to figure out," I say.

"Yeah," he says, his voice rough. "Good luck with the interview, I guess." Pete opens the car door and I do the same. We've been sitting in his car for a long time, but after the last few minutes, I don't want to move. This car feels like my last connection to what Pete and I had. This extra bland un-Instagrammable car. Which I fucking love. Along with the man who drives it.

"And I'll just bike down to Turtle Beach this afternoon for Alana's party. You don't have to leave work early if you don't want to."

It's petty, but I want to provoke him. He never wants me going places alone.

"Yeah, that's fine." he answers.

What the fuck? What happened to my complete happiness? I didn't ask for that. He volunteered it. Why bother saying that to me if he can turn it off so easily? I turn and start to make my way back to the hotel. Alone and completely miserable.

Chapter 22

THE THING ABOUT HAVING ADHD is that you're easily distracted, right? That's sort of the whole freaking thing about it. I have a hard time focusing. Certain simple tasks can feel like I'm doing them in thick mud, or one of those crazy ball pits. An idea I had will slip out of reach before I had time to complete it, or it's physically painful for me to pay that bill that's been sitting on my counter for over a month. But the real bullshit of it—like the real motherfucking bullshit about having a distractible mind—is that once I get stuck on an idea or subject or the thought of this guy who I've had a crush on since college and have been having the best sex of my life with and now I very much am not, well, I can't get off of it. I can't distract myself when I'm already distracted.

I order an extra-large coffee from the lobby café and try to fight back tears when the young guy behind the counter automatically adds oat milk and hands me two sugars, a tiny reminder that I was starting to settle in here. I pop one of my daily extended-release pills and pray it does it's freaking job. I get a bagel, too, because I can't risk coming back down here for a snack and running into Pete. I need a few hours to sort this out.

When I get up to my room, I hate it. I hate the piles of clothes that could have been so easily tossed into my suitcase, wheeled into Pete's car, and unpacked at his cozy house. I'm so mad at the big empty bed I've slept in maybe three times since I've been here.

"Guess you and I are going to get better acquainted, bed. You piece of Pete-less garbage," I mutter as I grab my computer and climb up on the bed. I stuff all the pillows behind me, punching them a few times because if I don't, I'll likely punch something else, then lean back with my computer on my lap. I take giant scalding gulps of my coffee and let the caffeine do its thing.

I have a couple of emails that I will force myself to focus on. First up, I reply to Blair Martindale at Covast and tell her I'd love to discuss the opportunity at her company. Maybe waiting a few days to answer her will hurt me in the interview process, or maybe it'll make them want me more. I guess I'll find out. I'm making my way through a few emails with no emotion attached to my responses. I write back to commenters and DM's. I follow back the smatter-ing of people who have followed me in the last twenty-four hours. None of this equals income, but the activity keeps me busy. I don't know how Quincy makes money doing this. I can't believe how foolish I was, thinking I could swing in here and fake my way into their world.

I go to my friend's Instagram to take a closer look, but before I can begin my scroll, Quincy's most recent post stops me in my tracks. The caption reads: These are my struggles. What are yours?

When I read through the post, I'm overwhelmed with a sense of pride for my friend's bravery. She's written a very personal post about what she's been going through with Monrow, the toll it's taken on her work with her blog, and the pressure it's put on her marriage. She ends it by asking her followers to write, if they feel comfortable, something in the comments that they've been struggling with, and when I scroll down, I see hundreds of responses. I click the comment slot and exhale as I start to add my own words. Quincy knows I don't love talking about my ADHD, but it was on my suggestion that she wrote this post, and I'm hoping it was cathartic for her to do this. Man, could I use some catharsis after the morning I've had.

> I still struggle with my ADHD as an adult. I make impulsive decisions that damage my relationships. I've always thought of my ADHD as my problem, and it wasn't until recently that I considered how it affected the people around me. Realizing that my impulsive choices impact others has helped me aim to do better in the future. We all have to grow up some time! Right, Mom?

I could have posted that from my personal account, but Quincy is risking a lot being open and honest about her struggles, so the least I can do is back her up with mine.

I try to focus again on my emails and push thoughts of Pete away by deleting a few junk messages when I see the reply from Blair at Covast. She doesn't seem at all fazed that I took a while to express my interest and suggests we meet on Monday to discuss things further. So, without any idea how I'll get there or where I'll stay, I agree to an interview in LA at 1:00 p.m.

My heart twists, wringing out the emotions of the last few

hours, as I think about leaving Peacock Bay and my friends here. But what other choice do I have? I said I'd stay a month and my time is up. Even if Pete did feel the same way I do, I wouldn't know where to begin making a life here.

With the details of the job interview settled, I lean back against the pillows on this Pete-less bed and scroll through my feed absent-mindedly for a few minutes, letting the endless images soothe my racing thoughts. I try to let myself get lost in images of beaches far away and children with artfully messy topknots, but everything I see reminds me that none of those beaches are as wonderful as the ones I've spent the last few weeks on, nor are the kids as cute and charming as Claire.

My phone starts to ring as I stare at the screen, and I answer right way when I see who's calling.

"You have to take it down," Alana says, after we greet each other.

"Take what down?"

"Your comment on Quincy's Insta post."

"Why? I do have ADHD. It does make things hard for me and the people around me sometimes." This is one of the first intentional, nonfail things I feel I've shared online, and I'm not sure why Alana is so freaked out about it.

"I'm trying to minimize the damage here. Quincy is refusing to take the whole thing down even though she knows how off-brand it is for all of us. You can't encourage her."

"But I want to encourage her. I think opening up about Monrow is a good thing for her and anyone else dealing with the same stuff."

"Millie. Haven't I helped you? Hasn't my support gotten your tiny little account off the ground? Shit, encouraging you to do that

Instagram Husband stuff got you the best dicking of your life, am I wrong?"

I roll my eyes even though she can't see me.

"So I should just hand over my passwords to you? Let you post for me?"

"It's not just what you're posting. I've got Sage hashing out her divorce—"

"She's not posting about it, and I don't think you can blame me for Sage's divorce."

"And now Quincy is getting Monrow evaluated for special needs. You came here on whim, but this is our fucking livelihood. Not all of us want to look like a joke."

My heart nearly stops. "I never wanted that either! How can you say that?" I can feel the quiver in my voice and blink away the tears threatening to fall. I know Alana is scared too. She found a way to make things work as an influencer, and that's not an easy thing. I'm sure it feels fragile to her, but I never wanted to look like a joke. Not to her, or Pete or anyone. Alana confirming that everyone thinks I'm a joke and Pete telling me to focus is more than I can handle right now. I know I have to get out of here and walk away.

"Don't act like I made this so hard for you. You're out here chilling and banging away on Pete's deck with no kids to worry about. You're completely unencumbered and can move through life however you feel like it. I've asked you to do one thing. One. Just stick to the program, and you couldn't even do this one tiny thing. I've been letting it slide that you keep posting your screwups, but this isn't the same thing."

"But it's been a lie. And a stupid one. Plus, it has gotten me exactly *nowhere*. With anyone or anything. I still need a job and a way to support myself. I want to help the hotel and everyone, but I can't keep pretending to be married to Pete hoping that it helps. Even posting my mistakes has reached its limits. At least I've got the 'fake husband' reveal in my back pocket. That's going to be a banger to go out on." I exhale into the phone, letting my own words hit me. I'll do this last post soon, and then I hope to god I can make things work in LA.

"Alana, I have to go back to work. I got an interview for a marketing job in LA. I'm leaving in a couple days. So, you don't have to worry about me screwing with your utopia for much longer. I'll just gather my spaz and take it elsewhere." Saying it all out loud is the punishment I deserve. Not for what I said on Quincy's post, but for trying to lie my way up the Insta ladder and into Pete's bed. The cold truth makes my stomach feel hollow, but there's nothing else I can do. I went after the things I wanted, and for the slightest moment I could almost feel the crest of the wave of those things catching under my feet, but because of the bungled way I went after everything, here I am still adrift with no Pete to speak of.

"Now you're moving to LA? Geez, girl. You really bounce around."

I shrug. "It's not by choice. But I don't see you offering me a job as your personal assistant."

"Definitely not," she says, which I wasn't really asking for, but still? Definitely? "Well, I'm pretty sure I can get you a place to stay down there. A hotel in Malibu has been offering me a few nights there in exchange for a post, but who the hell is watching all my kids while I go to Malibu? Anyway, I'll email them now and tell them I'm sending you as my proxy."

"You think they'll be okay with that?"

"Who cares." She sighs and I can just picture her rubbing her swollen stomach, worn out by my existence in her town and this conversation. "I mean, I'm sure it'll be fine. I'll let you know the details tonight at my baby reveal. Which you better still come to."

Now it's my turn to sigh. "Where else would I rather be?"

"LA apparently," she grumbles, but I can tell she's calmer than before.

We hang up and I look around my hotel room. Okay, I can do this. I have a place to stay in LA and an interview for a new job. Leaving Peacock Bay isn't what I want, but I can't stay here and wait for my heart to be more thoroughly broken.

Chapter
23

I'M GETTING READY FOR ALANA'S party when I realize what I need more than anything is to talk to the people who get me the most. Of course there's Quincy, but it's always a bit weird when it comes to talking to her about her brother. She'll make a joke or not take it seriously, which most of the time would be make it all feel like no big deal. The thing is right now, it feels like a very big deal to me. Before I can type out a plea for help to my friends, my phone rings with a call from my mom. I almost decline it because I don't know how to avoid whimpering about my problems with Pete, but something makes me click Accept instead.

"Hi, Mom," I greet her.

"Millie, hi." She exhales slowly, and I get that familiar pit in my stomach that I always get when I know I'm about to get a lecture from my mom. "I just saw your comment on Quincy's post."

"Oh yeah, I did mention you. I'm sorry. I probably shouldn't have done that on such a personal comment like that. I didn't tag you or use your name. No one will know you're my mom. You don't have to worry."

"Millie, I'm not worried that people will know I'm your mom. Is that why you think I'm calling?"

"I don't know." God, I'm so deep in this Instagram world of tagging people and who said what that it's become hard to see things from other people's perspective. I clearly need time off-line. I'm looking forward to stepping away from it all.

"I'm really proud of you. Recognizing that your actions affect others is a big part of being an adult. But I want you to know that while we worried about you, we probably would have done that even if you didn't have ADHD. It's just want parents do."

My eyebrows pinch together. "But I'm such a mess." My voice catches in my throat.

"Oh, sweetie. You're hardly more of a mess than anyone at your age. And even when you get everything together, it doesn't mean things stay that way forever."

"Great, so I'm never going to get my shit together?"

"I just mean life has its ups and downs. You get through the downs and then you enjoy the ups. The important thing is to have people that will stick with you for both, and you have that. With your friends, and with us."

Of course, she's right, but hearing her say that shifts something big in me. My parents worry because they're my parents, not because they think I'll never get it right. Even if I get it wrong sometimes, they're still going to root for me, and knowing this makes all the difference. We talk for a few more minutes until I feel ready to say goodbye. When we do, I look at the text I was about to send to my friends and actually laugh. I can't believe what a ridiculous situation I've put myself in these last few weeks, but knowing that I have the kind of friends who will be there no matter what foolish thing I do online or off gives me hope everything will be fine, eventually.

I send up the flare to Kate and Bree in the form of a text message begging for a confidence boost.

> **Millie:** About to blow the lid off the whole Pete Santana-is-my-husband thing.

> **Kate:** But why? It seems like things have been going so well.

At least I can take comfort in the way it looks from the outside. We've been believable, so that's something. Of course, it's easy to be believable when it's all real to you.

> **Millie:** I have an interview in LA on Monday. Time to go back to the real world. I have to post this one last personal fail before I go, and now seems as good a time as any.

This is always what we'd planned. The big reveal to cause a stir just in time for the tourist season to pick up again. I grind my back teeth, thinking of the Pete-hungry tourists who might plan their trips loaded with the knowledge that he's single again. But this was the deal. Time to fall on my face one last time and head for the hills.

> **Bree:** Are you sure you're not trying to force the issue a little?

FOUR WAYS TO WEAR A DRESS   255

Maybe it's the fact that I'm already thinking of the hordes of women flying in to get a glimpse of Pete and that's why my reply is so defensive.

> **Millie:** There's no issue to force. We're not a couple. We just play one on the internet. I have no life here. I'm just a visitor. Pete's made that as clear as anyone possibly could.

> **Kate:** Well, if my date today goes one-fifth as well as your taco night with Pete, I'd be happy. Though I don't have a lot of hope for romance at his dodgeball league.

I can tell Kate is trying to change the subject so Bree and I stop bickering, and I let her. I feel like all we've talked about lately is my drama, and it wouldn't hurt to be a better friend. I'm about to majorly screw up one part of my life. I'm going to need my friends more than ever now.

> **Millie:** Let me know how it goes. Too bad you don't have our dress for your date. Though it's not exactly dodgeball ready.

> **Kate:** That makes two of us!

I wasn't going to point out how much Kate dislikes all sports. Clearly, this guy she's been dating hasn't picked up on that or didn't care to ask. Not exactly a great sign.

> **Millie:** All right, I'm off to ruin my life. Love you guys.

I add an emoji hoping that shows I'm kidding and totally fine with everything, but I don't think either of them buys it.

> **Bree:** Let the dress work its magic for you out there a little longer, Mills. We're here if you need us.

I sigh in relief, knowing she still supports me. I'm not sure I could purposely let myself fall on my face like this if I didn't have my friends to pick me back up when it's over.

Bree is right about the dress though. I pull it out of the suitcase I had started packing, step into it, and ask for a little more magic while I end this internet farce I've been participating in. While I adjust the straps to lay where I like them on my shoulders, I think about all the moments this dress has seen, not just in California, but even before I brought it here.

We all know this dress isn't really magic. It's just a connection to our collective histories and friendship. But there's magic in that. Something to remind us we're never really going it alone when we reach our lowest points. Something that makes us a little less homesick or helps keep each other close when one of us is celebrating a victory without our best friends to share it with. The dress doesn't make any magic on its own, that's all up to the wearer, but it's along for the ride to watch us create our own magic.

Ready as ever, I scroll through my photos to find something to use in a new post. I try not to think of putting this out in the open as self-sabotage. This was the plan all along, to pull back the curtain and let my followers know it was all for their views. Even if I wanted more, or hoped something good would develop, I knew the likelihood of that was extremely small and now I have to face what's next. I can't control how people are going to react to this post, but at least I can start moving on. I told Pete this, though maybe not eloquently, and now I need to share it with my followers. Alana isn't going to like it, but seeing as how I'm not going to be a part of her utopia anyway, there's not much she can do about it.

I use a picture Pete took of me from his deck a few days ago. I'm wearing the dress, but my back is to the camera as I look out at the beach. It's a perfect image to go out on. I write up a caption that admits Pete isn't my husband. That it was just an arrangement between friends for likes and views. I own up to knowing how foolish it was, but that sometimes internet pressure affects us more than we'd like it to. I add that I'm going to step back from Instagram for a little while to explore some different options, but I'll check in occasionally. I end by thanking everyone for their support and then hit Upload.

With a deep sense of dread, I watch the little upload line creep across the screen loading my words to my grid. I can delete it, sure. But I can't delete my feelings for Pete or this beautiful little town and the fact that I want to be a real part of it. I have to do this. Alana might be trying to promote the idea to onlookers that Peacock Bay is a utopia, but it's really been like that for me. At least it was for a little while, and that had nothing to do with followers or thousands of likes churning up a wave of dopamine in my brain. Surfing, the friendships I've created, and those breezy nights on Pete's deck were better than any number of likes or comments. But it's time to get back to the real world. A real job and real life.

While I apply a few hints of makeup, I check my notifications a few times. I didn't realize how addicted I've become until I decided to step away. I have a handful of DM's and comments about my post asking what's going on and why I'm taking a break. Most of them are fine, sympathetic even, but some really are not. I think some of these people don't realize I'm going to read what they're writing...on my own Instagram post.

> I'm so sorry you're having a hard time, but can you recommend a surfboard for a beginner who's 5'5"?

> Who really thought they were married? He's way too hot for her.

> I never thought that was her husband. Honestly, I hope he's not so I can fly to Peacock Bay while she's gone and bang him.

So, this is fun. All the encouraging and friendly followers who cheered for me while I got my balance back on the board or watched the sunsets with me are now turning into Pete-thirsty monsters.

I can't even get that mad at the mean commenters. Except for the ones talking about screwing Pete... Those ones may get a block. But from most of them, I get it. They watched me go from not knowing what to do with my hands when I pose to acting like I know everything about surfing with a hot (fake) surfer husband.

I can remember what it was like watching Quincy and Alana live what looked like aspirational yet somehow attainable lives and feeling jealous. It seemed like I could have so easily been them if I just made a few small changes, like bought those pants or drank that weird smoothie in a mason jar or moved my entire life to California with a fresh Instagram of my own. Now here I am, with thousands of followers in just a few weeks, a once fake husband who probably hates me, and not even a surfboard to call my own. I have really made a mess of things.

I head down to the lobby where I've planned to meet Quincy to ride with her to the beach. She's promised the Bronco is running and said she only has baby Clay because Ari is bringing Monrow later.

"Oh shit, Millie is not here to mess around tonight," Quincy says when she sees me. Maybe I put a little extra effort into my look tonight, seeing as how it might be one of the last nights I'm in the same place as Pete. I'm giving our dress one last chance to work its magic. *Please don't turn your back on me now, dress.* I know I'm praying to a piece of clothing, but I don't have that much to cling to right now. This dress and a few encouraging texts from my friends are about it.

"I never mess around," I quip as I climb into the passenger seat. I wonder if she's seen my post or heard from Alana about my job interview. I know she'll support whatever I feel is best, but I still dread talking about it.

When we're on our way to the beach, I keep glancing at Quincy as her hair whips around her face unsecured by anything. She side-eyes my expression a few times before she calls me out.

"Why didn't you tell me you were using my brother to get to me? I'm a married woman, Millie." She fakes a scowl.

"You should be so lucky," I reply, looking down at my feet. "But that's not it. I don't think the Instagram life is for me. I'm glad I tried, but it's not like I can keep up all that…" I don't want to say fakeness, even though that's what I mean. What Quincy does online isn't fake and she's even taking steps to be more forthcoming now, but for me it wasn't right. The only thing that was sincere was how I felt about Pete, and that was doomed from the beginning.

"But I thought things were going well."

"It was going okay, except for having no money, embarrassing my parents… And how long can I keep pretending with Pete? I can't ask that of him, and I can't keep coming up with ways to make myself look like a spaz. It's exhausting."

"Who was pretending?" She looks at me wide-eyed. "You guys are so hot for each other that we could've blamed you for rapidly rising ocean temperatures."

"Way to work in a climate-change joke," I mutter. She's right about it being real for me, but he sure didn't argue when I was calling it off. "I have an interview in LA on Monday. I can't pretend this is going to work out for me anymore."

"Oh, you *are* doing that? Alana wasn't sure."

I just told Alana about it. How does Quincy know already? "Alana told you about my interview?"

"Yeah, she asked me to do it first, but how am I supposed to get down to LA with everything else going on?"

"Hold on, I don't think we're talking about the same thing."

"The *LA Times* interview. Did I miss something?"

"Yeah, I was talking about a job interview. For a marketing position."

"Oh weird, you said Monday and LA, and I know that's when Alana said the *LA Times* wanted to talk to someone about Peacock Bay, so I just figured."

"She can't have wanted me to do it. I'm nowhere near the same level as you two."

"I think she was getting pretty desperate." Quincy laughs. "She offered to do most of the interview over the phone, but they really wanted someone to come down and surf with them in Malibu as sort of a comparison to the Bay, from what I understand."

My head whips around to look at my friend. "What about Malibu?" She wouldn't.

"Just that's where they wanted to surf…"

"That sneaky little liar." I shake my head. "I can't even be that mad. The woman is smooth."

"What are you talking about?"

"I spoke to Alana this morning and told her I needed to step back from all the Instagram stuff and that I had an interview in LA but no place to stay, and she said she could hook me up with a place to stay in Malibu."

"Wow, that is pretty crafty."

"What did she think would happen? A reporter would show up for a surf lesson and I would just raise my hand and volunteer?"

Quincy rolls her eyes while she turns the steering wheel to round the corner.

"She's been known to stop at nothing to get her way. She probably just thought you'd do it since it came from Pete anyway."

Now she really has my attention. "What do you mean, it came from Pete?"

"You should really ask him to be sure, but I think the article is about surf hotels on the California coast, so they might include the Waveline. You can see how that would be good for all of us. Good for our platforms, Sage's store, obviously the hotel."

"And I'm sure Pete really wants it to happen."

"More like needs it to happen," Quincy says as she pulls the Bronco into a spot in the beach parking lot and puts the car in park. "You know how rough it's been for the hotel the last few years. Pete's been doing his best to turn things around after everything that's happened, but it's been slow going. A chance to be included in an article featuring the best surf hotels in the state isn't something he can turn down."

I know something like this could be a big win for the Waveline, of course, and my gut tells me Pete doesn't know Alana is setting me up to fill in for her. Still, why didn't she just ask me instead of trying to trick me into it? If I'm down in LA anyway, I don't have a problem talking up the Waveline to a reporter. It's not so out of my comfort zone after my time in marketing. Why did Alana feel like she had to be sneaky about it?

I'm trying to push aside all these thoughts as we walk onto the beach. Alana has layered colorful blankets all around with cushions piled on the corners for people to recline against. I see a few guys I recognize from behind the counter of the Waveline café near the bonfire playing guitars. They're both wearing crisp white button-down shirts, making them look more professional, and I'm guessing Alana hired them to be the musical entertainment. It's another reminder that even though this is party for Alana and ultimately her blog, these events serve the community. She's able to hire a few people, order food from local restaurants, desserts from a bakery, and in a town this small, that can make a difference. I want to talk to her about the interview. To get her side of the story before I jump to conclusions, but when I see Alana frantically barking orders at different people about where to put the elaborate multicolored balloon arch, I decide to wait for a better moment.

I trade a look with Quincy. "Let's give her a minute, huh?" she says.

"Yeah, I want nothing to do with that line of fire." We walk past the firepit on our way toward the water. Some of the older kids are roasting marshmallows, though whatever beef the girls had with each other still seems to be in full effect because they're yelling at each other across the bonfire. They're well trained, though, because whenever the photographer comes by, they stop and pose adorably for a picture. At one point they're in mid-insult.

"Your burnt marshmallow looks so gross," one says.

"Better than your face," the other says.

But when the camera comes by, they throw their arms around each other and show big smiles.

"Do those girls really hate each other?" I ask Quincy.

"Who? Alana's girls?" She shrugs. "They're sisters." As if it's that simple. And who am I to say anything really, since she's speaking as someone with sisters and I'm an only child. I'll have to take her word for it.

"But you and Amelia never fought like that."

"Uh, no, we were worse. But by the time she was in high school we'd grown out of it. I think Alana is hoping they'll just get over it. You know how she is. She wants them to figure it out on their own.

She pushes people, but not hard enough to make them think they have no agency of their own."

"So, you're saying I should stay out of it?" I eye her.

"Do what you want, but I don't think sisters who fight are that big a deal. Did *Little Women* teach us nothing?"

I nod to her point. "Louisa May Alcott was no liar."

Speaking of sisters, Amelia joins us slightly out of breath, with Claire on her hip.

"Hey, girlfriend," I greet my little friend. To my surprise, she reaches for me to hold her. I've never been so flattered in my life.

"Okay, so I'm here. I've said hello to Alana and now I have to leave." Amelia sounds exhausted. "Quincy, if Monrow goes to Vera Lake next year, can we please figure out a car pool? This drive is killing me."

Quincy's mouth twitches in what is supposed to be a smile, but her eyes shift around to see who might be listening. "Yeah, of course. But we haven't decided anything yet."

"I know, yeah. Do you think nine is too young to take an Uber alone? Even if you're with your brother? Because I'm seriously considering letting them do that. Poor Claire spends more time in the car than she does playing these days."

"You can leave her with us," Quincy says.

I nod in agreement. "I'm happy to hang with her. She's like the easiest baby ever. Is it weird that I like her more than most adults?"

Amelia laughs. "She is the cherry on my kid sundae." She squeezes Claire's hand and squishes a big kiss on her cheek. "It's why I feel so bad that she has to deal with this stuff. But the boys are thriving at their new school, so there's not much I can do about it." She sighs. I have a weird pang when I think about leaving when she does this. I like being able to help Amelia with Claire when she needs it. I wish there was a way for me to make a life for myself here, but I'm not sure I could do that knowing Pete wouldn't be a real part of it.

Amelia thanks us, and the relief on her face is so real as she goes to say goodbye to Alana and head back onto the freeway to pick up her boys.

Quincy and I put Claire down to play in the sand near the blankets where we can keep an eye on her and go to greet Alana now that she looks like she's not going to explode with her balloons. She sighs when she sees us and pulls us both into a hug.

"Thank god, you guys are here. I seriously don't know what I was thinking."

"About this party or the pregnancy?" I joke.

"Fuck. Both." She smiles. "But I've got to keep those clicks coming." She rubs a hand on her stomach as she looks around. "This all looks fine, right?"

"It looks great," Quincy says. "The pictures will be beautiful."

Alana looks at me to confirm. "For sure. And I'm sure the food will be…" I look around, trying to compliment whatever she's put out, but aside from a few cupcakes, I don't see anything.

Alana shakes her head, her stress level apparently spiking again. "Jeff is supposed to bring food with him from the restaurant. I think Pete was going to help him. Can you text him and see if he's on his way?"

"Oh, um, sure. I guess." I pull out my phone and try to compose a text to Pete that doesn't give away any of the complex emotions simply pulling his name up in my messages brings up for me.

Millie: Alana asked me to check your ETA with the food. Send a smoke signal so she doesn't go into early labor from stress.

My phone dings in my hand with his reply, and my heart twists as I search his words for any clue of hope to cling to.

Pete: On my way.

Not exactly the sonnet I was hoping for. This is going to be a fun party.

When Pete and Jeff finally arrive carrying trays of intricately arranged food, I watch his face for any clue to what he's thinking. But it's hard to tell how someone feels about you or the future of your relationship based on facial expressions alone. Especially when that person has a beautiful but unreadable face on a good day. Those thick, dark lashes aren't giving away any hints, that's for sure. I have keep my hands busy so I don't inadvertently find them tracing the ridges of Pete's muscular back, which may not be as welcome as it was a day ago, so I do this by helping Alana arrange everything on the picnic table she's covered with Baja blankets.

I pour the containers of sangria and nonalcoholic punch she made into beautiful glass pitchers to add to the buffet. Once Alana is satisfied with how it all looks, she gives us the nod, and Quincy and I stand on the picnic table benches to get the perfect shot of the food for our stories. I take my pictures, but don't upload them anywhere. Maybe I can share them with Sage when she gets here

and she can use them. It all looks beautiful and delicious, and Alana
finally looks a little calmer as a few more guests arrive.

"Okay, I think we're okay," she says, arms crossed, as she surveys
the party landscape.

"More than okay," I reassure her. She nods and blows out a long
breath. She links her arm with mine and gives me a squeeze. If I'm
going to bring up the *LA Times* interview, I need to do it now, when
she's relaxed and grateful.

"Did you have a chance to reach out to that hotel in LA you
mentioned? My job interview is Monday afternoon, so I need to
figure out a place to stay as soon as I can."

"Yep, you're all set. I'll email you the details today," she answers
and scans the party, checking the details one more time. Or avoid-
ing me.

"Thanks. I really appreciate your help," I tell her. I wait for her
to add something, but when she doesn't, I press on. "So, is there
anything you need me to pick up for you while I'm down there?
Any errands I could do for you?"

Alana eyes me warily. "Who told you?"

"Told me what?" I challenge her.

"About the interview. Look, I don't even know if they'd want to
talk to you now that you're 'going off the grid.' You're not exactly
the local expert they're looking for." I'm not sure if she's phrasing
it this way to try to make me want to do it or if she means it, but
either way it's pretty irritating.

"I'm not going off the grid," I tell her. "I just can't keep pretending things in my life are one way when they're not." My eyes
instinctually glance to where Pete is chatting with some of the other

guys. He meets my gaze, and I wonder if he overheard what I just said. He gives me a heart-wrenchingly bland head nod that tells me nothing except how little I likely mean to him.

"Fine. Don't pretend then. Stay off the internet forever for all I care. But doing this interview is the very least you can do after you screwed with everything we do here." Alana waves her hand at the beautifully decorated table.

"What did I do?"

"Oh, I don't know." She rolls her eyes and starts to list on her fingers. "Quincy is blogging about her kid's potential special needs, Sage is getting divorced and shipping her kids to Colorado. And look at Pete…" My head whips to read his face, but his expression hasn't changed. "He's more miserable than ever now that you're leaving. So maybe while you're down in LA, you could help us out and chat with this chick about how great it is over here in the Bay."

"The Cove is better," I grumble.

"Fine, say that. I don't care. But you're doing this interview. We all tried to help you when you wanted to be a part of this. Now you want to do something else, and I found you a place to stay while you try to get a new job. We supported you the whole time, so could you help us out with this one thing?"

I want to be outraged by the way she's yelling at me, but Alana's main speed is yelling so I don't take it that personally. She also, annoyingly, has a point. While I can safely maintain I had nothing to do with Sage's divorce, I was the one to out her to her friends due to my inability to keep anything to myself, and that wasn't right. I did encourage Quincy to write about Monrow's evaluation and I stand by that one. The stuff with Pete, I don't know. I never set out to make him miserable, but there's no arguing that he doesn't look happy now. It was stupid to try the Instagram Husband thing, and I'm sure he hated having to be so visible online. Admitting to what we did was the right thing to do. Now he can go back to being a quiet hermit and never have to go on fake dates for the sake of Instagram.

I don't get a chance to say any of this to Alana because Quincy tromps over in a hurry with a weird look on her face.

"Hey," she starts, and my stomach is already clenching from her tone. "Did Amelia come back and get Claire?"

I start looking around for the adorable tiny face I was responsible for. "I don't think so, why?" I keep looking. And looking. "Where is she?" I start moving around. I must just not see her where I'm standing. "Quincy, where's Claire? She was right here."

Chapter 24

PETE COMES OVER. HE TAKES the drink out of my hand and sets it down on the table with his own.

"What happened?"

"I put Claire down right here and now she's gone." I can barely squeak the words out. My heart is pounding where it's dropped in the pit of my stomach. "Oh my god." My throat tightens as I stare at the ocean. *No. No way is she in there.*

"Split up," he calls to the group.

I stand, nodding. We have to find her now. "I'm going this way," I say and point toward the longest stretch of beach. I will run until my legs fall off. Until I find her. This is my fault. I was supposed to be watching her, but I was too busy worrying about my job interview and chatting about my love life to see that she had disappeared. How could I let this happen? What kind of person can't watch a small child for more than a few minutes? What is wrong with me?

"I'm coming with you," he replies. We trudge through the sand a few feet, and then he turns to me. "This does *not* go online, Millie.

This may be your fault, but you don't get to post about this like it's some funny mistake."

My jaw goes slack and I shake my head, trying to process what he's saying. "Nothing about this is funny," I say. And it's really not.

I'm only partly aware that Pete is a few feet away calling for his niece. His niece who's not even two years old and probably can't even say her own name yet and definitely can't answer us. I had no business thinking I could babysit her. I can't even focus on her properly for thirty minutes without losing her. Alana was right. All I've done since I got here is use people and give nothing in return.

No wonder Pete isn't interested in anything serious with me. I'm not a serious person, and nothing proves that more than the fact that I just lost his sister's only daughter. Pete takes everything seriously. There's not a single casual bone in his body. No one like him could ever take me seriously when I can't hold a job or keep track of a human being. But how could he think I would use this as something for my feed? Is that really how he sees me?

Tears burn in my eyes. The heartache of Claire going missing— and now my anger at myself when I realize I've made this about me and Pete's feelings toward me—is pushing me over the emotional edge. I want to sit down and collapse into my tears, but I won't stop moving until we find Claire.

"Millie?" I hear my name and whirl around, thinking somehow even though the voice is from an adult, Claire will be standing there calling for me.

Somehow, I'm right. Sort of.

A young woman I've never seen before is walking toward us from near the parking lots. She has the broad shoulders of a lifelong surfer and dark-brown hair. She's holding Claire in her arms. I rush toward the two of them, but Pete is closer and gets there first. The woman hands her over with a smile.

"I thought that was you. I found Claire making her way to the parking lot and thought I should bring her back. I recognized her from Instagram." She laughs and I choke out something that might sound like a laugh, but is more of a sob. "I follow you and Alana and everyone." She's smiling at me and I'm so relieved, I burst into tears. She's here. She's safe and she's here.

"Thank you so much for finding her. We were so scared," I whimper. I run a hand over Claire's soft hair, but Pete starts walking away with her. Which is kind of rude to this woman who is basically a hero. "What did you say your name was?"

"Justine. I actually came here on a surf trip with some friends because of your Instagram. Which sounds a little lame when I say it out loud." She laughs. "It's really cool to meet you."

"Oh wow, well. I'm really glad you did." I laugh and wipe the tears from my eyes. The adrenaline starts seeping out of me and I know I'm losing it, but I'm still riding the wave of relief that Claire is okay.

"Do you think we could take a picture together?" she asks, as if there is anything this woman could ask me that I would say no to right now.

I wipe my eyes and take a deep breath to calm myself. Claire is okay. No mistake I've made or stupid thing I've done seems as important now that Claire is okay. "Of course. Tag me in it and I'll repost it," I tell her. Even if I'm not going to use my account anymore, I can do this one thing for this person who saved Claire from who knows what.

"Wow, that would be so awesome. Thank you."

"No, thank you. I don't know what would have happened if you hadn't spotted Claire."

She runs back up to the parking lot and grabs a friend to take a picture. It doesn't take long, and when we're done, I hug her and thank her again.

"I'm going to post it right now," Justine says. "I won't say anything about Claire getting lost. I'll just say I ran into you on the beach."

I nod. I'm not sure how Amelia would see it, but I need to apologize to her first before she hears about this from someone else.

"Thanks again for bringing Claire back. You'll never know how grateful we are." I'm not going to be rude like Pete, but I'm done here. I'm walking away as I call to her, "Post that picture and I'll repost it like I said." I have to catch up with Pete and see for myself that Claire is okay.

I have to run. Pete is nearly back at the party. He beats me there anyway.

"Oh my god, where was she?" Quincy asks, holding her arms out to her niece. She hugs her tightly when she has her, swaying back and forth. She kisses her head over and over. I want to hug her, too, but I better not. She's with her family where she belongs.

"She found her way to the parking lot," I manage. How am I ever going to tell Amelia about this?

"One of Millie's followers found her," Pete says with zero humor in his voice.

I eye him, then add, "She follows all of you."

Quincy laughs, I think mostly from relief. "And they brought her to you?"

"Well, thank fucking god for Instagram followers, huh?" Alana says. People around me laugh, but I can't even force a smile. I'm looking at Pete and watching for any sign that he doesn't completely hate me. Not that I blame him. I'm not such a fan of myself right now either.

Pete starts stalking away from the group. I double-check that Quincy has a tight hold on Claire before I follow him. I thought maybe he was just going to get a drink, and I could use one too, but he's not. He's heading to his car. I have to run to catch up with him again.

"Pete, please," I call. "Just wait one second." He stops, but doesn't turn toward me. He's rubbing his face with one hand. "I messed up. I shouldn't have taken my eyes off her for a second. I'm going to apologize to Amelia. I know I screwed up."

Pete drags a hand over his face. I swallow hard, preparing for what's coming.

"I bet you think I should be happy. Grateful that you and everyone else have posted Claire's picture everywhere, making her so recognizable that complete strangers know who to return her to."

"I'm not going to tell you how to feel…" I tell him.

"But I don't want that. I don't want Claire to grow up being used for social media notoriety. I don't want to pander to influencers so our family business has a chance at survival. I don't want this. Claire isn't another person you can pretend to care about for hits."

I know the emotions of the last few hours have been a roller coaster, and I don't expect him to forgive me this second, but this feels more like something that's been pent up in him and is only now erupting because of what happened with Claire. I understand that he's upset that I wasn't watching his niece as carefully as I should have been, but how could he think I would use her on purpose?

"I would never use Claire like that. She's just cute, and it's fun to take pictures with her. And you should know I put an end to our fake relationship online. You don't have to deal with that anymore. Or me." I try to smile, like it's funny. There has to be something funny here somewhere. I just can't seem to find it yet.

"Millie, you didn't. This is why they canceled. Shit," he mutters, shaking his head. I thought he would be relieved, but he looks panic-stricken. I'm so confused. "Did you tag me or the hotel?"

"Why would I tag the hotel in something like that?" Pete doesn't answer me, but he turns away, muttering something I can't hear. "We were lying, Pete, and I didn't want to leave here with that hanging over me. Or us. I thought you'd be happy to have it cleared up."

"The surf camp called and canceled all the rooms they'd booked this morning. They said they're 'reorganizing their company,' but I couldn't figure out why they would bail. Now it makes sense."

My stomach drops. Did I really do that? I know it was impulsive to put everything out there this morning, and maybe I didn't think how it would affect the hotel, but I never agreed to take full responsibility for the revenue of his family business with my Instagram account. I may have suggested we start this up, but he agreed to it, and we both agreed it would end eventually. Didn't we? I know I said it would only be for a month, but that was to take the pressure off of him. I didn't think he could handle it without knowing there would be a finish line he could look toward.

"You're the one who didn't want to do this in the first place!" I don't want to mess with the survival of his business, and in a way

I can understand if a women's surf camp would take offense at my deception. But he can't put all of this on me. Speaking of this... "And what about the *LA Times*? Did you know Alana asked me to do the interview or surf lesson or whatever it is?"

"She did? No, I had no idea." He looks like this is the first he's hearing of it, and I believe him. "Are you going to do it? It would be a big help for us." He takes a step toward me. I take a tiny step back. Who's *us*?

"I'm not sure. I have a job interview that day. I'll have to see."

"Right, your job interview," he sneers. "I know how important that is to you."

"Um, yeah, it is kind of important that I get a job, Pete."

He shakes his head and balls his hands into fists. So frustrated with me. I watch as each of his knuckles turn white.

"Yeah, I know. I'm sorry. I offered to go down and do the lesson myself, but they really wanted one of the influencers from the area. I'm kind of surprised Alana asked you, actually."

Ouch. "Right. Because I've made myself such a joke as an influencer," I scoff. *Jesus.* I thought the only risk I was taking coming out here was maybe setting myself back a little career-wise. I had no idea how I would screw up everything I've always wanted. The fact that I've disappointed and embarrassed Pete hurts so much more. It's one thing failing in a job when it's only me that will deal with the fallout. Having Pete so close to witness the wreckage makes the pain so much more acute.

Pete looks at me, tenderness coming back to his eyes. "You know that's not what I meant." He moves like he's going to pull me into his arms, but I step away. I can't do it. I can't let him hold me when I have no idea what it would mean. Does he actually care about me, or is he trying to win me back to his side so I'll do the interview?

"Pete, let's not confuse things anymore. We never should have done the Instagram Husband thing, and sleeping together made things even more confusing. It was great, don't get me wrong, but I let myself believe it meant more than it did and that was a mistake."

"I don't think it was a mistake," he says.

I shake my head. It's too late. I'm leaving. I can't keep changing my mind and being irresponsible. I don't want to be the kind of person who can't keep track of a toddler. I want to be someone people trust, and I can't be that person here, clearly.

"Anyway, I've cleared things up online now, and I'm sorry if that complicates things for you at all, but it had to happen eventually. We need a clean break with me leaving for LA. I'm not sure where I'll end up after the interview. I should probably interview at a few places in New York while I'm waiting to hear back." I guess I really will be sleeping on Kate and Bree's couch for a little while. Oh well, it's a pretty comfortable couch. It's no oceanfront swinging daybed, but then again I don't think anything will ever top that.

"Wait, you're not coming back here after the interview?"

"Here? To Peacock Bay? No, why would I come back here?"

"Because…because… Mills." Pete sighs. "Really?"

"I don't live here. I don't have a job here, and I barely have a place to stay." A wave of loneliness hits me after saying this out loud. I wanted to come here and regain a sense of freedom after being cooped up in an office for so long, but now after a few weeks, feeling this untethered is strangely suffocating. I want to feel like I belong somewhere. To have a group of people who will watch out for me as I would do the same for them. To have someone to love. I know I have that with Kate and Bree at least, so if I don't get the job in LA, I know I have them to fall back on in New York. That's something at least.

I look at Pete, who looks like he's trying to come up with some argument against what I've said, but he's got nothing and the reality of it all is making me too sad to continue talking about it.

I turn and scan the parking lot, then remember I came here in Quincy's car. Shit. I need to find a way out of here.

"Millie, please. This isn't what I wanted to happen."

"I sure as hell didn't either," I call back to him as I stride toward the parking lot. I spot one of the hotel bikes on the rack at the entrance of the parking lot. I pull it out and get on. Whoever rode it down to the beach will just have to get a ride with someone. This is an emergency. If I stand here arguing with Pete much longer, what's left of my heart is going to crumble, and I can't let him see that. I can't let him see how much he fooled me. How in love with him I've fallen, and how much I'm hurting now that it's all fallen apart.

I pedal the stolen bike faster toward Pete's hotel. I can't stay there anymore. I can't run into him in the lobby for the next two days whenever I need to get something to eat or go anywhere. Sure, a part of me is hoping he'll come knocking on my door and say something that makes this all not a big cluster of fucks. But I'm not sure I would even trust him if he did. He already took a risk with me for the sake of his business. And look how well that turned out.

When I get to my room, I throw the rest of my things in my suitcase as fast as possible. I'm not sure Pete will come looking for me, but I'm not sure he won't. Or send Quincy in his place. I manage to escape without someone from the Santana family questioning me. I carry my stuffed suitcase through town until I find one of the little motels so popular with the spring breakers. The Waveline it is not. There's no view. No sound of the waves to lull me to sleep. Just a small bare room with carpet that smells musty with mold and a door that opens to the parking lot. It's not where I want to be, but nothing in my life is where I want it to be right now. Not my location, or career, and clearly not with Pete Santana.

Chapter
25

"OF COURSE YOU CAN STAY with us if you come back. You know that offer still stands, but I still think there's no way he was faking things with you, Millie," Kate says. I'm on FaceTime with her and Bree first thing the next morning. They've just finished our old Saturday routine of SoulCycle and brunch and are piled on Bree's couch while she holds the phone.

"Ah, but alas, he was," I say. I don't really want to talk about this, but I can't leave my other best friends in the dark. "Or, I don't know. Maybe he wasn't faking things, exactly, but he was more in it for the sex and the potential publicity. I think at this point he's made that clear."

"I highly doubt it's as simple as that," Bree says. " But I guess there goes our fall trip to Peacock Bay."

"You can still come. I won't be here, but I bet Quincy would like to see you guys."

"What has she said about the whole thing?" Bree asks.

"Yeah, I'm sure she'll have more answers," Kate adds, with the hope of a baby lamb in her voice. Poor thing doesn't even know it's about to be slaughtered.

"I'm not going to get her involved. She has a lot on her plate already with Monrow's evaluation. I'm not going to ask her to sort out my love life too." She did text me when I disappeared from Alana's party to make sure I was okay. I said I was fine, that the thing with Pete had run its course and that it's probably for the best. She sent me a sad-face emoji, but didn't press me further. I know she believes in keeping up the utopia thing for the blogs, but she wouldn't have told Pete to hook up with me for good reviews.

She wanted us to be together because in her mind that would have been a piece of the perfect life that would have been real. I wanted it too. But it's over, and there's nothing more to do about it. I did tell her I checked out of the Waveline because I didn't want to run into Pete though. It only seemed fair since she had been so nice giving me that big discount on the room. I told her not to tell Pete where I was staying now and that I blocked his number. In a way, this is better. I can focus on getting a new job and starting over. Again. And while this isn't how I would have planned things, I'm heading out unattached and that's so much simpler. It's awful, actually. But it's simpler.

"So what are you going to do? Just hide out until you leave?" Bree asks.

"Online and IRL," I tell them. The comments on Instagram have not been kind, and while I'm trying to ignore them, I don't possess that kind of superhuman strength. I keep checking in, telling myself it's only to see if some need to be blocked, but then I get sucked into a shame spiral and have to close it all out again.

"I saw the post. I think you said it well. But the comments are pretty brutal. It's not like you photoshopped your faces into some wedding pictures. You were just using a hashtag," Bree adds.

"We did make it look like we were a cozy couple though." And it was starting to feel like that's what we were. "I'm trying to stay off-line as much as possible. I still have a few more calls to make, but I'll probably turn off my phone for a bit after this."

"But what if Pete tries to get in touch with you?" Kate asks with those Bambi eyes.

"I blocked his number and I don't want to talk to him." I sigh. I do, but I can't. He already had a chance to explain, and I didn't like the explanation. And I don't need to hear more about how I'm hurting the thing Pete's worked his entire life to build. "Anyway, it's only one more day. Alana has a car coming to pick me up tomorrow morning. Which I guess is another enticement to do the interview in her place. I'll be fine."

"It just feels wrong for you to end your time there on such a sad note," Kate says.

"It is what it is. We both really screwed up. I don't think there's any coming back from that." Especially since his screwup was pretending to be into me to increase hotel bookings. That seems like a tough thing to work around. My stomach drops as the realization of it hits me again. Wave after wave of this has been hitting me all morning. All those nights, and mornings, and surf sessions. In his own way, it was all for Instagram. His hands on me, the way his fingers traced the line of my side at night, all of it was part of a plan to make sure his grandparents' legacy comes back from a difficult economy. You can say this though. The man is loyal and dedicated. It turns out, just not to me.

I listen to some encouraging words from my friends for a few more minutes, trying to make them think I'm okay (I'm not, but there's not much they can do), then we say goodbye. I grab a sandwich from a tiny deli across the street and settle in for the night.

I turn my phone back on for a second to call Amelia to apologize for what happened with Claire. I ignore everything that buzzes and dings with notifications because I know there won't be anything good there. I should probably have called her sooner, but I was afraid if I did, I would start crying to her that her baby brother doesn't like me—and this should not be about me.

"Millie, please. She's a toddler. Do you know how many times one of my kids has wondered off at the beach?" she says after I give her a lengthy apology in a single breath.

"But she could have gotten hurt." Or worse, I think. The ocean is literally right there. "I'm so sorry. Are we okay?" I ask quietly.

"As long as you try not to lose my daughter again, we're cool."

"Well, yeah, don't worry about that because I'm leaving tomorrow."

"I mean, when you come back. We'll all still be here. You're not going to be gone forever, right?"

"It depends how the interview goes. I have to get a job, and there's not much here for me." I don't just mean the lack of employment opportunities, but I don't want to go into it.

"What about Little Goods?"

"What about it?"

"Oh, I thought Sage was going to talk to you about helping out at the store while she's in Colorado with the girls. She said she was going to talk to you at the party yesterday."

"I left pretty early yesterday," I tell her. "I didn't even see Sage." Though now that she mentions it, I remember Alana saying something about Sage and Colorado. "Maybe I'll give her a call."

"You should. Just so you know whether you have options when you're trying to figure everything out."

Options. What an idea.

"Give her a call. You lose one hundred percent of the business you don't ask for," Amelia says, a hint of teasing in her voice.

"How very Lean In of you."

After we hang up, I'm about to call Sage, but decide to text her instead. I haven't spent this much time on the phone in years, and I'm weary of it after just two conversations in a row. Plus, it'll be easier to take a disappointment in text form than hearing her say, yet again, that she can't hire me.

> **Millie**: Hey, Amelia said you wanted to ask me something at Alana's party and I should check in with you. Sorry I took off early.

After a few seconds, her response appears.

> **Sage**: Yes, I've finally given in and I'm letting my girls stay with my parents in Colorado so they can focus more on skiing. I have so much guilt and anxiety about it, but it seems like what they really want. 😫 Anyway, I'll be back and forth a lot, and since business has picked up so much, I'm going to need someone to help out at the store. Would you be interested?

Would I? If this were a week ago, I would have jumped at the chance. A chance to stay in Peacock Bay and build something unique with Sage, someone who values my ideas and wants my input. I could surf *and* have a job that isn't confined to a desk that makes me happy. But how can I stay here and see Pete and constantly be reminded that we ruined our friendship for a few likes and clicks. Still, I can't bear to let the door close on this offer completely. It's too good.

> **Millie:** I would. But I have this job interview in LA on Monday. Could I get back to you after I see how things go with that?

> **Sage:** That's fine. I still have a few weeks before our first trip to move them out there. Let me know after the interview. Is it bad if I don't wish you luck? For my own benefit?

I smile at the phone.

> **Millie:** Nah, you do what you've got to do. Business is business.

With that, I shut off my phone completely and head to bed. I'm not optimistic about my chance at sleep tonight, but like Amelia said, I lose one hundred percent of the business I don't ask for, and right now that business is sleep.

In the morning, I pack the last of my stuff in the bathroom, then splash some water on my face and apply a little sunscreen. I run a brush through my hair thinking maybe one bright side of this trip to LA could be a chance to get my hair highlighted. Though if I don't get the job I'll still have the problem of my rapidly decreasing funds, so I'm not sure if I can swing it.

I say goodbye to this sparse motel room and go to the office to check out. The woman behind the desk is older than me by about twenty years. Her dark hair is cut short, and her skin is a shade of brown that takes a lot of dedication to the sun to maintain.

"One second, there was something dropped off for you," the woman tells me after I've signed out. This motel is so old, I'm signing a form in triplicate. When I left the Waveline, I checked out on an app on my phone. I'm going to need to stop doing that. I can't keep comparing everything (and everyone) to the Waveline and its owners. It's not going to help me get over Pete. I know this intellectually, but emotionally I have no control.

I hear the sound of high-grade polyester rubbing against the floor as the woman slides a massive black surfboard bag toward me and leans it against the desk. I stare at it and then back at her.

"That's not mine," I tell her.

"Well, I don't know what to tell you. You're Millie Ward, right? It was dropped off this morning." She hands me a piece of paper with my name on it. It dawns on me that this is probably the board Alana kept saying was on its way. It must have come just in time. Tears prick my eyes at this gesture, and I shove the piece of paper in the board bag to read during the drive. I'm not sure I can process any more good moments here. I already know what I'm going to be missing. I can't add anything new.

Oddly, the travel bag it's in looks old, but maybe she put the new board in one of her bags because she knew it would be impossible for me to travel with the board otherwise. Alana Tatamo would think of everything. And everything includes adding a brand-new surfboard to the list of enticements to convince me to do the surf lesson/interview with the *LA Times*.

My driver arrives a minute later and helps me load my bag and the new board in the big black SUV he'll be driving me down to LA in. Once I get settled in, I realize this is the newest and nicest car I've been in for a month. There's something really off-putting about it, but maybe that's the guilt from accepting all these things from Alana when I still haven't agreed to do anything for her in return.

I pull my phone out and turn it on, ignoring all the buzzes and notifications, then send a text to Alana.

> **Millie:** Fine, you win. Stop plying me with gifts. I'll do the interview. When is it?

She texts back immediately.

> **Alana:** Tomorrow at noon. Addie Turner will meet you at the hotel for a surf lesson and a chat. It's really not that big of a deal. Just make sure you say how amazing it is in Peacock Bay or risk having the blood of a ruined town on your hands forever. Cool?

Actually, no.

Millie: My job interview is at 1 p.m. There's no way I can squeeze in all that before and still make it to Santa Monica for my interview. Can you change the time?

Alana: I don't know. UGH! I'll try. Maybe you can move your thing?

Millie: My job interview? No. Move yours or I can't help.

I know I sound inflexible, but there's not much I can do about that. It would be incredibly unprofessional for me to try to move my interview at Covast when this thing for Alana is a favor. She needs to make it work for me.

She responds eventually. I can feel her rolling her eyes at me all the way from her house on the Hill.

Alana: I'll see what I can do.

As the SUV rolls through town, I'm sad I didn't get to say good-bye to anyone in person. We pass the coffee shop and Little Goods, and my heart twinges at the sight of the closed-up store. I love the idea of running the shop while Sage is away. Then again, maybe it's better if she doesn't leave me in charge unsupervised. I wouldn't want to add her store to my list of careers I've burned to the ground.

The car passes the clothing store where I bought my new favorite pants and the dresses that drove Pete crazy. My throat catches at the memory of his hands pushing my skirt up my thighs. It wasn't real. I shake my head. My memories are fuzzy now. Did he really look at me with so much need and lust that he couldn't stand to be near me clothed for a second longer, or did I just make that up? Those nights when he held me close to his chest with his arm secured around my waist, was I just a warm body to curl up against? It really didn't feel like it in the moment, but now I can't be sure.

I wipe the tears from my eyes. *Screw you, tears. No one invited you here.* But it's like the tears know before I do that we're about to pass the Waveline. You can't see much of it from the road, but I know I'll be able to see the entrance. I'm not going to look. I don't even want to take the chance of seeing him for a second. I know I'll completely lose it if I do. It was one thing licking my wounds in the motel where no one could see me. I don't know if I can hold it together thinking about Pete going on with his life without even glancing over his shoulder as I leave.

I roll down my window and pull out my phone. I shoot a video of the landscape, the ocean side, rolling by. I do it just for me. There's no point in posting videos anymore. I lean my head on my bent arm out the window and shoot one of my face, eyes closed, a smile forced on my face, the wind blowing my hair into ribbons.

We're past the hotel now, and in a minute we'll leave Peacock Bay. I play the video back and my heart pounds as I watch the replay. I have to watch it three times just to be sure I'm seeing it right. Just over my shoulder in the driveway of the Waveline is the outline of a man I know well, his hands stuffed in his pockets. His head hangs down as he gets smaller and smaller. It's like seeing a ghost in real life because when I turn around, there's nothing there.

Chapter 26

THE NEXT MORNING, I REALIZE I haven't told my parents about my location change. I text my mom.

> **Millie:** I'm in LA for a job interview.

> **Mom:** That sounds interesting.

> **Millie:** Maybe. I'm not sure if it's something I really want to do, but I'm not sure I have a choice.

> **Mom:** I'm sure you'll figure it out. You always do.

Her response still rings in my ears as I'm giving myself a healthy dose of self-care by soaking in the massive bathtub in my Malibu hotel room. I never thought my mom believed I could figure things out on my own. Maybe instead of thinking about my constant mistakes, I should be thinking about my unending resilience. That's what I wanted my Instagram to be about, but I doubt there's a chance of that after my last post.

Admittedly, I haven't checked the comments because I'm too scared to see the angry posts that I thought I deserved. I did post a short hotel-room tour last night because Alana made me, stating that it was part of the deal, and I'm so tired of fighting with her that I just went along. I have, however, turned off all my notifications on all my social media, which has helped me keep my distance, but I constantly have to keep reminding myself not to open the apps. The muscle memory in my fingers seems to take me to the app every time I hold my phone, and it's been hard not to let myself be lulled into a mindless scroll.

Even though I'm trying to slow down on my phone usage, I have been checking my texts to make sure I don't miss anything from Alana. I'm guessing she'll move the *LA Times* thing to the late afternoon when the waves pick up again and my interview is over.

My phone buzzes just as I'm wrapping myself in a huge bath towel, and I check to finally see a message from her.

> **Alana:** They can move it to 11am, but that's the best I could do. Remember, the interviewer's name is Addie Turner. And don't worry, they said it's fine that you wiped out on Instagram. Just as long as you can surf for real and tell them about the town.

I stare at the phone, incredulous. At 11:00 a.m.? How am I supposed to teach someone to surf and talk up Peacock Bay in an hour and still get to my interview on time? My phone buzzes again.

Alana: Wipe out. See what I did there?

I roll my eyes and start replying.

Millie: This isn't going to work. I have to be in Santa Monica at 1 p.m.

Alana: It takes 45 mins to get there. I googled it. You'll be fine.

Millie: Well, if you googled it. 🖕. This is LA. The traffic patterns here are slightly less predictable than Peacock Bay.

Alana: Hey, don't be annoyed with me. I found you a place to stay and a ride down to LA. You have to figure out the rest. You also don't have to do this job interview at all. You can come back to the Bay and work at Little Goods. I know Sage offered you a job.

How can she suggest I blow off the job interview? That would be the worst kind of unprofessional, flaky move. No way. I'm going. I'm seeing this through. I'll just have to make it all work.

Millie: I'll figure it out. But don't expect this chick to learn to surf in one hour. I'm not that good.

I'm being self-deprecating, and when I see Alana replying, I expect some encouraging response to bolster me up before the interview.

Alana: Accurate.

And really, I should have known better.

I can't believe she's springing this on me at the last minute. She knew what time my interview was, and it feels like she barely tried to make things easier for me.

I text Quincy to vent.

Millie: I know this *LA Times* interview is a big deal, but Alana is screwing me here. I might be meeting with a surf brand, but I can't show up with salty hair wearing my wet suit!

It takes a few minutes for Quincy to respond.

Quincy: I'm sorry she's giving you trouble, but I suggest just going with it. Alana weirdly knows best.

I shake my head, annoyed with Quincy's unhelpful response and put my phone on the bathroom sink to start getting ready for the interview. Or interviews, I should say. I roll my eyes in the mirror. I'm just going to have to skip the surf lesson part of it and explain to the interviewer that I can only give her thirty minutes. She'll just have to understand. I'm sure she'll be forgiving if I appeal to her sense of supporting the sensibilities of fellow working women. Which hopefully is something she has and not something I just invented.

I go to rummage in my suitcase and try to plan an outfit that can take me from the beach to an office, but gimme a break. There's no fashion blogger on earth who could tackle this wardrobe request. Maybe Sage could—her style is the best—but I'd feel bad asking for her help dressing for an interview that's the reason I'm putting off taking her offer. Especially when I really want to take her up on it.

Wait, what?

I mean, yes, helping out at Little Goods was the most fun I've had in any workplace ever. And yes, I kept thinking of ways to help Sage and her business even when I wasn't in the store. But it would mean going back to Peacock Bay and running into Pete all the time. Plus, what if I mess up again? I can't do that to Sage when she would be putting so much trust in me.

But maybe it would be okay to text Sage and ask for outfit advice, and maybe I can hint that I'm seriously considering working with her. Just to feel her out a little more.

> **Millie:** Hey, how are things at the store? I just want you to know I'm still thinking about your offer and it's growing more tempting by the minute. But if you have a second to give me some advice... What does one wear to the beach and then to a job interview?

It takes her a few minutes to respond, and I'm laying out outfit options on the hotel bed when my phone finally buzzes.

> **Sage:** Things are really picking up! Could really use an extra set of hands. Especially ones good with social media outreach.

I smile and then she adds.

> **Sage:** Think dressy casual. But don't overdo it. It's LA. A dress that can double as a cover-up is your ticket.

I nod and look at the options I've laid out and realize, of course, there's really only one choice here. Maybe our dress isn't actually lucky; it just works for so many different occasions that we're bound to have important moments when we wear it. After my interview, I should really send it back to Kate and Bree. They deserve a turn with it and… When did I decide I wasn't going back to New York? Did that just happen?

Then my phone buzzes again.

> **Sage:** By the way. Pete's Insta. WOW. How's that ice in your blood, Millie?

Why is Sage talking about? Pete and Instagram? Those two words don't go together.

> **Millie:** I haven't seen it. I've been off all social media. Should I check?

My heart nearly beats itself out of my chest while I watch those little typing dots appear.

> **Sage:** Now might be a nice time to dip a toe back in if you've got a minute.

There's no way I can ignore comments like that from Sage, so I let my thumb follow its natural path across all apps and click on the camera icon. When I do, it's like the algorithm knows exactly why I'm there, and the scary thing is it probably does.

There is Pete. He's standing on his deck, holding a handwritten sign that says in bold black letters, DEAR MILLIE. He looks a little like he's being held for ransom and I'm the only one who can save him. A deranged part of my brain kind of wishes that were true.

My hands are shaking as I scroll to read the caption. A few things have happened recently. I said the wrong things and didn't get a chance to say the right ones. I made a big mistake, or maybe more than one. Most of all, I didn't say I was sorry, but I need you to know that am. And I learned to use Instagram. #PeacockBay #InstaPete #HeretoStayintheBay #comehome

He's using my hashtag. The one I made on the first day to chronicle my time in Peacock Bay. I included that hashtag on every post I made when I was in the Bay, but sometimes it was buried deep in a pile of other hashtags desperately seeking likes. I click on his profile, and there are three more posts in his grid. The first is a video of him panning the view from his deck. With #comehome and #HeretoStayintheBay right there in the caption line. The next is a selfie—a goddamn selfie, I don't even believe it—of him and Claire eating ice cream together in town. The caption reads, We miss @heretostay.

I look down at the dress I've been clutching in my hand and blink my eyes. "Did you do this?" I ask a piece of clothing my friend found in a used clothing store. I have to get ahold of myself, but there's no good explanation for it. I would more easily believe that this dress is magic than the idea that Pete would willingly post personal things on Instagram. I try to make sense of these posts as I climb on the bed. All that exists now is Pete's use of social media. After the picture of Pete and Claire there is one more. A photo of his surf rack, the one we defiled just a few days ago. The caption reads: If you know, you know.

And I do. Or I did. If I had seen these a day or two before, I might have thought he was doing this as a way to convince me to support the hotel and do the interview for Alana. But I've already agreed to do it. Alana must have told him I'm doing it. This doesn't seem like his way of saying thank you for helping out. Especially not the last one, the Dear Millie one. I can't explain that without letting myself hope that there's a way for us to fix what we broke.

I study the picture of his surf rack because something looks different then I remember it. Or something's missing. Pete has four surfboards in his collection. A shortboard he almost never uses, the huge nine-foot vintage longboard that was his dad's, his everyday Channel Islands board, and the amazing custom Robert August board he got when he graduated from college from his parents. The one I used to borrow. The one I coveted. The one that's missing.

I drop my phone and fly to the surfboard bag that's been leaning against the wall. The towel I still had wrapped around me drops to the floor when I start to rip the zipper down like a horny teenager on prom night. Or like me whenever I was near Pete Santana. My heart seizes in my chest when I see the board in my hotel room. I run my hand over the wooden nose and take a deep breath, as if I might be able to smell Pete's salty-sea-air scent. It's almost there. Just a hint of it. Why didn't he say anything? Why did he just let me leave if he wanted to explain?

I rub my eyes with the tips of my fingers. I did move to a secret hidden motel so he couldn't find me, and I blocked him. I didn't even look at the note the woman at the motel handed me when she pulled out this board.

With trembling fingers, I unzip the front pocket of the board bag. I was in too deep a state of despair to care what it said when I left. I thought it was just my name or a goodbye from Alana. I didn't care at the time. All I cared about was that Pete and I were over. How did I not realize it was a note?

I find it deep in the pocket and unfold it with shaky fingers. It reads, *You're taking my heart to LA, so you might as well take my board too. Surfers need surfboards, and I need you. —P*

It's just all too much. I don't know what to do now. I need to call him. Or screw that, I need to rent a car and drive directly back to Peacock Bay and throw him down on his deck swing.

Back up. That seems like an overreaction, but I'm having trouble connecting the dots from our fight a few days ago to him standing on his deck, my favorite place in the world, asking me for another chance. I look around my room for answers, but none appear. All I've got is a very magical dress, a custom-made surfboard, and a day double-booked with interviews. I need to deal with that first, and then I can figure out what's gotten into Pete.

I would make a dirty joke here, but there's literally no time.

Okay. I haven't even tried to push back my job interview. It might be last minute, but technically the reason I need to push it back is related to marketing, so maybe they'll understand.

I shoot Blair Martindale at Covast a brief email, explaining my friend Alana Tatamo of Surf Shack Dream House has asked me to speak with a writer on her behalf, and would it be possible to move back my interview time at all?

Am I dropping Alana's name to someone who works in marketing? Maybe. But I'm not lying. These are the facts, and I'll just have to wait and see how she responds.

I flop back on the bed and shake with laughter. I'm not sure what is going on, but my brain is spinning out of control. I take a few deep breaths to try to slow everything down. The next few hours are going to be insane, but if I take it piece by piece, I think I can handle it.

It's time to go big or go home. For real this time.

I'm supposed to meet Addie Turner in thirty minutes, and now I'm going into it with my head spinning. I have to calm down. I rush into the bathroom and splash water on my face. I brush my hair and then braid it so it'll stay neat while I surf. Which, now that I know it's Pete's board I'm toting around, I'm dying to do. I toss the newly crowned magical dress over my Roxy racer-back bikini that I know will hold me in securely and stuff my wet suit into the board bag with Pete's board. Without thinking, I pull the board toward me and plant a kiss on the wooden nose before closing the zipper all the way.

Okay, so I have to be losing it, right? That's not normal behavior, but I'm not going to look too deeply into that and just focus on getting through the next few hours. I turn on my damn notifications in case more posts from @waveline_pete decide to drop. This new Pete on Instagram thing has turned my world upside down. I can't make sense of it. My mind is racing, and I can't figure out what to do next—and that's not in the broad figure-out-my-life way. I keep walking into the bathroom to do something and then turn around because I forgot what I was going to do. Then I go back into the hotel room and can't remember what I needed in there. My brain is being assaulted by thoughts.

We had a fight. A bad one, but I could have let him explain. No. I didn't want him to explain more and get hurt. But didn't I kind of skip ahead and assume the worst? That's not unusual for me, it's true. But it just seemed like… It felt like… I'm not sure anymore. He's missing me. He's posting about me. He's telling me to come back. To come home. The idea of making Peacock Bay my home is intoxicating, and a giggle erupts out of my mouth at the very thought. But there is this nagging doubt in the back of my mind. He knows I'm about to do the interview with Addie, and I have to fight against the idea that he's trying to butter me up right before it.

I shake my head. It can't be. I know Pete, and he's not that cruel. I heard what I wanted to hear before because maybe it was easier to leave if we weren't together. I think I needed to see if he'd still want me if I wasn't a way to bring likes and tourists to the Waveline. When he was so concerned about me doing the *LA Times* interview, I took it to mean that's all he wanted me for.

Okay, breathe. In and out. Yoga breathe that shit right out of you. I have to get through this interview, and then I'll deal with the rest.

I drag the board down the hall and push the button for the elevator. I guess I could have called for the hotel to send someone to carry the board down for me, but now that I know what it is, I'm not letting it out of my sight. This board is a declaration. It's a connection to a place and a person that I thought I'd lost. It's an anchor. A lifeline. So, no way am I handing over my lifeline to some hotel employee who's likely more focused on selling his screenplay than not dinging up this board. This is LA after all.

When I get into the elevator, I feel my phone buzz in the pocket of the dress just as I lean the board against the elevator wall. It's a text from Quincy:

Quincy: I think you broke my brother.

My fingers instinctively move to Instagram, and the first picture on my feed again is from Pete. But I don't get it. It's not something or somewhere I recognize. It's kind of nothing. Just a plain white square, save for a lone letter H in black sitting in the upper-left corner.

Millie: What the hell is that?

Quincy: Dick pic?

Quincy: Sorry, reflex. I have no idea. What do you think it means?

Millie: How the hell should I know but I'm freaking out and I need to not freak out right now because I'm about to go meet Addie for the interview. Maybe go check on him? See what's going on?

> **Quincy:** Already tried. He's not here.

My heart pounds. I need proof of life. I need to know someone has seen him in person and confirmed that he wants to make things right with me. That this isn't just for show.

> **Millie:** What do you mean? His place or the hotel?

> **Quincy:** Both. Checked all the places. Texted him. Dude is nowhere.

The elevator doors open with a ding, and I shove my phone back into my pocket. *Shit.* Where is he? I grab the board and head out the big wide-open patio doors of the hotel that lead to the restaurant that sits almost directly on the beach.

If I unblock him now and text him, then what? I can't have him texting me during my interview. I will look like a complete asshole texting and grinning and possibly weeping into my phone at the slightest mention of Peacock Bay. I mean, I might anyway, but I have to at least try to set up myself for success.

Okay, let's do this. Get these two interviews done, figure out my next career move, track down the love of my life. Quite the to-do list, really.

Chapter
27

I HIT THE BEACH AND start pulling the board out of its bag. I still can't believe it's here with me, or that really any of this is happening. I assume the interviewer knows what I look like from social media, so I take my body through a series of stretches to warm up while I wait to meet her. After waiting for a few minutes, I get bored and check my email to see if there's an update about my interview time. My heart rate picks up when I see the Covast email address staring back at me. I hope for a simple "no problem" kind of reply when I click into the email. But of course, I find something a little more complicated.

> We certainly understand about the interview. We can push back our interview to 3 p.m., but that's the latest we can do because our CEO is leaving soon after for a meeting, and I know he wants to meet you also. He's very interested in your media contacts. We're such fans of all the Peacock Bay Bloggers!! So, we can work with you on the interview time. Please feel free to give me a call if you need to. We can

possibly do the interview over the phone or video call as well!

I let my hand and phone drop down to my waist, thinking about what I just read, then lift it again to reread the email once more.

I'm running all this over and over when a cheerful voice greets me. I turn to see a woman with brown hair cut neatly at her shoulders being followed by a hotel employee carrying a surfboard.

"I'm Addie." She holds her hand out for me to shake. "I love that this hotel has a surfboard valet service." She nods to the guy putting her board down. I smile at her, then look at Pete's board.

"That's really cool, but this board is a very special loaner. I can't let it out of my sight." I might sleep with it in bed next to me tonight, curled up against it, pretending it's the body of its true owner, but I'm not saying that part out loud.

"That's so nice. I wish more of my friends surfed. I went on a few trips with my family when I was younger, but I never kept up with it. I think the reason I got this assignment is because I'm one of the only staffers who've been on a board before, but you'll have to be patient with me today."

"I totally understand. When I first came out here a few weeks ago, I hadn't surfed in years. It took me a while to get back into the groove, and it was pretty embarrassing. It's one thing to try something new and fail, but it didn't feel great to fail at something that used to be easy for me."

Addie smiles. "Well, I might have to remember that when I'm writing up this article. You've managed to make failure look pretty good." She's still smiling at me, but I must look confused because she adds, "I think people have enjoyed your openness with your social media presence."

I shrug. "I was only open about some parts." I don't know how closely she's been following me. I know she originally wanted to talk to Alana and she got stuck with me instead, so I'm not sure if she knows just how badly I crashed and burned. I'd like to leave that out of the article, so I'm not planning to bring it up.

"I think openness and honesty on social media are having a powerful moment," she continues. "People know the photos they see aren't reality, and they're getting bored with it. How many perfectly clean kitchens or well-styled bookshelves can you see before you lose interest? I know my kitchen counter always has a forgotten dirty coffee mug on it, and I think that's why people have taken to your Instagram so much."

"Because I'm the dirty mug?"

Addie shrugs "Maybe, not exactly like that. People see themselves in you more than in an influencer who is wearing a floor-length dress while they unload clothes from the dryer."

Logically, I can understand what she's saying. While it's fun to dream life could be the way Alana presents things online, the average person isn't doing the vegan baking in handmade ceramics that she's doing. More people out there are trying to surf (or their equivalent) and crashing headfirst into the water. There's a problem with Addie's argument though.

"Even if I'm the charmingly dirty mug on everyone's counter, I think someone just knocked me off and cracked me. Instagram and I have gently parted ways is what I'm trying to say."

Addie tilts her head at me, her eyes narrowing in thought. "Really? I would have thought you'd be excited by the way people have been supporting you in the last few days."

When I stare back at her, blinking like a broken traffic light, she adds, "I think you were up to seventy-five thousand followers when I looked last. That can't hurt either."

I gasp and the air gets caught in my throat, making it impossible for me to speak. I cough and sputter and shake my head because that can't be right. I've purposely been ignoring Instagram. Even when I went on to check what Pete was doing, I ignored the numbers I saw there because I assumed it was all going to be backlash to my recent admissions.

"I haven't looked," I admit, my jaw hanging uselessly probably somewhere near my ankles. "I've been ignoring everything ever since I let it rip about the whole fake husband and ADHD stuff." I look down at my phone. I'm dying to look. "I don't want to be rude, but…" I tell Addie.

"No, go for it." She grins. "This will be fun to watch."

After a few taps, red hearts and numbers swim before my eyes. I'm not sure how I was able to avoid it before, but I truly did believe that any responses were going to be negative so I forced myself not to look. I scroll through what seem like endless comments. There are a few "delete your account" and "cancel @HeretoStay" messages, but for the most part people are being really supportive. Saying they appreciate that I was honest about everything. There's one comment in particular that catches my eye from a follower that says she (at least I think it's a she) understands what it feels like to have a brain that doesn't work the same way as everyone else's.

> Just because we mess up doesn't mean
> we ARE messed up.

That really hits home and is kind of what my mom was saying in her text earlier. Even if I mess up, I always try my best to make things right again. I write a quick thank-you back to that person. I want to dive into all these messages and respond to the people who are showing me support, but now isn't the time. It would take hours, and I need the time and a quiet place so I can really focus on each one properly.

I look up at Addie, shaking my head in disbelief.

"So, how many is it?" she asks with a knowing smile.

"God, I still haven't checked." I look back and blink as my eyes adjust again to the blue light. When I see the number, I stick the palm of my hand into an eye socket and drag it across my face. "Just like you said, just over seventy-five thousand. Holy shit."

I can't believe this. Maybe the people following all my mistakes weren't just laughing with me. Maybe, for some, it made them feel okay about their own mistakes. I thought the followers of Here to Stay were often rooting for me so I would produce more failures to keep them entertained, but now it feels like they looked at the things I was posting and felt less alone. And I did that by being my most honest ADHD and messed-up self.

"Like I said, I think people really like seeing someone honestly fail and then have the courage to get back up," Addie chimes in. I don't know her really at all, but I'm weirdly glad she was here for this.

"If it's failure they want, these fools have come to the right place." I laugh.

I can't wait to talk to Quincy about this—and Pete, if things really have a chance of getting back on track with him.

Pete. I glance back down at my phone and click into the app to check his profile for more posts. I have to scroll down a few squares to find one, but he's put another one up. Another white square with a black letter O and what is that next one? Half of something else, an M? Is he spelling something? What is even happening right now?

I click on his profile so I can see the posts together, and find there's a third one. The same white background, the same black lettering, this one an E, and it starts to come together. I shake my head again because this day isn't even half over, and it's truly been one of the oddest of my life.

Pete Santana is making a goddamn grid.

Chapter 28

SINCE I HAVE A NEW feeling of kinship with Addie Turner, I put a little more effort into teaching her how to surf. We start on the beach and I show her how to paddle and pop up on her board before we hit the water. She does remarkably well on the paddle out, and after a few tries with me pushing her into the waves, she manages to get onto her feet and ride a wave halfway to shore.

She's grinning ear to ear while she paddles, and I smile back at her, knowing I felt that same pride only a few weeks ago as I clawed my way back to my dormant surf skills. Still, the entire time I've been in the water, I can't stop thinking about Pete, and I'm dying to check Instagram again. I keep looking down at the board and grinning like an idiot. A few times I leaned down and wrapped my arms around it like a hug while I was waiting for a wave to come. Yes, that's strange, and I'm completely fine with it.

I wonder if he's posted anything new. What's he trying to spell? *Home?* Is that the whole message? Why is he doing this? I never asked him to embrace Instagram or cared if he wanted a life of social media darkness. I've wanted him for so long, and I was so afraid to show him that I hid behind a hashtag. But now it seems like he's trying to show me there's been more to his feelings then I knew, that we might have a chance of a future, and that's something worth paddling in to find out.

When Addie reaches me again, I let her know I have to wrap this up so I can get to my next interview. There's a tug in my stomach when I say it, but I try to shake it away. When we reach the beach, the first thing I do is dive headfirst into my beach bag and open my phone to check for more updates on Pete's grid. When I tap to his profile, I see the whole thing. Laid out for me and all of his thirteen followers to find. *Come home.*

For once, I'm glad to see the absence of hashtags. I'm glad this message is just for me. Me and the other thirteen lucky followers who I'm guessing are mostly family and a few friends. I want to take this message and press it into my heart. I want to wrap myself in it like a warm towel after a long day in the water. I want to be in Peacock Bay. I want be there for Quincy as she goes through the next phase of challenges with Monrow. I want to help Sage at the store and watch Alana hit one million followers. If anyone can do it, I'm sure she can. More than anything, I want to go home.

"Before you take off," Addie says, bringing me back, "I should probably ask you what you think makes a great surf spot."

I look down at the message on my screen and then back at Addie. "There are the obvious things. The dependability of the waves, what's at the bottom, sand versus coral or rock. That can make a difference if you plan on falling a lot or even if you don't." Addie laughs. "But it's just like anything else. What really make the difference is the people you surf with. You could be on the most

perfect break in the world, but if you're surrounded by assholes…
Sorry, I'm probably not supposed to swear," I say sheepishly, putting
a hand over my forehead and smoothing back my wet hair.

She grins. "I can edit."

"I just mean that if you're with people who are rude or disre-
spectful, you're not going to have a good time. But you could be on
shitty, choppy little waves with your best friends and still have the
greatest day."

"Sounds like you're on a mission to help people have better surf
days by connecting with each other."

I smile back at her and nod. "That would be something." I love
the idea of people connecting with each other because of something
I created. I'm not sure that's what the future holds for me, but it's a
nice thought.

"Do you think you'll return to Instagram now that your posts
are being so well received?"

"Maybe. I think…" I begin. "I think I want to go back to a lot
of things." I smile at Addie and then look out at the water.

"So, last question. Is Peacock Bay really as perfect as everyone
makes it out to be?" Addie has a glint in her eye.

"It is to me. Everyone has stuff they're dealing with in their
lives, even if they choose not to show it. Just because you don't
dump every detail out for everyone to see doesn't mean you're not
real. It's a weird world to navigate, and everyone has to choose what
amount is right for them to share."

I check my phone for the time. *Shit.* This is going to be close.
I knew it was going to be tight timing-wise to get to my interview,
but any hope I had of a shower before just flew out the window.

Addie and I say our goodbyes. I spent a little too much time with her, but if I hurry, I think I can still make it.

I carefully put the Robert August board back in the bag, pull off my wet suit, and throw on my dress so I don't look like a complete bum rushing through the hotel. It's a surf hotel, but it's a pretty fancy one, and I don't think they exactly want me running around in a dripping-wet suit.

I check the time again and something twists in my stomach yet again. This time, I know what it is.

I don't want to go to that interview. I don't want another job in marketing in a city I'm not familiar with. The thought on its own makes me so lonely I could cry. I know it looks better on paper to have the stable job and the apartment in a major city, but that's not what I want. And maybe it's seeing all my screwups clustered together on one little grid and knowing there are people out there—ones I know and ones I don't—embracing me for those screwups instead of walking away, but I feel empowered to make the choice I want to make. Not the one I feel looks best.

> **Millie**: Don't make any plans for the store without me. I want the job.

I text to Sage, and a thrill of excitement rushes through me. Not impulsive excitement, but true joy because I know this is what I really want.

While I wait for her to respond, I email the people at Covast and thank them for the opportunity, but explain I've taken another position.

I'm still standing in the lobby of this hotel, letting my bathing suit soak through my cover-up. I have to change. A shower would be nice too. But honestly, I have waited long enough to call this man who has been haunting me.

I push the button for the elevator, and while I wait, I get a response from Sage.

> **Sage**: You sure? I'm not trying to talk you out of it, but I know Peacock Bay isn't LA or New York.

I smile at her message.

> **Millie**: Thank god, it's not! And yes, I'm super sure. I can't wait to get back.

> **Sage**: I'm so glad!

I'm in the elevator, feeling like I can finally breathe big gulps of air again, when I open Instagram. The grid is still there. He hasn't changed it or added any captions or made any changes. I'm going to call him when I get to my room. I'll track him down. I'll rent a car and drive back to the Bay today. Right now. Or after a shower, at least.

The elevator doors ding open, and I lift the board out and drag it down the hall. It's so big and heavy, I can barely make it around the corner without banging into a wall. Jesus, this thing is so hard to maneuver, part of me is beginning to think Pete loaned me this board just to slow me down.

And then there he is. Sitting on the floor in front of my door, knees bent to his chest, one hand in his dark-brown hair. He looks up at me, and the relief on his face brings tears to my eyes.

Pete's here. My heart lurches into my throat as I let go of the board bag and launch myself at him. Our mouths collide in a kiss, and I wrap my arms around his neck, digging my fingers into his hair. His tongue dives into my mouth, searching and hungry. I push my tongue right back, taking what I need from him too.

"Get in my room," I order him, and he grins against my mouth. We keep kissing, but inch our way toward the door to my hotel room. I break only to unlock the door, but when I do, we both have the same thought.

"Your board," I say in reminder.

"Your board," he says. I shake my head, because there's no way I'm really keeping that thing. It's too massive for me anyway.

"No way. I can handle some big things, but that surfboard just isn't practical."

"I'd like to see the big things you can handle."

I shake my head at him. "Enough with the dirty jokes, dude."

Pete bows his head a little, then goes for the board. He grabs the strap and slides it into the room while I hold the door open. Then we launch at each other again. My hands are at the hem of his shirt, and his fingers hook in the straps of my dress. We break apart so I can step out on my own and he can pull his shirt over his head.

I run a hand over his chest and let the other find a place just under his jaw. I have to squeeze my eyes closed to keep them from tearing up. I don't even know where to start.

"What did I miss?" I grin at him.

"Everything," he breathes. He leans his forehead against mine.

"Yeah, you learned to use Instagram," I laugh, but then it comes out half a sob.

Pete smiles sheepishly. I know it wasn't natural for him to put himself out there like that. His fingers are probably itching to delete every post.

"And your Instagram is taking off."

I dip my head. "Apparently, failing is the thing to do now. Who knew? But that's not even the biggest news."

"There's more? Did you get the job?" Pete is doing his best to look happy and excited even though I can see he's dreading an answer that moves me to LA.

"Oh, I canceled that interview. But I did get a job." I grin. "I'm going to work at Little Goods while Sage is in Colorado."

Pete's lips tighten like they're trying to hold back an enormous grin. "Just to be clear, you mean the Little Goods in Peacock Bay, right?"

"Oh, no. Did you think I meant the one in Peacock Bay? I meant the one in Guadalajara. Was that confusing?" I smirk at him. "Yes, the one in Peacock Bay. I'm coming back."

"Thank god." He puts his hands on either side of my face and pulls my lips to his. I'm flushed with warmth up to my hair follicles, and I can't believe I was ever unsure of his feelings for me.

"Millie, I never should have made you feel the fate of the hotel was tied to your Instagram. Yes, it's important to me for the hotel to survive, but it's not going to come down to one blog or one article or Instagram post. The bloggers in town are important and they always will be, but Amelia and I have come up with a real PR plan to expand our outreach. You'd be so proud of our press release, Mills."

I laugh. "I'm sure I would be. But what about the surf camp that canceled? I feel awful if that was my fault."

Pete shakes his head. "It wasn't. I was wrong to make you feel that way, and I was wrong about why they canceled. They folded as a company. Which is too bad, but not in any way related to your Instagram activity."

"That really is too bad." My eyes widen with a thought. "But you know, the Waveline could host their own women's surf camp. Maybe Quincy or Alana would even host it."

"Or you." He smiles, but I shake my head. I'm going to keep blogging, but reaching that level of influencer isn't the end-all for me. I want the life that's real and true and built into perfect little moments like this.

"And just so we have everything cleared up, yes, I was freaked out when Claire was returned by a stranger that recognized her—"

"Don't worry, I was too," I jump in.

"But I shouldn't have said what I did, and I need you to know I was never pretending anything with you. Every single minute I spent with you was real. I went along with the Instagram Husband stuff thinking it was a way to show you how good things could be if we were together without having to risk looking like I was actually begging you to stay in my tiny, boring town with me. I wanted to help you succeed, too, because I thought if you became one of the influencers of Peacock Bay, well, then you'd have to stay there with me."

"So you were just pretending to be fake?" I tease, letting my fingers brush the scruff along his jaw. He scowls in response. "It was all real for me too. It always has been." Pete's body relaxes. He lets his forehead fall to my shoulder in relief. "But you kept talking about how I was leaving, and our deal, and I got scared to tell you things weren't going well online."

"They were going so well off-line though."

I can't believe this is happening. I'm ready to launch myself at him again, but before I do, I want to make something else clear. "I think it's safe to say this is the end of social media playing any sort of role in our relationship."

Pete smiles and his eyes relax. "I had to get your attention somehow. I wasn't going to wait around again. I'm a patient guy, but I couldn't let you slip away again. I wasn't sure you'd hear me out in real life, but I knew if I showed up in your feed, you'd see how serious I was."

I shake my head, looking down. He really put himself out there for me. Maybe that "Get out here" was what I wanted it to be after all.

"Hold on, what do you mean *again*?"

Pete wraps his arms around my waist, pulling me closer still. "Millie, I always assumed after college you would come out to California with Quincy. I never dreamed you would move to the East Coast. I graduated and took over the business from my dad and thought it wouldn't be long before you and Quincy moved out here together. I had a whole plan. I just didn't know it was going to take you so long to get here. I should have told you a long time ago how I felt, maybe even when we were at school together. I'm not sure."

"You've been into me since college?" I exclaim. He's been

holding out for me since he graduated. Maybe even longer. "Hell yes, you should have said something sooner." I grab his face in my hands and pull his wonderful soft lips to mine. He responds by pulling me in tighter, hands flat on my back, covering and touching as much of me as he can. And I am offering it all to him.

My entire body lights up at the idea that Pete has been holding onto the hope that one day I would make my way to his hometown and find him again. I kiss him hard, my hand brushing against the short strands on his neck. The mistakes we made before don't matter so much. If we're going to be together now, I'm sure we'll make mistakes sometimes in the future, too, but I know that we belong together and I know he knows it too. That he's always wanted it. Just like I have.

Oh my god. Goodbye, clothes.

I need to feel him against me now. I need him inside of me. I want to show him just how real everything is for me, and that I'm always going to feel like this. I get to work unbuttoning his pants and he follows my lead and unties the strings on my bikini. I sit him down on the bed and take a step back to let my eyes drink him in. He's here. I watch as he reaches into his shorts pocket and pulls out a condom.

"You were optimistic," I tease.

"If I hadn't been, I would have lost my nerve around Pismo and turned around."

"How did you know where I was anyway?"

Pete tilts his head in question. "Geotags. Come on, Mills."

"Sorry, I forgot you're Mr. Robot now."

With that, Pete hooks an arm around me and twists me onto

my back so I'm under him, his broad shoulders eclipsing my chest. One hand strokes me gently between my legs, and then he slips a finger into me. My head tilts up as I enjoy every stroke of his hand and kiss of his lips on mine. His fingers are gentle but urgent, and my body responds to the friction he's creating. I'm wet and hot, and I'm losing sense of where I am and everything else except for the way Pete is touching me and how close I am to losing control.

"Millie, I need you," he says. "I need you so much." With that, there's no holding back any longer. I lift my head to look at him as I put one hand on his hip while the other strokes the length of him before I pull him into me. I fall back against the pillows at the sensation of being filled by this man that I love.

"More," I whisper. Pete closes his eyes like he's never heard anything better, then pulls himself back slowly and sinks into me again. I let out a soft moan before I know it's happening, which makes Pete release his own sound in answer. He cups the small of my back with one hand, pressing me against him harder, but I want to be closer. I want to feel him deeper. He answers the need of my body by rocking into me over and over. I meet him hard and faster with each thrust because no amount of his is enough.

I feel the heat building in my body, the tight coil of pleasure about to explode. I know there's no controlling it, so I don't try. I let the feeling overtake me, and before I can give Pete a warning that I'm about to go over the edge, convulsions of white-hot pleasure rip through my body. The feeling of my body pulsing against his must take Pete to the brink, too, because I feel him give in to his release. I pull him to me and we let our warm, boneless bodies relax in a big pile of joy.

After a few minutes of pressing kisses wherever we damn want and letting me roam every inch of his body with my fingers, Pete gets up to throw away the condom. When he comes back, he pulls the sheet over us and pulls me close again.

"You know what we should do?" he asks between kisses.

"That again, a million times forever?"

"Yes, obviously." He smiles. "But really. I had an idea."

"If it involves clothes then, no."

Pete rolls on top of me and pins my arms to my sides so I'm forced to look at him and stop with my hilarious jokes. But if he thinks this is going to get me to stop thinking dirty thoughts about him, he needs to stop looking so damn good while he does it. Or anything.

"Seriously. We should go to Mavericks."

I laugh. Maybe he actually is trying to kill me. "Dude, I can't surf Mavericks. What is wrong with you?"

"Not to surf, just to shoot some content."

"The guy makes one Instagram grid…"

Pete laughs. "I'm serious. We'll drive up there before we go home. It'll just be a random day, but we could see if any women are there surfing. It would make for an interesting post."

My lips pull into a grin and I try to lift my head to kiss him but he's still holding me down. "I don't like this," I tell him.

"The idea or not being able to do whatever you want?" he teases. "Because there's something I like about this very much." He kisses my neck, then trails his tongue down to the hollow of my throat.

"Oh god," I murmur.

Still with a hold on my arms, which I'm not fighting at all

anymore, Pete takes my nipple in his mouth and sucks just enough to make me buck underneath him. He gives the side of my breast the smallest nibble, then works his way back up to my mouth again. He lets go of my arms, and I immediately capture him around the waist and hold him against me.

We're both smiling like fools.

"Talk more about content to me," I say into his kiss. But I have another reason to smile too. "How do you know I'm going home with you?"

"You caught that, huh? I thought maybe I could slip that by you and just pack you up with me before you noticed anything was happening."

I give a tiny shake of my head. "Nothing gets by me."

"So will you?" His eyes grow soft as he waits for my answer.

I roll onto my back and fold my hands across my chest. "Are you sure there's room for me?"

"Is that a comment about my size?"

I shake my head slowly. "Never. But I need to make sure my new place is going to meet my needs."

Pete trails his curled fingers down the side of my neck to my hip. My leg bends at the knee and he wraps his arm around it.

"I can assure you," he says, "your needs will be met."

This I can believe.

He sits up and the loss of his warmth has me following him like a shadow. He takes the bedsheet and wraps it over my shoulders when he sees my shiver. "So, what do you think? Should we go? Drive up to Mavericks and watch some surfers drop in on some monster waves? Then you can use the photos to create content for a few new posts. Just because you're working at the store doesn't mean the blog is done."

I can't believe how much he's thought this through, and I love the life he's describing. Working at Little Goods, blogging, and a little travel when I can afford it. And all of it with Pete.

I launch myself at him and we fall back into the bed again. "Say 'content' again," I laugh. "Really slowly."

"Content." He kisses me.

"Mmmm," I answer.

"Impressions." Kiss.

"Yes."

"Unique visitors."

"Oh god, more." I burst out laughing and kiss him hard. My tongue dives into his mouth, and we kiss each other hungrily until I feel the hardness of him press against my leg.

"Let's not leave right away, though," I tell him. "This is a *really* nice hotel."

Pete freezes and raises his eyes to look at me. "Excuse me? I think that's a typo."

"Don't worry. The Waveline is still number one in my heart."

He smiles. "You're damn right."

No contest.

Chapter 29

WE END UP STAYING ANOTHER night in Malibu. It is a really nice hotel after all, and I can appreciate it even more now that Pete is with me. We spend the entire day in bed eating an enormous breakfast and watching an old surf movie about Mavericks on his laptop. There's also lots and lots of sex.

It's the kind of day your friend would tell you about over brunch and you simultaneously want every detail, kind of hate them, but also don't believe it.

And it's happening to me.

So naturally, I need to call my friends and tell them about it. I also think it's a little odd they haven't checked in with me in the last few days. I had texted them briefly about reuniting with Pete, but got no response. Kind of rude, but they have lives of their own, I suppose.

I call Bree, but she doesn't answer. Which isn't that weird, but a few minutes later I get a text from her that makes me sit straight up in bed.

> **Bree:** Hey, in the hospital with Kate. She's okay, but likely tore her MCL. A dodgeball date fail. I guess she was lucky it wasn't the ACL, which would have been worse.

"Shit," I say. "Kate tore her MCL." I explain to Pete while typing my response.

> **Millie:** Are you sure she's okay? I feel so bad I'm not there to help. What's she going to do?

I didn't even know Kate went to another dodgeball date. I'm not even sure I asked how the first one went. It doesn't feel great thinking of these things happening without me there. How is Kate going to manage this in New York? Kate and Bree live in a third-floor walk-up. There's no way she can manage the stairs with this injury.

> **Bree:** She has surgery scheduled for next week. Her dad is on his way down from Vermont. She's going to stay with him while she recovers. Her boss is letting her work remotely.

I look around the room, wondering how fast I can pack and if I should start looking at flights to New York to go help Kate. I know Bree said she's going to stay in Vermont for a while, but it still feels wrong to be so far away when she's going through such a big thing.

As if reading my mind, Bree sends a second text.

Bree: She says don't come here. We've got it under control, and you're barely holding your shit together there.

Millie: She did not say that.

Bree: No, but that's what she means.

Millie: Okay, but I have to do something.

I search the room again, trying to think of a way to send my support to Kate even when I can't be there. When I spot the pile of yesterday's clothes that were tossed on the chair in the corner, it comes to me all at once.

Millie: Never mind. I've got it. Tell Kate I'm sending her a care package and to call if she needs anything.

I chew my bottom lip. I can't really afford to fly back to New York right now, but the least I can do is send something to Kate to lift her spirits in whatever tiny way is in my power.

"We have to run an errand," I tell Pete. "I have something I need to mail to Kate."

Pete locates a post office while I pack. It feels strange to leave out the one piece of clothing that has come to mean so much during my time in California, but the dress was never only mine. That's what made it so special. I don't actually believe it has magical powers sewn into its fibers, but there is something magical about carrying your truest friendships with you as you take on life's challenges.

That's what the dress did for me. It made me brave, it brought me comfort, and it reminded me at every turn or downturn, that I was never really alone. If anyone needs something like that right now, it's Kate.

"Who do you think will miss this dress more? Me or you?" I tease Pete when we pull into a parking spot at the post office.

"I was never after your clothes, Mills. Pretty much the opposite, to be honest."

"You're just annoyed you won't get your own turn to experience its magical powers," I fire back with a grin.

Pete looks at me as one corner of his mouth turns up. "I'm pretty sure I already did."

While I send off my little package to Kate, Pete waits patiently outside and takes down all the posts except the big *Come Home* grid. He has decided to retire from Instagram. I don't think he ever meant to dive into social media in the long term, but he let me take a screenshot of all of his posts before he deleted them. Even though his account to set to private, I think leaving such personal captions under those posts is uncomfortable for him.

I FaceTime Quincy while Pete drives. He texted her after the first night when we made up to tell her all was well, but I haven't answered her texts because I wanted to share the news in person. I'll settle for FaceTime.

"You dirty little hodad." She scowls at me through her phone. Which, given how little she surfs these days, is an unfair insult. "Where are you?"

"We're driving up to Mavericks to get barreled," I laugh.

Her eyes go wide. "Without me?" she screeches.

"We're not actually surfing. I like my life these days." I grin at the truth of it. "We're going to go check it out for the 'Gram."

"And then after that?" She grins.

"After that I think we're heading back to the Bay. Sage needs my help at the store and there's this guy there I'm pretty into."

"Oh god. I don't know if I should be happy or vomit, but for now, yay."

"What else is happening back there? How's stuff with Monrow?"

"Okay. The blog is getting a lot more traffic since I started writing about it. A few more sponsorships have come up, which is a nice surprise and will help with tuition at Vera Lake. I think writing about it has been positive for the most part. I still feel weird about sharing parts of his life, but when he gets older, if he wants me to stop writing about him I will and I can take down old posts."

"That's great. I think we're onto a whole new brand here. Failure is the new success. Though I'm ready to retire from my many failures, and nothing you're doing fits that category."

"I'm into it." She looks behind her, then leans in a little closer to the phone. "So what's the deal with you and my brother?"

"I don't know, but I think he really likes me." I grin and curl my fingers over my mouth as I raise my eyebrows at my friend on the phone screen.

"You can say that again," Pete calls from the driver's side.

"Cool, so, you guys are gross. I'm gonna go."

"Before you do, I just heard from Bree that Kate tore her MCL. She's having surgery next week and then heading home to Vermont with her dad to recover."

"Oh shit, that's terrible. What happened?"

"I'm not exactly sure, something about a dodgeball game. The guy she's been seeing kept inviting her to play in his league."

"And he didn't pick up on the fact that she hates sports? That relationship doesn't sound like it's going anywhere. Well, is there anything we can do?"

"I think Bree has it handled for now. I, um, sent her the dress." It seems like such a small thing, but hopefully it will bring a smile to my friend's face when she opens the package.

"That was a good idea. Plus, I guess you've gotten what you needed from it." My friend raises her eyebrows at me suggestively.

"Hey, all that time when you were teasing me about hooking up with Pete. You weren't joking because it was never going to happen. You actually meant it, huh?"

"You guys were meant to be gross together for a long time, Mills. So, tomorrow night? Can we hang?"

"You mean at four o'clock? I know what 'night' means in the Bay."

Quincy laughs. "Yeah, something like that. Anyway, if you're sticking around for a while, I think we'll have plenty of time for a proper catch-up."

"Yeah, plenty of time."

"Plenty!" Pete calls again.

After I hang up with Quincy, Pete grows quiet for a minute, and I can tell he's got something he wants to say.

"Spit it out, man. What do you have brewing over there?"

"Just, when you were on the phone with Quincy. I don't just like you, Millie. That's not what this was about. I wouldn't have done anything close to this if I just liked you."

I smile so big at Pete. "You fucking love me, don't you?"

"Jesus, with the f-bombs, Mills."

"What, did you bring a baby so I can't be mad at you again?"

"Can we return to the original post for a minute here?" Pete grins.

I can't believe he has no idea. "I love you too. Big time."

"Well, thank fucking god for that!" We both laugh, and he reaches over and grips one of my hands in his. Pete drives like he can't get me back to the Bay fast enough. It's the first time I've ever seen him break the speed limit. But I think he must feel like I do, that we've waited long enough to go home.

Acknowledgments

There are quite a few people to thank for helping make this book happen. First, my agent Joanna MacKenzie. When I first received her request for my query I thought to myself, "Let's do this, Joanna MacKenzie." And after a few years, many drafts and her endless support and encouragement, we did. Joanna is savvy, tough, fair and bold. The best kind of agent and I'm so lucky to have her in my corner.

To Rachel Gilmer and the entire Sourcebooks team. Thank you for seeing the potential in this book and these characters. This book wouldn't be what it is today without your creativity and thoughtfulness.

A very special thanks to the ones who rooted for me when I locked myself in my house writing things that would never see the light of day and still wanted to be friends with me while I did it. Melissa Post, my original reader and cheerleader; Alex Metz, my pretend psychic who helped me through the really tough "is this ever going to happen for me" times; Jennifer Katzner, for always being there to talk through ideas and plot points; Miryha

Fantagrossi, who said "you got this" when I really didn't think I did; Danielle Natarajan for being proud for no reason; and Emily Rosnick, Natalia Feinstein, and Papri Harkey who were always and sincerely rooting for me.

Ashley Lavin and Carlynn Finn, my earliest beta readers. Ashley stays up all night reading my terrible drafts and gives me feedback faster than anyone should ever ask of her. You can't have her. She's mine. Carlynn, one day, one of those books with your name in it will get out there. Thank you both for all your help.

To my Asheville School friends, Kaleah, Katrina, Frances and Krissy, thank you for cheering me on and helping me with Zoom outfits (and how to use Zoom).

To Mia Libby, just for being the best and my working mom role model.

And finally thank you to my family, to Matt for holding it all together and my parents to whom this book is dedicated and the ones I do it all for, Sutton and Henry. Sutton, I started writing to fill the time while you napped and you'll never know how grateful I am for not only your existence, but for that rigid schedule that taught me how to produce a lot of words in a short amount of time. Henry, thank you for using your birthday wishes on me. I'm so glad you both have grown up watching me struggle to achieve this long held goal and that you remember that relentlessness is often the answer to getting to the finish line.

About the Author

Gillian Libby left New York City after many years and many jobs. She worked in PR/marketing film/TV and was a SoHo shopgirl. She tried her best to become a traveling surf bum, but it didn't stick. She now writes books in Connecticut where she lives with her husband and two children near a beach with no waves.